Not So

Broken

Love Grows Series, Book One
By

Renee Regent

Thanks to all my writer friends for their support, especially Amy, Elaine, Dodie, Kat, and Eliza for their invaluable feedback. Thanks to Chris Hall of The Editing Hall for her editing expertise, and T.E Black Designs for her awesome cover work. Special thanks to Danny Lankford, for imparting his wisdom about the beverage industry; my sister, Karen, for her enthusiastic support; and for Eric, my very own hero.

Not So

Broken

Chapter One

Gibson

*I*t's amazing what a man can do when he has no choice. Like chopping wood with a big-ass axe. I'd run short of firewood a few times last winter, and the old pot belly stove in my cabin needed to be fed on a regular basis once the cold set in. Winter in the North Georgia mountains was short, but it could be as moody as an angsty teenager. That's why I was drenched in sweat, and my arms were beginning to ache as I split log after log. But I welcomed the pain. It was a penance, of sorts.

Four p.m. on a hot day in mid-August probably wasn't the best time to be chopping wood but keeping my hands busy calmed my mind and kept me from returning the phone call I was dreading.

I hefted the axe and swung, enjoying the sharp cracking sound the log made as it split. This was some real lumberjack stuff. I tossed the wood on the growing pile and adjusted the plastic glasses I wore to protect my eyes from flying debris. Considering my attire—jeans, work boots, the lightweight plaid shirt, not to mention my bushy blond beard—I probably looked like a modern-day Paul Bunyan. All that was missing was a woolen cap and suspenders.

The truth was, I was beginning to enjoy this simple life—chopping wood, living in a rustic cabin in the middle of a forest, and earning a living by working with my hands.

I didn't miss being a billionaire at all.

1

My cell phone buzzed in my pocket, mocking me. I didn't have to look to know who it was. I knew when Dad's voicemail came through six hours earlier that it would be another round of pointless arguments. Cell reception was spotty this deep in the woods, and I'd been too busy working all day to return the call sooner.

Well, that was my story and I was sticking to it. I caught the call just before it went to voicemail.

"Hey, Dad. What's up?"

"Right now, I'm about to have dinner with a client so I'll get to the point. I need your final answer soon. You've had enough time to nurse your wounds, Gib. Time to man up and get back to work."

Damn. He doesn't get it. I set down the axe and walked up the steps to my cabin. It gave me a moment to squelch the anxiety swirling in my stomach.

After my world fell apart, I took off on my motorcycle and ended up here in Tilly, Georgia. It's the perfect place to hide out. Small town, gorgeous scenery, and tons of solitude. I may stay here forever, as Gib Cole, local handyman. I was born John G. Colebank III, heir to the Colebank fortune, but that person no longer exists. At least in my mind. But my father hasn't accepted that fact yet. I took a calming breath and stilled my growing anxiety.

"You forget I'm a grown man, not some lovesick teenager. And frankly, I'm appalled you'd make light of the situation. You know what happened. It's nothing to joke about."

The moment of silence on the line followed by a sigh, told me my point had hit home.

"I'm not making light of it, son. It's just…I can't give you much more time. Our line of work demands constant attention, especially now that it's booming. I need to know if you're on board for the long haul or not."

My reply died on my lips. This was so not the way I'd wanted my life to go. It had been over a year since that awful day when my world shattered. I had made a decision that ended in tragedy, and I had since taken full responsibility for it.

It didn't mean I was ready or willing to go on as though it had never happened. I also knew I probably wouldn't stay in Tilly for the rest of my life, but I couldn't see going back to being who I was before.

I cleared my throat of the lump that was forming and took a breath.

"I can't give you an answer right now. I'm sorry. I'm just starting to feel like myself again."

That was a lie because I no longer felt at all like the man I was long ago. The eldest son and heir to a luxury resort and vacation rental empire; an ambitious, power-hungry player who lived for the conquest, be it financial or sexual. That man had faded into the ethers. Gone were the fine suits and devoted staff to take care of my every need. I no longer had women falling all over me, eager for a moment in the spotlight or for the pretty things I'd toss their way.

Now I wore jeans and work boots and cooked my own meals. I had no interest in relationships and kept pretty much to myself. Hell, I didn't even have Internet at the cabin, and my phone was a cheap prepaid thing. I was better off alone since I had nothing left to offer anyone.

Exasperation laced my father's tone, but his next words gave me what I was hoping for—more time.

"You have until your birthday to decide. If you're not on board by then, I'm cutting you off."

It could be an empty threat, but with my father, any outcome was possible. John Colebank II hadn't become one of the richest men in Atlanta by playing nice or by making idle threats. I was one of the few people who would stand up to him, and only when necessary.

It seemed this was one of those times. Still, I tried to rein in the sarcasm in my voice. No need to be disrespectful.

"I've already done that myself, haven't I?"

"You know what I mean. Don't be a smart ass. I have to go. We'll talk later."

The crisis was averted. For now. My next birthday, my fortieth, was several months away.

I let out a long sigh, more of a groan really, and entered the cabin. The now-familiar scent of musty wood enveloped me like a favorite old blanket. I laid the phone on the counter and walked to the kitchen. I had no appetite so I grabbed a beer from the fridge and took it to the back deck.

A panorama of colors greeted me. Rolling hills as far as I could see peppered by a mosaic of changing leaves. Deep green with flecks of orange and red were a preview of the spectacular display that would be here, come October. A breeze rustled the nearby trees, cooling me. The mood had changed again.

I had cut myself off from my family and their fortune the day I called to say I wouldn't be coming home, nor keeping my position at the company. They had been furious, shocked, confused. My grief over the death of my wife and our unborn child was understandable. After all, my family had been grieving too. But it was obvious my sudden withdrawal from the world made no sense to anyone else but me.

It was simply something I had to do.

I'd wandered in to Tilly one day, a broken man. For some reason, the place called to me. Sanctuary was what my soul needed, and the mountains provided that in abundance. I used some of my own money to rent the cabin, and then to buy an old truck and some tools, paying cash for all of it. From then on, I have lived on what I made from odd jobs around town and haven't touched the millions stashed away in my personal bank accounts and stock portfolio.

Just like that, I started a new life. It was as though the tragedy of my past had never happened.

Now if I could only convince myself to believe it.

~*~

Sacha

It's amazing what a woman can do when she has a goal.

I was in the midst of packing my suitcase for yet another road trip for work, when a knock sounded on the door of my apartment. It wasn't just any knock but *the* knock. My neighbor Melanie and I had a specific knock, three short then silence, followed by two more knocks. That way we knew who was at the door. Living alone, you couldn't be too careful.

I opened the door to let her in, and she blew me a kiss as she went straight to my kitchen.

"Hey, girl. What's cooking?"

Melanie's question was rhetorical, but I answered anyway. "Nothing. But I have some cheese and crackers laid out on the counter and some wine in the fridge."

"That's why I love living next door. You always have the good stuff."

It really was the good stuff. But then, I'm a liquor and wine sales rep so I have an edge. Plus, a trip to the gourmet section of my local market that afternoon had been a success. I'd scored some aged fontina, sour cherry chutney, and garlic salami. Melanie sniffed the tray, her dark eyes lighting up.

Not So Broken

"This will go perfect with that bottle of Shiraz, won't it?"

"You bet. Go ahead and pour us some, I'm almost done packing."

As I reached the bedroom door, I heard Melanie ask, "Where are you going this time?"

Travel was one of the things I liked about my job—sometimes. The long hours on the road would often make me lonely. But when I visited a new town, there was excitement about the possibility of writing a high-dollar beverage order. Of course, there was also anxiety over striking out. But there was always hope.

This time, though, I needed to score big. I'd set myself a monthly sales goal that was nearly impossible, not only to gain extra pay but because I was vying for a promotion to regional manager. I was on a mission—I had a dream to finance and failure was not an option.

"I'm going to this little town up in the mountains called Tilly. Have you heard of it?"

"Yeah, my band played in a bar there once. Years ago."

Melanie entered the bedroom and handed me a glass of wine. Then she sat on the bed, crossed her long legs, and took a sip from her own goblet. Dressed in yoga pants and a faded tee shirt, with her long, dark locks in a ponytail, she looked nothing like her onstage rock diva persona. I adored her. Her band, Sparker, was really good, and she sang like an angel gone bad.

"You recall the name of the place?"

"Nah. I heard it burned down or something. But the town itself is cute. Like a little European village smack in the middle of the North Georgia Mountains."

I threw some lingerie and a sleep shirt in the case and zipped it shut. I tend to travel light.

"I've heard it's nice, but I'm only staying for one night. The last guy my company sent up there came back virtually empty-handed. No chain restaurants, and the bars in town are run by locals who are not fond of newcomers. But the city recently passed an ordinance that relaxed the liquor laws, so I figured maybe it was time to try again."

"Maybe. Well, if anyone can do this, it's Sacha Rowan, the Queen of Liquor Sales in Atlanta. But take time to have some fun while you're there."

I picked up my glass from the nightstand and held it up in a toast to Melanie's confidence in me. "Well, I'll be working most of the time. Not going there for fun. C'mon, let's eat."

Renee Regent

We stood at the kitchen counter, talking as we nibbled. I'd almost cleaned out the fridge, so there was an assortment of veggies and fruits to go along with the cheese and crackers. I listened to Melanie gossip about the neighbors while I glanced around my apartment. It was small, but I loved everything about it—the dark wood floors, white walls, and eclectic décor that had taken me months to find. It was decorated to suit me and no one else. One of the perks of living alone.

But those perks were few, and I had a long-term plan to change my status. I was doing everything in my power to make my dream come true, and if it did, I'd never be lonely again.

~*~

Friday morning, I called a few clients to make sure their orders had gone in correctly before the weekend. Even though I was used to driving all over Atlanta, it was a welcome change to be heading away from it for a few days. Between increasing traffic and non-stop road construction, my days had become torturous. I wasn't getting any younger, and the hours I've been putting in sure weren't getting any shorter.

The drive to Tilly was uneventful, except for the phone call from my mother. Julia, bless her heart, loved to keep track of everyone she knew on social media, including my ex-husband, Kevin. I rarely had the time or patience for it, but she told me anyway.

"Mom, you know you're gossiping, right?"

I was born in New Jersey, and we moved to Georgia when I was in middle school. I'd lost my northern accent, except for a word or two. But my mother's "Jersey voice" made every story she told sound dramatic.

"I swear, Sach, I'd bet a million bucks she's pregnant again. Not even trying to hide the freaking baby bump."

"What part of 'I don't care' do you not understand?"

It was a bald-faced lie, but I'd never admit it. I actually did care that Kevin's new wife was pregnant again. Even though it was none of my business.

It was because of *her* I was now listening to my mother discussing the cause of the worst year of my life.

The fact that Julia was hundreds of miles away didn't slow her down much. She still called me, her only daughter, nearly every day. Even so, I missed her. Especially the past few years while I was going through hell with Kevin and his antics. Lately, with work and all the traveling, I rarely had time for social media, thus the phone calls from her to keep me updated.

"Well, I thought you'd like to know. Where are you going now? How are you ever going to date if you're always on the road?"

"I'm not worried about dating. And I like my life the way it is."

Another lie, but I was working to change things.

When mom remarried five years ago and moved back to New Jersey, Kevin and I had already been married for two years. I thought we were happy, working together at his catering business, buying a house, the usual married life. I'd wanted to have kids right away, but there always seemed to be a reason why it wasn't the right time. He never came out and said he didn't want children, but he never seemed excited about the prospect either.

Mom's voice on the car speaker was skeptical. "Really? Like your job and that tiny apartment are enough. I know you better than that."

"It's fine. For now."

"Mmhmm. Well, I still can't get over how he treated you. It's been almost two years since you split up, but still. Now, to hear they're having *another* baby…"

I gripped the steering wheel, forcing down the anxiety that reared every time I discussed having children. My mother wanted a grandchild as much as I wanted to give her one. What she didn't realize was how it hurt to be reminded that I would likely never be able to conceive. I couldn't bring myself to admit it out loud, though, and she had never addressed it directly, either.

"Yeah, I know, Mom. This will be their third child. Not our concern, really. I have to go now. Call you tomorrow."

I didn't want to be reminded of how my marriage ended, but now the memories came flooding back.

Eventually, I had grown tired of waiting for the perfect time to start a family and told Kevin I was no longer on the pill. After a huge argument, he agreed we'd try to conceive. I was happy and hopeful, but somewhere deep inside I could sense his heart wasn't in it.

We tried for two years, with no luck. My periods had always been irregular, even when I was on the pill, so every month it was a continual cycle of raised hope and bitter disappointment. Kevin began to avoid my sexual advances, saying he was too tired or not in the mood. I chalked it up to the stress of trying to conceive and decided we needed to take a break. I left for a two-week vacation to visit Mom and see some old friends. I thought some time apart might rekindle our spark, and when I returned home, we'd be happy again, and I would finally conceive.

Maneuvering my little compact car up the winding mountain road, I realized now that vacation had been the beginning of the end. It was a decision that at the time had seemed to be inconsequential. I had never been so wrong about anything in my life.

~*~

Gibson

Friday morning, I worked on a deck repair job at a cabin across town. It wrapped up by lunchtime, so I headed to Nickel's Diner on my way home. When I arrived, the parking lot was almost full with trucks, jeeps, and beat-up late model compact cars. A memory flashed of pulling the Lamborghini or the Ferrari, or maybe even the Jaguar, depending on my mood—into my reserved parking space at CB Resorts International headquarters. Then I'd take the private elevator to the thirty-fifth floor and plop my ass in an overstuffed chair in my corner office, overlooking the Atlanta skyline. On my agenda would be endless meetings and phone calls, maybe a lunch meeting in a swanky Buckhead restaurant.

I still recalled the last conversation I'd had with my father, the day before I left Atlanta for good.

It had been my job to scout locations to add to our portfolio, from identification through to acquisition. The best part was the time I spent away from the office, in the field. I loved making deals, but I'd always longed to handle one of the projects hands-on, designing and building a resort from the ground up. But Dad insisted we contract out any building or remodeling projects.

"We can't afford to lose momentum by having you off in some remote location, watching guys sling a hammer. Our investors expect quick results, and growing our portfolio is top priority. The less renovation, the better."

My answer was the same as always, though he never wanted to hear it. "Finding a turn-key resort means paying top dollar too. Even then, there's always something that needs improvement. That's what I'm good at. Finding the hidden gem among the crap."

It was true, and I no longer had much opportunity to use my

talents to improve the properties we bought. I had studied architecture in college and spent many a summer in my youth building and remodeling homes for charity. But no amount of discussion had swayed Dad's opinion that I belonged right where I was, at his side.

Stepping from the truck, I shook my head to clear the memories away and took a deep breath of fresh mountain air. The scent of pine was bracing, edged with the first notes of decaying leaves. It was intoxicating and so was my freedom.

As I crossed the parking lot, the aroma of frying burgers took over. My stomach rumbled as I entered the diner, but no one heard as I made my way to my usual booth. It was the one with the long split in the red vinyl seat, covered with duct tape. Nickel's was in desperate need of renovation, yet no one seemed to care. The food was good, the service acceptable, and for many of the locals, it was a second home.

A server, a girl named Dahlia, was wiping down the table as I scooted onto the seat. She was pretty, with a round face and permanently pink cheeks. She was always the friendliest server at Nickel's. Well, at least she was with me.

"'Hey, Gib. I was hopin' you'd show."

"Where else would I eat lunch?"

"My place is much cozier than here. You should try it sometime. For breakfast."

I said nothing but gave her my most charming smile as she poured me some coffee. With a wink, she was off to tend to another table. I'd been tempted to take her up on her flirtatious offers a time or two, but never followed through. I hadn't so much as kissed a woman in the past year, not since before I arrived in Tilly. Despite the rumors to the contrary that seemed to surface about me now and again.

Hey, it was a small town.

I took a sip of the coffee, which was nothing special. There was a time when I commanded the best of everything—coffee, food, wine, and women. Not much had been out of my reach, and I'd taken it for granted. I watched the faces of the other patrons as they talked, ate, laughed. Each in their comfortable little world. Now this was my world too.

The tinkle of a bell on the door announced another customer had arrived, and the din of the crowd faded to silence. I looked to the door and stifled a groan.

It was Marvil Crouch, my landlord. He lived down the hill from me in his own cabin. His unofficial nickname was "Crouch the Grouch" and for good reason. He had no friends in town, having pissed off nearly every resident at one point or another over the thirty years he'd lived in Tilly. The man had no filter, no conscience, and didn't care who he insulted. He stood in the doorway, looking like an elderly ogre, with his broad shoulders, short neck and round, balding head.

"Dammit. No seats. Don't you all have someplace to be?"

Murmurs among the crowd were the only response, so I waved. When Marvil's squinted eyes rested on me, his frown eased into a smile for a moment. Then it was gone, replaced by his semi-permanent scowl.

He muttered under his breath as he sat opposite me in the booth. "Didn't hear your truck go by this morning. Must've been when I was in the john."

I sipped my coffee to avoid a smirk. "Hello to you, too."

"Eh." The single word was followed by a wave of his gnarled hand, followed by a shout to the restaurant in general. "Some coffee would be nice. Today, if possible."

Dahlia hurried over and filled a cup for the old man, then refilled mine. There was gratitude in her gaze. For some reason, I was the only one in Tilly who could handle the "cantankerous old fart" as Dahlia had described Marvil on numerous occasions.

But she never met my grandfather, John Colebank I, who made Marvil Crouch seem like a cuddly kitten.

He was still grumbling into his coffee cup when I lifted mine in salute. "So, Marvil. What's on your agenda for today? Besides terrorizing the general population of Tilly, I mean."

The tug at the corner of his wrinkled lips was the only indication of a sense of humor. His dark, beetle-like brows knit together, and his frown returned.

"I gotta go to the post office. Some kind of certified letter there for me."

We ate mostly in silence. I don't know why, but the old grouch was growing on me. Maybe it was the similarity to my grandfather. He was a challenge at times, but I often found Marvil to be amusing. Besides, the poor guy had no one else. His wife had died years earlier and they had no children.

I'd finished my burger and motioned Dahlia for the check. She gave a pointed look at Marvil, and I nodded. I didn't mind paying for his lunch. As a landlord, he'd been more than fair, despite the rumors he was hell to work with.

The door chimed again, and a young woman entered the diner. She was wearing a light blue pantsuit, like she'd just come out one of my endless meetings in Atlanta. She glanced around the room, as though she was casing the joint or looking to buy it. Then she walked to the cash register where Dahlia was ringing up my purchases. I strained to hear her over the din, curious as to what brought her to Tilly.

"Hi, I'm Sacha, with Queensmark Beverages. I know you don't sell alcohol here, but would you mind telling me what's the most popular bar or restaurant in town?"

Dahlia shut the register and reached into her apron pocket. She handed the woman a business card.

"The best restaurant is Charlie's Steak House. That's the one overlooking the river. But the best bar in town is the Frisky Beaver. They don't open until around three, though."

The woman looked at the card then smiled and held out her hand for Dahlia to shake. "Thanks, I'll check them out."

Dahlia shook her hand and pointed to the business card the woman now held in her other hand.

"My brother's band is playing at the Beaver tonight. You should go if you're staying in town. There's a stamp for a free drink on the back of the card."

"Thank you. I'll try to make it."

The woman slipped the card in the pocket of her pantsuit, brushing a lock of long brown hair from her shoulder. She turned to leave and caught me looking at her, green eyes flashing interest. I grinned and nodded, which she returned with a quick smile. Her demeanor was all business, but a woman with a wiggle in her walk like that had to have a wild side.

I stood, realizing maybe I'd been holed up in my cabin alone for far too long. Now I was fantasizing about random women, a visitor in town who I'd probably never see again.

"C'mon, Marvil. I'll walk you to your car."

"I can see myself out. I'm not feeble."

I ignored his comment and waved to Dahlia as we passed. She hurried over and pressed something into my hand.

"I meant to give that to you earlier, Gib. It's a ticket for a free drink at the Frisky Beaver. Why don't you go watch my brother's band play? You deserve it after buying lunch for that guy."

She cocked her head at Marvil's retreating figure, making me laugh. I turned the card over in my hand. "Thank you, Dahlia. That's sweet of you. Care to join me there?"

I had no idea why I asked her, but it seemed like the polite thing

11

to do. Her face lit up, dimples and all.

"I will if I can find a sitter. I've got my son this weekend."

"Great."

I walked out, wondering what I would do if Dahlia actually showed. I hadn't seriously thought of going out with her before, but maybe some company would be nice.

What if one thing led to another, and we ended up in bed? I wasn't ready for that type of date, but it had been a long time. If an attractive woman came onto me, would I be able to resist?

My parts still worked extremely well, and I couldn't swear that I wouldn't respond.

My love for my late wife, Bianca, would never be diminished. Being intimate with another woman wouldn't change the way I felt. I'd only slept with one woman since being widowed, a wild weekend in Atlanta, which I tried to forget.

But right now, maybe some attractive female company wouldn't hurt. The local pharmacy was at the other end of town. It would be wise to have protection, just in case.

Chapter Two

Gibson

I'd just made it back to my cabin when my cell phone buzzed. This time, I didn't mind taking the call. My sister Audrey and I were close, but that didn't mean she gave me any slack.

"Hey big brother. How's it going in…What's the name of that town again?"

"Nice try, sis. You're on a need to know basis. And you don't need to know."

Audrey was three years my junior, but she still thought she knew everything, including what was best for me. It was rare when she didn't lecture, so I put the phone on speaker while I changed out of my work clothes.

"I didn't call to lecture you," she started, and I was glad she couldn't see the way I rolled my eyes. "Mom and Dad's anniversary is in a few months. We'll be having everyone up to the house for a party. I think you should be there."

"I don't think so. My being there will become the talk of the event, with everyone asking why I left and where I went. Don't want to take away from Mom and Dad's special day. I'll send them something."

She snorted. "Oh, get over yourself. Everyone knows what happened. And you could be easily found if we really tried. But I don't think anyone will have the balls to bother you. Except maybe Spencer. He has no shame."

Now it was my turn to snort. Spencer was our least favorite cousin, though we had all been close when we were young. He and I always seemed to be in an endless competition now that we were adults. Spencer also reported to my father at CB Resorts International, as the Director of Marketing and Sales, and he'd made no secret of his ambition to take over the company one day.

"Yeah, truth. I'm sure he's enjoying my absence. Hey, how are the kids?"

It bothered me that I hadn't been around when Audrey's last child Nathan was born, my newest nephew. But I couldn't admit to her that seeing her baby would have ripped my heart out, so I stayed away. Audrey and her husband, Richard, didn't need to be dealing with my sadness at such a happy time.

"They're still driving us nuts, now that we have three to deal with. But it's a good kind of crazy. Oh, and now Nathan is sitting up on his own."

"That's great." I didn't know what else to say.

Then Audrey's voice changed, indicating she was wrapping up the conversation.

"So think about it, huh? Make an appearance. You don't have to stay the weekend or anything. Mom has been so worried about you, and if you want to know the truth, I think Dad's not doing so well. He's under a ton of pressure, and he's not getting any younger. He tries to act like everything's fine, but he doesn't seem the same, you know?"

"I don't know. The man can afford to find someone to replace me, but he won't."

"Stubborn old fool."

"That he is. He told me yesterday that I have until my birthday to come back for good, or he'll cut me off."

Audrey whistled. "Bet you're scared now, considering you've done that already."

"That's what I said. He didn't think it was funny."

I ended the call, saying I'd think about coming to the party. As I hung up, I realized it might also be a chance to see if my father was serious about his threat.

And a test to see if I was really ready to give it all up for good.

~*~

Not So Broken

Sacha

After checking into my motel, I kicked off my shoes and collapsed on the bed. I'd managed to pick up more orders than I expected, and the largest one was from the dive bar the girl at the diner had told me about. I'd have to stop by and thank her tomorrow.

Between the drive and all the meetings, I figured I deserved a break. I lay back on the pillows and flipped on the television. Then I picked up my phone. Ignoring a tinge of guilt, I opened up the social media app Mom used to keep tabs on Kevin.

Why am I torturing myself like this? Lord knows I've got better things to do.

Yet I kept clicking through his posts, and sure enough, there was one formally announcing they were expecting. It was obviously a joyous occasion for them, with tons of people offering their congratulations in the thread.

It made me want to throw the phone across the room.

Guess his sperm count wasn't the problem after all.

I shut the app and tossed the phone onto the bed, but it responded with a buzz. I picked it up to see Melanie's smiling face on the screen.

"Hey Mel."

"Hey yourself. Are you there yet? You said you'd call the minute you got there."

"I just checked in. I was about to call but got distracted."

"By what? Or should I say, who?"

I hesitated. I didn't want to admit to what I had been doing. "Well… You're on the money, as usual. By Kevin's new wife's baby bump."

"Ew."

"Yeah. Apparently, they're both really fertile."

"Apparently. Why are you doing this to yourself?"

She was right. Why did I torture myself like this? "My mother called and got me going. She stalks them online regularly. All it does is piss me off."

"I don't blame you. The less you see of them, the better. Focus on what's ahead."

"Right."

Melanie was the only person I trusted with my plans for the future because she wouldn't judge, or tell me what I should do. She was

15

also the only one except my mom who knew the sordid details of Kevin's betrayal.

Triggered, no doubt, by the images of Kevin's page, the scene played out in my mind. When I had returned from my two-week stay at my mother's, I had no reason to believe anything was wrong. The recollection of what happened next was pissing me off all over again.

I was known for my quick temper, which I normally tried to control, except with the people who were close to me. It never seemed to bother Melanie. She understood my need to vent, so I did. "Was I really so blind, Mel? There must have been signs. You don't throw away a marriage on a whim."

She sighed. She'd talked me off the ledge of my anger many times before. "There may have been signs, but your focus was elsewhere. You had no reason to suspect anything from what you told me. He took advantage of the fact you were preoccupied with having a baby."

"Yeah. I was clueless, I guess. When I'd returned from my trip, I was ready to start all over and work on getting back the spark that had brought us together. Instead, I came home to find him waiting for me with that stern look on his face, like someone had died or something."

Images of that awful moment still made my stomach clench. "Kevin, what's wrong?"

His next words were a punch to the gut, one I never saw coming. "I'm moving out."

"What? Why on earth… What happened?"

He didn't look at me then but *through* me. As if he couldn't bear to look me in the eyes and tell me the truth.

"I'm with someone else. We're in love."

Not that it even mattered, but all I could stutter was, "Who is it?"

His new love was someone I didn't even know, someone he'd met online. The fact he would go behind my back and start a relationship was devastating enough, but it was his last words that sliced my heart into shreds.

"She's pregnant."

My stunned response seemed funny now, but at the time it was a wonder I could even get the words out. His manner was so cold, not at all the man I'd married. He'd already detached himself and was expecting me to accept it without warning. Once I got over my momentary shock, we had a huge argument about the situation. But it was useless. The bottom line was, he was leaving me for another woman who was having his baby.

Not So Broken

The baby that should have been *mine.*

I heard Melanie's voice, bringing me back to the present. "Sacha? You okay?"

I'd been silent for too long, reliving a day I was trying to forget. "Yes, I'm good now. Let them live their lives, and I'll live mine."

"Amen, sister. That's the right attitude."

I sat up a little straighter against the pillows. I was determined to handle life my way from now on. My history was simply that—history. My heart may have been broken, but I wasn't.

"You're right, I need to focus on my goal. I don't need a man in my life to accomplish that. My mom raised me alone, and I turned out fine."

Melanie's throaty chuckle made me laugh too. "You'll be more than fine, you're going to kick ass."

"Damn straight. That's why I'm in Tilly. If I can drum up a few good accounts, I'll be that much closer to a promotion and more money. If today is any indication, I have an excellent chance."

"You got this, girl. I believe in you."

"Thanks Mel, you're the best. I gotta run now."

I hung up and pulled out my tablet to review the orders. If I hit my sales numbers this month, the monetary goal I set for my savings account might be within reach. Then I'd have enough money to finally realize my dream. I'd already set the wheels in motion, and nothing could stop me.

I was going to adopt a baby and raise it on my own.

~*~

I must have dozed off while reviewing the orders. I woke around six p.m. with a growling stomach and decided a night out was in order. I'd go stir-crazy sitting in this tiny room thinking about the past.

I took a quick shower and dried my hair. I looked at my reflection in the wide hotel mirror. Not bad. I'd lost a few pounds since the divorce. A new, longer hairstyle showed off my chestnut waves, and contacts made my green eyes pop, instead of being hidden behind glasses. Not bad for thirty-seven. *And counting...*

My stomach nudged me for food again reminding me I hadn't had much of a lunch. A quick salad at one of the bars was all I'd had time for. The evening stretched ahead with nothing much to do, so dinner and a stroll through the shops in town sounded like a plan.

Ten minutes later, I was dressed in a summery skirt and blouse, my feet clad in wedged sandals. Who knew? Maybe later I'd even stop at that bar and listen to some music. Once I became a mother, these kinds of excursions would happen less often, as would dating. If I even dated at all. At Melanie's insistence, I'd signed up for one of those online dating sites months ago, but so far, I wasn't impressed. I'd met a few guys, went on some dates, but it was a waste of time and energy, to be truthful.

The adoption was all I really thought about these days. Becoming a mother, having a little one to love, was all I needed. I'd thought of in vitro, but with my history, there was the risk it still wouldn't work. Giving a good life to a child in need seemed to me the best possible outcome.

Though I had to admit, the idea of having one last fling before taking on the responsibilities of parenthood was tempting. It wasn't likely to happen, but perhaps if I met a nice guy, I might. But that was just another dream.

Shaking off the silly speculations, I grabbed my purse and walked out the door, into the night and an unknown future.

Chapter Three

Gibson

*I*t was close to sunset when I woke. The darkened cabin was silent, though a storm of images and sounds still raged in my mind. I'd fallen asleep on the sofa in front of the television earlier and had the dream again.

I sat up, rubbing my eyes, and the images faded. I needed air, desperately. I walked to the back deck and stood leaning over the rail, gulping. It was still humid, but without the sun beating down, not as stifling as it had been earlier.

I stared out over the ridge, illuminated in the deep orange glow of sunset. Soon the moon would rise and cast silvery shadows over the terrain. The mournful wail of a whippoorwill started up, echoing my mood, drowning out the last of the late summer cicadas buzzing in the trees.

It must've been the helicopter I'd heard while chopping wood yesterday that triggered my recurring dream. Every damn time I hear the staccato roar of a chopper's blades, I cringe. I've tried not to react, but it still gets to me.

I'd even dropped the damned axe, missing my foot by only an inch. Will I ever get used to that sound?

Probably not.

I needed a drink. I walked to the kitchen and grabbed a beer from

19

the fridge. The icy brew felt soothing as I chugged it down. My gasp of relief was followed by an ungentlemanly belch as I returned to the deck.

Scenes from the dream kept repeating in my mind, and the beer hadn't dulled my senses one bit. I propped my feet up on the railing and leaned back in my chair, closing my eyes. Best to let it play out, so I can get on with my evening.

Bianca. She was the love of my life. In the recurring dream, she was searching for me, calling my name. I'd answer but could never find her. I kept running, looking for her everywhere, hearing her cries. The sense that she was there, close but out of reach, was maddening. I'd wake up expecting to see her standing over me or lying by my side.

We'd been wed less than a year before I lost her. After a lavish wedding at my family's Atlanta estate overlooking the Chattahoochee River, we embarked on a month-long honeymoon. I showed her my favorite places—Tahiti, then Paris, and finally Switzerland. She'd never been out of the country, and I enjoyed her innocent sense of wonder and her excitement about seeing new places. It was like discovering them all over again.

After we returned, she moved into my high-rise condo near the office. She continued her graphic design work from home, so we were rarely apart. Whenever I traveled to scout locations or meet with prospective clients, she came along. We were inseparable. I had put my billionaire player lifestyle behind me the day I met her and couldn't be happier.

I leaned back in my chair and stretched, releasing a long sigh. My anxiety was easing at the thought of those happy times with Bianca, and a smile crept onto my face. The best day of all was the one she told me she was pregnant. We were going to be a family. We celebrated by staying in bed all day, watching family-style comedies and dreaming of how our lives would change.

I'd never dreamed that change would happen the way it had played out. All because I put work first, instead of her, and our child.

For that, I would never forgive myself.

~*~

Heading to the bar that night, I felt a twinge of guilt. I wasn't really interested in Dahlia that way, but when we flirted, it felt good. Was that so wrong? After debating in my head, I decided to go and if it didn't feel right, I'd politely excuse myself and come home. No harm in being friends. Besides, if I stayed home, I'd be feeling sorry for myself, and I

Not So Broken

didn't want to be that guy.

The Frisky Beaver was a funky dive bar on the outskirts of town, where the rows of shops and restaurants ended. Not the kind of place I was used to frequenting, but it had a fun vibe. The place was dark, crowded, and noisy. That was to be expected on a Friday night, and it seemed even the namesake stuffed beaver on the wall had a bucktoothed smile on his face.

It was well after nine and I'd been occupying a high-top table near the bar for a half hour. Dahlia hadn't showed. She probably couldn't get a sitter, so all my angst had been for nothing. With no one to talk to, I ordered a scotch and nursed it. I'd already eaten a sandwich on the way over, so I wasn't starving.

A microphone buzzed, and I looked to the stage.

"How's everybody doing tonight?"

The band's singer, who I guessed from the resemblance was Dahlia's brother, tried his best to engage the crowd. The music wasn't half bad, a mixture of rock and country. But I was more interested in people-watching. I had a game going in my head, trying to determine who were the locals, and the tourists. There were a few hot looking women, and some checked me out in return. It wasn't a bad way to pass the evening.

The alcohol was kicking in a bit, and so was the band. I hadn't been out like this in months, so it felt good to relax and forget about everything else. The scotch tasted damn good, even though it wasn't a premium brand, so I ordered another shot.

By the time the band took a break, I was ready to leave. I'd just reached for my wallet when a commotion started on the other side of the bar. A woman's voice rose above the crowd's chatter.

"I said *no*, dude. No thank you."

Looking in the direction of the voice, I saw a slender brunette attempting to evade the attentions of a drunk guy. The same woman I'd seen earlier in the diner, though she was dressed in a skirt and heels. No wonder the guy was interested. She was gorgeous. I looked around and saw several other guys in the bar had noticed her, too.

The drunk guy was tall, built like a linebacker, and stumbling as he tried to follow her. He grabbed her arm, causing her to spill her drink. She looked like she was about to punch the guy, but she shoved at him instead with her free hand. Then a blonde chick appeared out of nowhere and shoved the brunette onto one of the barstools.

"Back off, bitch! That's my man."

Brunette look stunned for a moment then recovered her balance. She placed her now-empty glass on the bar and faced her aggressor. In a voice sweet as Georgia tea, she cooed, "You can have him, honey. He's all yours."

Blondie was almost as tall as her man, who was watching the proceedings with a stupid leer on his face. She took a step closer to the brunette and got right in her face. She was ranting, probably drunk as well. The brunette's lips were drawn tight, and I could imagine what she was thinking.

The next thing I knew, I was walking across the bar. I leaned in between them, smiled, and placed an arm around the brunette's shoulder.

"There you are, Darlin'. I've been looking all over for you."

The stunned look was back on her face and on the blonde's face as well. The drunk guy let out a loud guffaw, and his girlfriend elbowed him. I maneuvered us through the crowd, back to my table before someone else could claim it, still holding on to my new friend. She let me lead her, leaning over to whisper, "Thank you."

When we reached the table, she still seemed shaken, so I gestured for her to sit. Once she was settled on the stool, I introduced myself.

"I'm Gibson. Welcome to Tilly."

She shook my outstretched hand but arched a brow at me. "Thank you for getting me out of that mess, but how did you know I'm from out of town?"

"Gut feeling. Besides, most of the people here on the weekends are tourists."

"I suppose you're not, then?"

"No. But I haven't lived here long. And you didn't tell me your name."

She seemed flustered for a moment, her cat-green eyes wide. "Oh, yes. I'm Sacha."

"Nice to meet you, Sacha."

I managed to catch the server's attention, and Sacha ordered a margarita, since her drink had been spilled. I also ordered another scotch. It seemed I'd found a reason to stay a little longer.

I watched her as she turned to look at the band, which had returned to the stage. She definitely had the air of a business person, one I might have met in downtown Atlanta for martinis. Not the type of woman one would expect to find in a dive bar, getting into a brawl. She had been sexy in her pantsuit, but in a skirt, she was dynamite. Her long

brown hair framed a heart-shaped face. "Sweet" was the word that came
to mind, but I sensed a toughness beneath her feminine exterior.

The silk of her blouse draped over her curves, and as she crossed
her legs, I was treated to a bit of thigh at the side of her skirt. When she
turned her head back toward me, I glanced up at the band, but her sly
look told me I'd been caught.

"So, Gibson. What else does your gut tell you about me?"

Her smile was taunting me, but I liked it. I liked it even more
when she sucked on the straw in her margarita then licked her lips,
though she probably didn't realize the effect the innocent gesture had on
me. I leaned over the table so she could hear me over the music, and it
was close enough to smell the scent of her perfume. Vanilla, with some
spice.

Like her.

"It's telling me you've been working way too hard for too long.
You need to relax, get a little wild tonight."

It was suggestive, but I wasn't faking it. Something about this
woman was drawing me in. I had no idea who she was or where she was
from, and for once, it didn't matter. Maybe the rush of rescuing her from
the clutches of Drunk Guy and his jealous girlfriend had made me feel
something I hadn't felt in a long time.

Like pride, and hope. And desire.

She cocked her head and gave me a strange look. "That's funny.
I was thinking the same thing earlier."

"Well, I'm happy to help."

We clinked our glasses together and she laughed.

The crowd was getting rowdy, and the dance floor was packed.
She'd finished her drink, so I ordered her another. When the band
changed songs, she clasped her hands together. I knew that cue.

I leaned over, close to her ear. "You like this song?"

"I love it. It's my jam."

"Let's dance then."

I held out my hand. She slid off the stool and let me lead her
to the dance floor. I hadn't danced with anyone since my wedding, so I
had no idea what had possessed me to offer. When I was single I'd gone
to dance clubs, but I'd have an exclusive room or table for entertaining
guests or clients, and no time for something as frivolous as this.

But here we were, moving to the sultry beat of an old blues tune
the band had rocked up. Sacha was inches away, as the crowd left little
room for movement. Her hips moved in a sensuous swirl, which I found

23

intoxicating. Her eyes were closed, and for a moment, she was lost in the song.

We moved in tandem. Her arms were raised above her head, swaying back and forth. Though I was getting elbowed and bumped into every other minute, there was no place I'd rather be. I placed my hands on her hips to keep her from getting plowed over by an enthusiastic dancer behind her, who ended up pushing Sacha against me. Her eyes opened wide, and then a slow, sensual smile graced her lips. She stayed right where she was, even after the other dancer moved away.

Maybe it was the scotch, or maybe I had been pent up too long. I found myself hoping for much more than a dance with this woman tonight.

~*~

Sacha

I couldn't recall how long it had been since I'd danced. Kevin never would, so it must have been somewhere in my mid-twenties the last time I was at a club, enjoying myself with abandon.

Abandon. That was a perfect word for what I was feeling right now, with this handsome stranger smiling down at me. It was really tempting me to let loose and shove my conscience aside for once. He was right, I had been working too hard for too long, and I deserved a little fun.

Didn't I?

Three margaritas hadn't hurt, either. I hardly even tasted the first one since that idiot spilled it.

But I'm so glad he did that…now.

Gibson, my rescuer, was tall and well-built, but not overly stocky like the drunk guy. He had a full beard, but it was neatly trimmed, and his blonde hair was slicked back. He looked the typical small-town worker guy, but something about him was…different. Despite the way he was dressed, in flannel and jeans, there was nothing "rough" about him. Watching him, I sensed an intelligence. There was power in the way he held himself. He radiated more CEO than blue collar.

As the song ended, his arms were still around my waist and he pulled me up off the floor. He held me up in the air, inches above him. Not at all the move I was expecting.

Not So Broken

I let out a gasp. "Oh!"

As he gradually released his hold, I slid down his body until my feet touched the floor again. I grabbed his biceps for balance, surprised at the hardness beneath my fingers. There was no denying his well-muscled physique was firm, causing a spear of heat to my center. The room spun for a second as I gained my equilibrium and stepped back.

I was sure my panties needed changing.

He hadn't completely let go of me yet, and as the band launched into a fast song, everyone around us started moving. The crowd was writhing and bouncing, yet he stood holding me, his head bent down, his lips inches from mine.

Oh, hell, why not?

His lips were warm and tender, an introduction. The pressure increased as his lips parted, and I opened as naturally as if I'd kissed him a million times before. The familiar taste of scotch tingled on my tongue as he deftly explored my mouth, making me drunk with excitement. I leaned into him, losing control. Before I could even think about what was happening, I heard someone in the crowd prompt others to watch us.

I honestly didn't care. The world had fallen away and all that mattered was this man, now claiming my mouth with his. His tongue was exploring, tasting me, and I couldn't escape the sensation of how thirsty he was for it. And how utterly hungry I had been for some attention like this.

My senses began to kick in and I drew away. He gave me a wolfish grin and led me back to the table. The pounding of my heart began to slow, but I was still quivering, recovering from that kiss.

Cross that one off my bucket list, because Gibson the mountain man is the best kisser ever. *What else can he do with that mouth?*

I pushed the thought away and looked back at him. There was a glow in his eyes, and his lips were curved into a wicked smile. It was almost a smirk. He knew I liked kissing him. Well, I did. Damn it.

I was about to suggest calling it a night before I completely lost my mind and my virtue, when the owner of the bar, a middle-aged man named Stuart, appeared at our table. I'd met with him earlier and he had placed a good-sized order. He had kept me there for almost an hour, telling me his life story and how he came to own the Frisky Beaver.

"Ms. Rowan, I thought that was you. Let me get you and your friend some drinks."

The band was on another break, so we were stuck while Stuart chatted on about nothing and everything. He kept getting interrupted as

25

patrons who knew him stopped by to say hello or clap him on the back as they passed. I accepted the drink, another margarita, to be polite, but only sipped at it in between nods at Stuart as he rambled on. My head was already starting to swim from the alcohol and being ravaged by Mr. Hot Beard's lips. I was usually a lightweight, and the few times I'd gotten really drunk, I had blacked out. So, it was better to quit while I still had my wits about me.

When Stuart finally moved on to another table, Gibson gave me the strange look I always get when people discover my profession.

"So, you sell booze?"

"I prefer the term, 'liquor distributor', thank you very much."

I was joking, but sometimes it did irritate me when people inferred my job was questionable. Alcohol had been around for thousands of years and wasn't going to disappear anytime soon. Someone had to sell it.

I gave him a look of faux indignation, to prove my point. He laughed.

"Well, you must be good at what you do. That guy seemed pleased."

"He got a hell of a deal, too. I was only up here for the day and he was my best client so far."

He downed the last of his drink, and I took another sip, though it was unlikely I would finish it, the way I was feeling.

"So where are you from, Miss Sacha?"

"Kennesaw. It's near Atlanta. A few hours from here."

For a moment, his gaze seemed fixed far away. Then he nodded. "I've heard of it. I actually used to live a bit south of there."

"Oh. So, how'd you end up here?"

The band was starting up again, so the music almost drowned out his words.

"I came for a visit and never left."

Chapter Four

Sacha

I ended up finishing that last margarita while he told me about Tilly and his favorite sights in the area. I had a hard time concentrating on his words when he was looking so damn good. I figured he was about my age—near forty, there were crinkles at the edges of his eyes—but he was still in great shape. If anything, that added to his appeal. He seemed to be a man who had been around, despite his casual appearance.

High cheekbones and aquiline nose gave him a regal bearing, but his deep blue eyes had a naughty sparkle. I sensed he was a man who appreciated the fine things in life and wasn't afraid to go after them. His choice of words, the way he spoke, everything but his clothes and slightly unkempt hair indicated he wasn't working class stock. My curiosity about him was growing, along with the annoying heat in my lower belly.

When he stopped talking, I had to ask, "What do you do for work?"

"Odd jobs, handyman stuff. I fix decks, install ceiling fans, that sort of thing."

I must have involuntarily raised a brow because he frowned. "There's enough of that type of work to keep busy up here?"

"Yeah. Lots of second homes, rental cabins, and retirees who don't want to do it themselves. I make enough to get by."

"That's great. Tilly seems like a nice place."

I pushed my empty glass to the side. His hand reached across the table and clasped over mine. "I wasn't even going to be here tonight, but I'm so glad I came."

I stilled as his thumb brushed provocatively over my knuckles. That and the look he gave me promised much more. His hand radiated a heat that sent waves of excitement rippling through me. My stomach fluttered like I was a damn schoolgirl talking to her crush. Or was it the tequila?

"Me too," I croaked. I cleared my throat and gave his hand a squeeze before withdrawing mine. "Thank you again for saving me. It was my first bar brawl, you know."

He chuckled, and I slid off the chair. I took a moment to steady myself, gathering my purse. Somewhere in my head, a pent-up, sexually frustrated version of Sacha was seriously contemplating asking him to my room for a nightcap. But the future mom, soon to be promoted salesperson, and ever-virtuous good girl Sacha was shaking her head and wagging a finger in warning.

As I walked through the bar to the exit, Gibson placed a firm hand at the small of my back, and I had a feeling I knew who was going to win the argument in my head.

~*~

Gibson

We were standing outside the bar. I hated for the night to end so soon but couldn't think of a cool line to say to keep her from leaving. Before, all I'd do was tell a girl my name and what I did for a living, and I couldn't pry her off me.

Not knowing what would happen somehow made it more exciting.

Sacha stood there, looking up at me, as though deciding what to do. "I think I need to get back to my motel. The margaritas have done me in."

Damn.

"Well, I wouldn't be much of a gentleman if I didn't see you safe. I'll escort you."

Not So Broken

To my own ears, my voice sounded thick, so maybe I was a little drunk too. I'd sleep it off in my truck, if necessary, but I'd rather hang out with her. The wary look she was giving me said she was thinking otherwise.

"That's okay, it's just over there."

She pointed to the motel across the street, but the gesture caused her to wobble on her heels. My arm came out instinctively to catch her before she fell.

"Whoa, I've got you."

She mumbled, "Thanks" but kept leaning on me, so I hooked her arm through mine and started in the direction of the motel. There was no way I was going to let her walk off on her own.

In minutes, we were at her door. She fumbled in her purse for the keycard then looked at me.

"Do you want to come in? I don't think you're in any shape to drive."

Dear God. I wanted to be with her more than anything at the moment, but I had to be sure it wasn't just the tequila talking. She was sexy as hell, but I wasn't going to take advantage of her and regret it later.

"Only if you want me to."

Her eyes said she did. She stood there, her keycard in hand, back against the door. She hadn't turned me down yet, so I inched closer. My hand came up to cup her face, and she didn't move away. Her delicate pink lips were slightly open, and her bottom lip quivered as I bent down to taste them again.

It was another scorching kiss, one that seemed to go on forever, but I really didn't want to make out in the hallway. I pulled back but only an inch or two, my breath quickening. She hadn't answered me yet and the wait was excruciating.

"Sacha, if you want me to come in, I need to hear you say it."

Her words were barely a whisper. "Yes. I do."

I said nothing more as she opened the door. Once inside, she flipped on a light and placed her purse on the desk, next to a cut-crystal bottle of amber liquid.

"Whoa, what is that?"

She held the bottle so I could see it. "A boutique label, small batch, rare whiskey. I offer samples to impress clients with our high-quality merchandise."

She popped the elegant crystal-topped lid off, and the aroma set my mouth watering. I hadn't had any of the really good stuff since I came to Tilly. No way did I need any more alcohol, but this I had to sample.

"May I? Only a taste."

She nodded and picked up a plastic cup. "Sorry I don't have a proper glass."

"It's okay."

The scent of honey and wet wood hit my nose. As I sipped, my tongue burned for a split second and then warmed. There were notes of cedar and orange, with a faint herbal finish. Delicious.

"Well?"

Her hopeful gaze almost made me chuckle, but I was too busy savoring. Warmth spread immediately from my neck down, not that any of it needed warming.

"Wow. That's nice."

"Thank you. Now, where were we?"

I set the cup on the desk as she grasped my hand and led me to the bed. My heart was doing flip-flops in my chest, and my head was buzzing so much I began to fear I'd had too much alcohol. Sacha sat on the bed and I eased down next to her.

She kicked off her shoes and I did the same. With a shy look, she lay back on the bed. I leaned over and lay next to her, propped up on one elbow.

"I think we were right about...here..."

I wrapped my free arm around her waist and leaned down to kiss her.

There was nothing more to say. There was only one reason we were here, together like this—desire had taken over and reason was out the window. It may not have made sense logically, but if felt so damn right.

She might be gone in the morning, but we'd always have this one passion-filled night to remember. I planned to make it one she'd never forget.

Though I was still tipsy from the drinks, I had enough control of my senses to go slow with her. It took some effort to resist the urge to rip her clothes off, but I made a point of taking my time. She was moaning and her breath was ragged, so it seemed she was enjoying it. I kissed a path along her jaw, then her neck, and worked my way down to her collarbone. As I licked the sensitive flesh at the base of her throat, a memory flashed of Bianca. I opened my eyes, so I could focus only on Sacha and not the intrusive memory.

Her eyes were closed. She seemed lost in sensation, so I kept my hands moving across her skin. I sat up and tugged at the edge of her silky blouse. She rose up enough to take it off, revealing an equally silky peach lace bra. Her breasts were not large but well-shaped. After a moment to admire the view, I placed a kiss on the curve of one breast, eliciting a gasp and a shiver from her. My other hand was inching its way under her skirt, caressing her thigh, and moving higher. As my fingers touched the satiny material of her panties, she took in a sharp breath.

"You like that?"

"Yes," she whimpered.

Making circular patterns with my fingertips on her mound, I used the other hand to unhook her bra. She needed no prompting, easing out of the bra to toss it aside. I lost control right then because my mouth *needed* to taste her. I immediately took one pink peak and nibbled it. Sacha grabbed my head, holding me to her chest, on a low groan of pleasure.

Her other hand was under my shirt, teasing my nipple with her nail. Our legs were intertwined, and her thigh moved to press against my crotch. My erection moved in response, and my resolve to go slow crumbled. If we didn't get these clothes out of the way soon, I was afraid I might come right there.

Her next words nearly pushed me over the edge.

"I want you inside me. Now."

I stood to take off my jeans, and as my clothes hit the floor, I wondered where I'd put the condoms I'd bought earlier. *Crap.* They're in the truck. I'd figured if I actually did hook up with Dahlia, we'd go back to my place. A midnight tryst with a sexy stranger at a motel was never on the agenda.

As much as I wanted to bury myself in her right now, I couldn't. I stood there naked, evidence of my desire standing at full attention. Sacha was naked now too, spread out before me on the bed and looking at me like a cat about to lick the hell out of a bowl of cream.

Fuck.

"I can't. I forgot my condoms."

~*~

Sacha

Renee Regent

The room was tilting. How much tequila had I consumed? Too much, obviously.

The hottest thing on two legs was standing over me with a pained expression on his face. He looked like some kind of bronzed god, or maybe more like a Viking, due to the beard. A very horny Viking from the looks of what was between his legs, though now it was starting to flag. He was waiting for me to say something, but all I could think of was the raging heat radiating from my core. This was so not like me, to get carried away with lust like this, but I didn't feel like myself at all tonight. I seemed to be living in some kind of perverse dream.

Reason was slowly returning, so I sat up and put my hands to my face and rubbed. When I looked up, he was still watching me. Then the import of his words began to make sense to my lust-addled, inebriated brain.

"Sit," I commanded, patting the bed.

He sat next to me. "I'm sorry. I wasn't expecting—"

"Neither was I. I don't ever do this kind of thing."

He looked down at his hands. He smiled without looking at me, his cheeks pink above his blond beard. "Truth be told, I haven't been with anyone for a long time. I guess I'm a bit rusty."

It didn't sound like a line. How many guys would stop mid-makeout like he just did? Not many, unfortunately. My racing hormones were beginning to calm, and I felt some empathy for the guy.

"It's okay. I'm a bit rusty too. I haven't been with anyone since my divorce, over a year ago."

He gestured to his chest with a thumb. "Widowed."

An awkward silence followed. We were both naked, so what was there to hide now?

"Well, I still don't think you should drive. Where do you live, anyway?"

His eyes shifted away for a moment. When he looked back at me, they were a soft, warm shade of blue, like faded denim.

"I have a cabin up the mountains. About twenty minutes from here."

When was I ever going to get a gorgeous guy like this naked in my bed? No strings, purely enjoyment. A last blast before I became a parent. Isn't that what I'd wished for earlier?

How could I kick him out now?

"Well, it's probably safe to say we're both clean, but even without the condoms there are things we can do, right?"

32

Not So Broken

It sounded like someone else saying those words, not me. His face lit up at the suggestion, but I caught a flash of wariness in his eyes. "Right, but...are you sure? I want you in the worst way, but we both had a bit too much to drink."

I wanted him too. No denying that. It wasn't only the alcohol making me feel that way, either. "I'm sure."

Before I took another breath, he had pulled me onto his lap. His mouth assaulted my lips, and I grabbed onto his full beard with both hands and slammed my mouth against his. I couldn't get enough of his taste, and the shock of skin against skin was thrilling. Crisp chest hair tickled my nipples as I pressed against him. His erection had returned full force, rubbing me exactly where it counted. By instinct, I responded by grinding against it. I was about to explode from the friction when he stood up, carrying me along with him. He turned to face the bed and laid me down.

I scooted back so my head was against the pillows. He was on all fours above me, inching his way down my body by placing kisses, bites, and licks as he went. I couldn't remember the last time I'd done this, especially since my ex wasn't fond of pleasing me this way. Anticipation had my heart banging against my ribs, and I had a moment of worry about how it would taste to him. As soon as he settled in between my thighs and began, every thought in my head dissolved.

That first lick was like a shock to my most neglected part. Nerve endings sprang to life, shooting sparks of bliss with every touch. He was gentle at first, exploring my folds with lips and tongue, with one hand splayed across my stomach to still my writhing. I couldn't help it. My voice sounded far away, but it was moaning, grunting, and sputtering. Not quite eloquent, but I didn't care.

Neither did he, apparently. He doubled his efforts, nibbling on the sensitive bud, swirling his tongue in an exquisite manner. When he suddenly nipped at one of my larger folds, I cried out. Pain and pleasure intertwined, taking me to a new level of desire. Clutching the bedsheet, I spread my legs wide to accommodate his onslaught. Seconds later, I stiffened as my climax neared, followed by wave after wave of release. I heard myself crying out something unintelligible, and then a gasp as I fell from the precipice of sensation.

He withdrew and I rolled onto my side, legs drawn up. I was still convulsing with aftershocks of pleasure. It was the longest orgasm of my life.

I felt a hand on my hip.

"Sacha, are you okay?"

"Yes. I mean, I will be. Oh my God."

He chuckled, a smug sound. "I guess you liked it, then?"

I turned to face him, now that I could breathe again. "Hell, yes."

I could still feel some of the effects of the alcohol. Now I felt drowsy from the release, too, but he had pleased me so well, I wanted to please him.

He was lying on his back against the pillow, so I raised myself to straddle his lap. I kissed him, embarrassed and aroused by my musky scent on his lips. Mimicking his earlier movements, I began a journey down his torso, licking, nipping, and tasting as I went. A quick look at his face and I saw surprise in his eyes. I stopped, and he touched my face.

"Darlin' you don't have to just because I did that."

"I want to."

I really did. I wanted to experience as much as I could this night. I'd never see him again. We were two souls who needed each other, coming together in a perfect moment that would never be repeated. No strings, no expectations. Sharing a night to remember after we'd parted.

I bent to my task, eager to please him the way he pleased me.

~*~

Gibson

The effects of the alcohol still made my head swim, but it hadn't diminished my ability to feel every delicious thing Sacha was doing to me. In fact, I think it had dulled my sensitivity just enough that I didn't come too soon. Which was fantastic because I didn't want this to end.

For a woman who said she was "rusty" at sex, she was doing a damn fine job. Her enthusiasm while going down on me was impressive, as was her technique. She took her time, beginning first by licking and biting my thighs, and then teasing her tongue across my balls. Working her way up the shaft to the tip, varying her strokes from gentle to vigorous—it was an exquisite torture I was happy to endure.

She couldn't take my entire length in her mouth, but she gave it a hell of a try. The way she was using her lips, hands, and tongue, I was surprised I held out as long as I did. When I warned her I was about to come, she got even more excited and doubled her efforts, pushing me over the edge. She kept her mouth on me, taking in everything I had to give.

I was grateful, satisfied, and humbled. I had wanted to make the night memorable for her, but she had definitely done the same for me. I felt like an ass for forgetting the condoms, but as I took her in my arms and turned out the light, her soft sigh let me know I had been redeemed.

~*~

It was one of those dreams again, where I could feel, see, and hear everything. This time, I even smelled her—Bianca. She'd always worn the scent of gardenias. It was spicy, sweet as vanilla, and intoxicating. She knew it drove me crazy and purposely wore it when she wanted to seduce me.

I pulled the warm feminine body closer, spooning her. She made a noise, a cross between a sigh and a moan, and pressed her soft bottom against me. I hardened immediately. My free hand caressed the curve of her hip then slid over the softness of her breast. It fit neatly in the palm of my hand, so I made lazy circles over the peak with my thumb. She made a guttural sound, which only served to make me harder. When she pressed her ass against me again, I moved forward and found her wet, hot opening. The impact almost made me cry out.

Then the warm female body next to me stiffened.

"What are you doing?"

I came awake, startled by Sacha's voice. My dick was still hard, poised at her slick entrance. Embarrassment and shock rippled through me, and I pulled back.

"I'm sorry. I was dreaming, I guess. I didn't realize…"

She turned to face me. In the darkened room, I could see only the outline of her form. I didn't know if she was angry, so I held my breath. Her voice was slightly above a whisper when she finally spoke.

"I didn't hate it."

"Neither did I."

That was an understatement. My erection had softened slightly, but her words brought it to life again. The temptation to take her was strong when she was warm, naked, and so close. I leaned forward to kiss her, intending to tell her it was okay if she didn't want to go any further. Even though it was killing me to resist.

Instead, she muttered, "Oh, what the hell," wrapped an arm around me, and kissed me hard.

Sacha lifted her leg up and hooked it over my hip to allow me access. I pushed forward with a gasp, feeling her tightness swallow me up. Her soft moans fueled me on, wanting to please her but needing to take her roughly at the same time. Each thrust brought immense pleasure, and some part of me thought it might still be a dream. It felt unreal, but at the same time, nothing had ever felt so right.

Her hips were bucking as she ground against me. Our ragged breath, in tandem, was the only sound. I struggled to hold off my orgasm, waiting for a sign that she had reached a peak. A few seconds later, she cried out, her insides clenching repeatedly. I lost control and shuddered as I groaned my own release.

A sheen of sweat broke on my brow as I collapsed back onto the bed, withdrawing from her body. I had no regrets, as long as she was pleased. As my heart began to slow its pace, I reached out to touch her face in the dark.

"You okay, darlin'?"

She let out a "whew" noise. "Yes. More than okay."

"Good."

I turned on my side and pulled her against me. This was a night to remember, for sure.

Chapter Five

Sacha

*N*oisy people in the hallway jarred me awake with a start. Sunlight edged the dark curtains of the motel room, and I had to blink to focus. My head was pounding. There was a churning sensation in my stomach, and for a moment thought I might be sick. I sat up, only then recalling I wasn't alone.

He was tangled in the sheets and snoring lightly. There's something about a naked man wrapped in a white bedsheet, especially a hot, Viking-ish one. I studied him like one would a strange, beautiful creature in a zoo, wanting to remember every detail later.

His blond hair stuck out in tufts and his broad shoulders rose and fell with his soft breathing. He hugged the pillow like a child with a teddy bear. I smiled. His strong, muscular back and sculpted arms were all grown-up man, but asleep he was like an innocent child.

Well, not so innocent. Reminders of his prowess lingered on my lips, which were bruised from hard kisses and irritated from his beard. The things his lips and tongue had done… I'd never forget. I was still wet between my legs.

Like, weirdly wet. And sore.

A fragment of a dream flashed through my alcohol-muddled mind. Being taken by some fierce warrior, grabbing my breast, breathing his hot breath on my neck. Had it been a dream? If so, it was a realistic one. But we had both been a little drunk. I could hardly recall getting from the bar to my room. It had to have been a dream because I did remember Gibson saying something about not having condoms.

Then it hit me.

We *had* made love, in every way. Too bad I could only recall fragments of it because I had the sense it was enjoyable. Even so, it was probably not what we should have done. I looked over at my snoring companion and sighed.

"Too late for regret now."

I doubted there would be any complications from this, except for maybe some guilt. I had just finished my period two days earlier, and since Kevin the Fruitful hadn't been able to get me knocked up after a year of trying, I wasn't worried about getting pregnant.

Naked, I slipped out of bed and carefully walked to the bathroom. There were circles under my eyes, and my mouth felt like I'd been chewing on sandpaper. I brushed my teeth, washed my face, and donned a robe. When I came out, my guest was up and making coffee.

"Good morning, you."

His smile was bright, so despite my still-pounding head, I smiled back. "Good morning. Sleep well?"

"Like the dead. I always do when I've been drinking whiskey. Puts me out cold."

"I was out pretty heavy myself. Must be the mountain air."

He poured some coffee and handed me a cup. While we finished dressing, an awkward silence ensued. What do you say to a stranger the morning after? If there was some sort of protocol, I couldn't recall.

Gibson cleared his throat so I looked up at him. He set the coffee mug on the desk and buckled his belt. "Well, I guess you need to be getting on, so I'll be out of your hair."

"Well, yes. I need to get home. Have to check out soon."

We stared at each other for a moment, and then he opened his arms wide.

"A hug? It was a wonderful night."

I crossed the room and fell into his arms. It was a good hug, not exciting like on the dance floor, but friendly and warm. "Yes, it was."

He released me but stood still like he had more to say. He was gorgeous, but the sooner he left, the better. The last thing I wanted was to start wondering where he was or what he was doing. I had no place in my life for a man.

He moved toward the door then turned back to me. "I would say I'll call you, but that wouldn't be fair."

I felt my mouth drop open. Heat infused my cheeks, and the last of the hangover fled as my temper soared. What an ass.

"Not if you don't mean it. And that's rather presumptuous of you. Who said I expected to see you again?"

Now his mouth was open. When he found his voice, he stammered. "I didn't mean it like that. I was simply being honest. I didn't want you to get the wrong idea. I'm not ready to see anyone, even though I think you're awesome."

I could not contain my sarcasm. "Well, thanks for the compliment. And I know what a one-night stand is. I also know when someone is being a dick. So, bye-bye, so long. Farewell."

His face was pained again, like it had been last night. His deep blue eyes had a downward tilt to them, making him look like a sad puppy. I ignored it and opened the door for him.

He paused. "I'm sorry if I upset you. Good luck with your work."

Once he was in the hallway, I slammed the door.

After a shower, some aspirin, and two cups of coffee, I was feeling human again. I also felt bad about how our time together ended. He had seemed so nice last night. Had I overreacted? Had guilt prompted my bad temper at his words?

After all, he was just being honest. I knew what he'd said was true. But who wanted the truth after a drunken night of lust?

Better to chalk it up to experience and move on.

Once I checked out, I said goodbye to Tilly, Georgia. Somehow, I sensed a new chapter of my life was beginning.

~*~

Gibson

On my way home, I stopped at the diner for a hangover-curing greasy breakfast. Dahlia wasn't working, and the surly waitress who brought my food seemed to be in an even worse mood than I was. Who could blame me? My anger at Sacha, for giving me the bum's rush after such a great night together, had bothered me more than my aching head and sour stomach.

No one had ever kicked me out before, and I wasn't sure what to make of it.

Once my belly was full and the caffeine began to kick in, I decided it was almost amusing. If she took my words the wrong way, there was nothing I could do about it now. I couldn't even apologize, since we never exchanged numbers. Maybe I should have kept my thoughts to myself and said goodbye.

In any case, it had been a memorable night, but it was history now.

Before I reached my cabin, I pulled up to Marvil's place to check on him and to drop off some of the firewood I'd chopped and left in the back of my truck. I stacked the bundles in a pile on the side of Marvil's deck, which was covered, so it could dry out for use in the winter. The old man was too cheap to pay the tourist prices in town for firewood and too stubborn to admit he couldn't chop it himself. So, I had taken to dropping a few bundles into his pile now and then.

It was the least I could do for a friend. Though Marvil vigorously lived up to his reputation for being a grouch, he seemed to like me. That didn't mean he pulled any punches when it came to giving his opinion, which he did as soon as he saw me on his deck.

"Why aren't you at work by now? You act like a damned tourist on vacation."

Still dressed in his robe and slippers, his bone-thin legs were uncovered. They were hairy but not as fuzzy as his slippers, which resembled two large, furry bear claws. Marvil had a sense of humor few people saw. But I knew.

He handed me a Styrofoam cup filled with dark, fragrant coffee. It was a small gesture, but it spoke volumes about the decent human being beneath the crusty façade.

"Thanks, Marvil. There's a chill in the air this morning."

"Yes, there is. You know, it's too late for me, but you ought to find a woman to keep you warm this winter. I saw how that waitress at the diner was eyeing you."

He winked and I smiled, feeling my cheeks heat. "If I need matchmaking services, there's plenty online. But thanks."

Marvil waved his hand in distaste. "Bah. Computers. I've lived fine all these years without one. Not going to start now."

I leaned against the railing and sipped from the cup while Marvil rambled on about various topics. I nodded, or made affirmative noises, but said nothing. I knew better than to debate with the man. He was a product of his time, like my father and grandfather. I'd never told Marvil the real reason I'd come to Tilly, and he hadn't pried. But he'd throw out a probing question every now and then, catching me off guard. I couldn't blame him for being curious about his tenant.

I handed Marvil the empty cup. "Well, I better get going. I have to meet with a guy about a job I'm starting soon."

"You up for fishing, maybe next weekend?"

"Sure. Let's do that."

I'd never had an interest in fishing in my former life, but Marvil's enthusiasm for the sport, and his companionship, had slowly changed my opinion. We had a secret spot on the river where the fish seemed to bite often, and we'd go every few weeks. It was the only exercise the old man got, and I found the ritual of it soothing.

The rest of my day went downhill from there. I waited at the job site but the guy who was supposed to meet me never showed. He'd finally texted a half hour after the appointed time to say he wasn't going to make it. Then as I was leaving, my truck tire picked up a nail in the gravel road, so I had to change out the tire.

By late afternoon, I was cranky and tired. If I couldn't start the job next week, the delay would put my finances behind. I refused to touch my savings. I wanted to prove I could survive on my own. When I was living the high life, there had been plenty of stress—multimillion-dollar deals could get fucked up all sorts of ways, costing the company big time. I was used to monumental pressure. But this was different. This was living how most people lived, hand to mouth, not knowing what was going to happen tomorrow. It was humbling and made me grateful for every good thing that had happened in my life.

Exhausted, I pondered this and more as I trudged up the steps to my little cabin, my current sanctuary. If I ever returned to my family and the job at CB Resorts International, I'd do things differently. The many nameless people who worked for us had lives, hopes, dreams, and families they loved. I would make it a priority to show appreciation for them more often. Having money didn't automatically make you a better person, and sometimes it made things worse.

When it came right down to it, my family's entire fortune hadn't been enough to save Bianca and our baby.

But now, I was surviving one day at a time until I could decide what I was meant to do with this life.

~*~

Much to my frustration, even after a week had gone by since that night with Sacha, I couldn't get her off my mind. Perhaps it was guilt over my poor choice of words when we parted, or maybe it was plain old lust. My rusted-over libido had been jumpstarted that night, and erotic fantasies had been haunting my dreams and tormenting me during the day as well.

I knew I really should forget her. We hadn't exchanged phone numbers, and I was unable to find her online. I didn't know why I'd even bothered to look, she'd made it clear she didn't want to see me again. I could probably get her number from the owner of the Frisky Beaver, but what would I say? Even if she accepted my apology, we lived too far apart to start dating.

It was best to let her go. We had a moment, and it was over.

A peach-colored sky showed through the trees as I made my way down the hill to pick up Marvil. It was Saturday and we were heading to his favorite spot on the river to fish. It was several acres of prime land right on the Chattahoochee, apparently owned by someone Marvil knew. He'd never mentioned the owner by name but warned me to keep our visits a secret. I wasn't sure we even had permission to trespass there, but I figured if the old man was willing to risk it then so was I.

It was a miracle the land had sat vacant all these years. It was gorgeous—a gentle slope to the river, which tumbled over small boulders with a waterfall effect. It was the kind of place that should be pictured on a calendar or a motivational poster. But I had to admit, it was a damn good fishing spot, so I was glad it was undeveloped.

Except my years of experience and business acumen told me it was also the perfect spot for a resort, and I couldn't help imagining what that might look like. There was room for a hotel, cabins, a pavilion, gardens, and even a luxury home up on the hill, overlooking the whole thing.

But I was no longer in that line of work and besides, CB Resorts International had plenty of options. They wouldn't miss out by not having property in one little mountain town.

"Ready?"

I called the question to Marvil, who was standing in front of his old log cabin. The man's comical fishing outfit made me laugh, a sound that was ignored as Marvil climbed into the truck. His beat-up fishing hat was weighed down with lures and buttons, as was his multi-pocketed vest. Baggy jeans and an old gray sweatshirt with Mickey Mouse on it completed the ensemble.

He snorted and looked straight ahead. "Shut up and drive. The fish have been up for hours already."

"Yes, sir."

I put the truck in gear and maneuvered around the giant rut in the road, which Marvil refused to fix. As we bumped along, I complained, though I knew it wouldn't do any good.

"Marvil, when are you going to add gravel to this road? Some grading would help tremendously."

"It ain't free unless you want to pay for it. Plus, it keeps out nosy strangers."

He had a point. No one would take a drive up this rough mountain road unless they had to. It was another reason why I had yet to bring a woman back to my place.

When we arrived at the property, we had to park the truck and hike the last quarter mile or so. Once our poles were in the water, Marvil's questions began.

"So, did you go fishing as a kid? Your dad probably took you, huh?"

Immediately, a memory flashed of the one time I had fished with my father on a deep-sea expedition off the California coast. I was sixteen, and by that time, Dad had started the family business with several investors. One of which had his own yacht, so we had been invited for a weekend trip to Catalina Island.

"Yeah, once. But it was ocean fishing. In California."

"Is that where you're from? La-la Land?"

The old man smirked at his own joke then threw his line back into the water. He'd been casting and trolling, while I let my pole be.

"No. It was a vacation. I'm from Atlanta originally. But it may as well be California these days."

"Never been to either of them. Here's where I'm from, here's where I'll die."

I had met many people from Tilly who had expressed the same sentiment. It amazed me how they were content to stay close to home, with no desire to see the world. But then, I was used to traveling and had been blissfully unconcerned with the cost. For some of the folks I knew now, a day trip to Atlanta would be considered a splurge. It didn't make them lesser people. Some of them worked harder and had more determination and integrity than half the people I knew in my former life.

Had I been one of those people? Had my success been earned or simply handed to me?

The solitude of the fishing spot tended to bring these deep questions to mind. Thankfully, Marvil was here to distract me. He cleared his throat and launched into another inquiry.

"So, are you ever going to tell me about your new lady friend?"

Ice shot through my veins. I hadn't run into anyone I knew when leaving Sacha's motel room, but it was a small town. Hard to go unnoticed when you wanted to. I played dumb, hoping to find out who talked.

"What lady friend?"

"The guy who works at the drugstore has a cousin whose niece saw you at the Frisky Beaver last Friday night, getting cozy on the dance floor."

Of course. The random-guy-cousin-niece connection. I should have known.

"There's nothing else to talk about in this town?"

"Oh, sure. But I've already heard the gossip about them. You're still new, don't ya know."

"Hmmpf."

Marvil snickered. "I guess that's a no, huh?"

It was all I would say. I definitely didn't want to talk about a casual encounter and draw more attention to myself. The rumors were already rampant, though I'd kept a low profile.

I'd just leave it to their imaginations and move on.

Chapter Six

Sacha

Nearly two months had passed since the trip to Tilly, and I was on a roll. It seemed since I'd allowed myself to let loose and have a one-night stand, my luck really had changed. My attitude certainly had as well—now I no longer doubted I was meant to live the life of my dreams.

It had been announced at work that a large corporation was taking over the company soon. The merger meant more product lines, and hopefully a chance for smaller territories. As it was, I drove all over hell and creation on a regular basis. Melanie, when she actually saw me, joked that I was living in my car. It wasn't far from the truth.

"But that's what it takes to gain accounts. I've added several in the past few months, and they are consistent buyers so far."

Melanie had countered with the one argument I couldn't refute. "Your car is not a great place to raise a kid, though."

"That's why I need this promotion. Or at least a smaller territory."

I'd heard rumors that I was on the short list for the Regional Manager position opening up in Atlanta. It would mean more responsibility but less traveling.

That would be perfect. I'd already contacted a few adoption agencies where single parents were welcome. The approval process would take time, but I was moving forward, and that was what was important.

I had a rare Saturday with nothing planned, so Melanie and I went shopping that morning at a nearby outlet mall. I knew it was premature, but I couldn't help browsing the children's clothing and furniture shops. As we "oohed" and "aahed" over tiny baby clothes, Melanie made an observation.

"Your mom would love to be here doing this, you know."

I shrugged. "I know. I'm not ready to tell her until it's set. Otherwise, she'll be asking for updates every five minutes."

"I get it. But maybe she needs some hope too. I'm sure she was disappointed about not having grandchildren. God knows my mom has been pretty vocal about it, even though my sister has more than her share already with three kids."

I set down the pair of tiny baby shoes I was holding. Why was I tempted to buy them, when I had no idea how old the baby I adopted might be? This was becoming an unhealthy obsession. "That's just it. I don't want to get her hopes up. What if I chicken out? Or I don't get approved?"

Melanie touched my arm, a reassurance I desperately needed. "You'll do fine. You're going to be a great mom."

God, I hoped so.

If I wasn't a great mom, it wouldn't be for lack of preparation. I had everything planned out, from what foods we'd eat, to day care options, to which pediatricians were nearby, to which school my child would attend. But was I really emotionally ready to be a parent?

Is anyone ever ready for that?

I turned back to Melanie and touched her arm. Her faith in me was inspiring. "Thanks, Mel. I'm still nervous, but I know I'm meant do this."

We left the children's store and passed a lingerie shop. Melanie winked at me, pointing to a racy red plaid ensemble on a mannequin.

"So, have you heard from your mountain man yet?"

"No. And I'm glad. He was an ass."

"I thought you said he had a great ass. My mistake."

She was giggling, and I was trying not to. "He did. And he was. Case closed."

"Too bad."

I hadn't told Melanie I'd already searched for him online but came up empty-handed. I recalled his name was Gibson, but he never told me his last name.

It didn't matter. I'd almost forgotten him after my initial search. Until we parted, it had been fun—what I could recall of it. Exciting images of nakedness and pleasure comingled in my mind with fragmented moments of nausea and room-spinning. It was a wonder I hadn't thrown up on him.

There was a reason why I rarely drank, besides being surrounded by alcohol and in bars constantly. I was a lightweight.

"Well, it was a fun one-night stand. Nothing more. Now it's out of my system, I can forget about men and focus on becoming a mom."

Melanie high-fived me. "Right on, sister. And I'm going to be Auntie Mel."

Yes, things were falling into place just the way I wanted them.

~*~

I spent the rest of the day not doing a damn thing. I was in my pajamas at four in the afternoon when Melanie stopped by to borrow an iron. She held up a wrinkled satin blue dress that looked like it had been in her closet since the 'nineties.

"You sure you don't want to go out tonight? We're checking on this club where we might be having a gig soon."

I was searching in my closet for the iron, something I'd used only once since Mom gave it to me as a housewarming gift when I moved into the apartment. "Nah. I'm so tired today. I guess all that running around we did has caught up with me."

"Are you sick?" She made a cross with her fingers in warning. "Whatever it is, I don't want it."

The iron was still in its box, and I laid it on the coffee table. "Nah. It's like my period keeps trying to start but never does. I'm all bloated too. Another reason to stay home."

Melanie threw the dress over the back of a chair and flopped down on the sofa. "Well, it's good to see you relaxing for a change. Have your periods been erratic? Maybe you're getting into menopause. I mean, like pre-menopause. That's an actual thing."

"I doubt it. I'm not that old. Am I? And my periods have always been erratic."

The idea of getting old had been weighing on my mind lately. My biological urge to have a child had been strong for years, and I knew time was running out. That was also a reason to adopt instead of trying in vitro. But was my body really starting to change?

Melanie laughed. "Well, neither one of us is getting any younger. But at least I can still fit into this dress from my college days."

We were interrupted by a knock on the door. I looked through the peephole and let out a squeal of delight.

"Oooh! My Chinese food is here. I've been craving it all week."

After the delivery guy left, so did Melanie. I dined in front of the television and binge-watched Game of Thrones. I'd opened a bottle of wine but found it tasted sour, though it was one I'd had before and loved. Must have gone bad. I opened a can of ginger ale instead, and it helped to settle my stomach.

I hadn't told Melanie about the text I'd received that morning from my boss. He'd requested a meeting first thing Monday morning, at his office. He didn't disclose the reason, so my imagination had been working overtime. Either I was getting the promotion or being fired. Both scenarios caused anxiety, which I was trying to assuage by more binge-watching. It wasn't helping.

I didn't sleep much Saturday night. My anxiety had been so bad I even threw up a few times. Finally, I dressed and did some grocery shopping Sunday morning to get my mind off the upcoming meeting, but my stomach acted up again with all the sights and scents of food.

I'm falling apart. So not the time for this.

I was being ridiculous. Several people had told me they thought I was one of the hardest-working reps at the company. That reputation had been a challenge to earn, being a woman in what was traditionally a man's profession. I had overcome opposition and outdated attitudes among my co-workers, and even some members of management.

There was no way this meeting was going to be a bad thing. It had to be good news. I totally deserved it.

~*~

Gibson

Sunday, the day of my parent's anniversary party, I decided to make a surprise appearance. Maybe it was the guilt again for disappearing, or maybe it was plain old curiosity over how they were getting along without me. Still, I was not ready to reveal everything, so I parked my truck in the Walmart parking lot and waited for a shared ride. I was dressed in jeans and a button-down shirt, and had my hair and beard trimmed, but those were the only concessions I made for this trip home. The less they all knew about my new life, the better.

That conviction didn't ease the queasiness in my stomach on the drive to Colebank Manor. That wasn't a real name, but a nickname Audrey and I made up years ago. It was not the only house my parents owned, but it was the one they'd had the longest. It was their base of operations and not far from the CB Resorts International headquarters in Atlanta.

It was also my personal favorite since I grew up there. My nervousness gave way to nostalgic anticipation as we entered the gates at the bottom of the long driveway. The main house sat up on a rise, overlooking the river on one side and the Atlanta skyline on the other. My driver, who was probably a college kid, muttered in awe under his breath as we entered the flagstone circular parking area, bordered by three garages. Each one held three cars, and the doors were made of elaborately carved wood. A fountain graced the center of the circle with three stone mermaids in the center, pouring water from clay pots they held.

Yeah, my beat-up old pickup truck would have looked just fine here.

I handed the driver a twenty for a tip, though it hadn't been a long ride. After gathering my bag from the trunk, I steeled myself for the onslaught. I watched the car disappear down the drive and felt a moment of panic. I was trapped.

I can always call for another car. Best to get this over with.

"Gibbie!"

It was my mother, Angela McDonough Colebank. I knew despite her cheerful greeting, I was about to get an earful. I ascended the few steps to the front door, and she pulled me into a hug. She patted my back affectionately and whispered in my ear.

"Oh, how I've missed you." Then she took a step back and gave my cheek a good pinch. "That's for being gone so long."

It didn't hurt much, but I got the message. "Nice to see you too, Mom." I rubbed my cheek and followed her into the house.

As we entered the foyer, there were shouts from the other rooms as assorted relatives and friends came to see me. In moments, I was surrounded, and the faces had various expressions from joy to skepticism to a downright scowl. The last was from my father, standing a few feet away, his arms crossed over his chest.

I didn't meet his eye. Thankfully, my aunt swept me into a distracting hug. She was my father's sister, and they were always in competition over something.

"Aww, poor Johnnie. How are you holding up?"

I returned the hug, which lasted longer than I wanted. "Um, I'm fine, Aunt Margaret. And no one calls me that anymore."

At the age of fourteen, I decided to use my middle name, primarily to avoid forever being called, "Johnnie Three" after my father and grandfather. It was only years later, I began to wonder if it ever bothered my parents that I'd rejected the moniker. They hadn't said anything, but they'd also teased me about having an independent streak.

It was Audrey who rescued me from Margaret's clutches and steered me to the kitchen, where a crew of white-coated workers were laying out food for the party later. Audrey opened the fridge and, with a wink, handed me an artesian water bottle.

"We'll have something stronger later. I'm sure we'll need it."

I winked back, suppressing a laugh. No doubt, we'd need something stronger by evening. If I made it that long. The urge to flee was strong, but I was here now and that was half the battle.

The next few hours passed as I sat in the living room, dodging questions. After the third round of answering, "I'd rather not say," I decided to turn the tables on them and ask the questions.

"Mom, enough about me. What's been going on with you? And Dad?"

The furtive movement of her pale blue eyes told me I'd struck a nerve. Something was up with Dad and she knew it.

"The usual, darling. Work and more work. But he hasn't been traveling as much. Spencer's stepped in since…"

She didn't finish, and her eyes flashed.

"Since I left? You can say it, Mom. I know someone has to do my job. May as well be Spencer."

The slight groan from Audrey's lips was lost on everyone else, but she was next to me on the sofa so I heard it. It was her go-to reaction anytime our cousin's name was mentioned.

"I may as well do what?"

As if on cue, Spencer appeared, looking the same as he had the last time I saw him—tawny-haired, tanned, impeccably dressed, and smug as ever. His polo shirt and khakis were neatly pressed, and as he moved through the room, his cologne hung heavy in the air.

Margaret stood, her arms outstretched for the requisite hug. It didn't hurt that Spencer was her favorite.

Not So Broken

"Don't think you're passing me by, young man." He hugged the frail woman politely, and she clung to his arm after he let go. "We were just talking about how great it was that you could cover for John—uh, Gibson while he's been away."

She'd emphasized the word *away*, as though it was a curse or some mysterious code word with a cryptic meaning. It was obviously disturbing her not to know what was really going on.

Spencer smiled his famous too-charming smile in response. "I'm happy to help. Take as much time as you need, buddy."

He looked directly at me and saluted. The condescension was almost more than I could bear. My hand twitched and fisted, but Audrey pressed her elbow to my arm in a silent warning. I'd have to ask her more about it later when we were alone.

Soon I pleaded exhaustion from the trip, since they had no idea how far I'd traveled. I really wanted to see my old room, to find out if it stirred any memories.

"Just a quick nap, unless you all need me for something?"

I asked the room in general and got several waves of approval. They would be sitting around talking until the party, anyway.

My old room had been converted to a guest room long ago, but it still comforted me the second I entered. Mom had kept the décor masculine with a nautical motif. Sailboats and lighthouses were everywhere, and the pale seafoam green and navy blue tones were restful. I lay back on the bed and in minutes was asleep.

I had the dream again, but this time I wasn't searching for Bianca. It was another woman, the one I'd met that night in Tilly. The one I tried to forget, only to find intimate memories of her would hit me out of the blue.

Sacha.

In the dream, I was chasing her through the woods. I kept stumbling over logs and rocks or catching my coat on branches. I called for her stop but she kept running, always out of reach, darting out of sight. But I knew it was her.

Later, the party was in full swing when Audrey approached me. Behind her was a young woman who looked vaguely familiar.

"Gib, you remember Valerie, don't you? She and I were friends in high school."

Tall and lithe, the brunette was stunning. She extended a hand, which I politely shook. "I think I do. It's been a while."

There was a minute of small talk, and then Audrey excused

51

herself. I knew a set-up when I saw one, especially since Mom and Aunt Margaret had both introduced me to young ladies in the past hour. They were trying to give me a reason to come out of exile, but it wasn't working. They were all nice and good-looking. But that wasn't what I was here for. I chatted with Valerie for a few minutes before making the excuse of needing the restroom.

My father's office was next to the closest bathroom, so I couldn't help but look in as I passed. He was at his desk reading, when he should have been mingling with his guests. I wasn't surprised.

"Dad, you're missing your own party."

"I could say the same about you. We both have our ways of hiding out when we need to."

I leaned against the desk and folded my arms, mimicking his earlier stance. "If you've got something to say to me, say it."

The papers Dad was reading hit the desk with a thump. "This whole disappearing act is not like you, son. I used to be able to count on you, more than anyone. Now you're off doing God knows what. Living off your savings until it runs out?"

"No, I haven't touched my savings. I sublet the condo, and I've been supporting myself, earning my own money."

He took his glasses off and looked me over, as though I was a stranger.

"Doing what?"

"It doesn't matter. And don't worry, it won't reflect badly on the company. No one there knows who I am."

He shook his head then looked back at me with his stern gaze. It was a look I'd seen many times, and it still gave me a shiver. "Son, it does reflect badly that you're not where you should be. Spencer is happy to do your job, but he doesn't have the same drive as you. He thinks it's a non-stop vacation. He's learning, but he's not the closer you were. I can replace you if I must, but I don't want to. And I shouldn't have to beg my own son to work for me."

This was the conversation I'd been avoiding for months. My sense of duty was strong, but it was not enough to change my mind. Not yet. I had to make him understand why this was important to me.

Which was hard to do, when I hadn't really figured it out for myself yet.

"I don't expect you to understand what I'm going through. All I know is, losing Bianca and the baby changed me. How could it not? It was my fault. I made the decision, which put events in motion that ended up killing them, and for that, I will never forgive myself."

My voice faltered on the last few words. My throat had seized up as it did every time I talked about my role in the accident that killed my wife. I closed my eyes, pinching the bridge of my nose to stem the tears that threatened.

I would not let him see me fall apart.

"Gib, you can't keep beating yourself up. You had nothing to do with it."

His voice had been calm, reassuring even. I knew under his anger over my actions, he did care. I straightened up to face him, shaking back my shoulders with a deep breath.

"I don't know what it's going to take to get me through this, but I have to do it alone. After the funeral, I just couldn't go on with business as usual, or with my life as it was, without them. I couldn't."

I had spoken the truth. *My truth.* Dad's blue-gray gaze went from stern to sad then looked away.

"Well… I suppose I can wait a little longer. But this situation can't go on indefinitely. Maybe more counseling—"

I cut him off with a wave of my hand. "I tried that before I left town. I'm not mentally unstable. I need some time."

Before he could counter, Mom appeared at the door.

"There you are, boys. I'm not leaving until both of you return to the party, so whatever it was, finish up. Quick."

He gave me a helpless glance, and then shrugged. The conversation was over, whether we agreed or not.

"Yes, Mom. We're coming."

She turned on her heel and we followed. There was so much left unsaid, but it would have to wait.

~*~

Dad and I went our separate ways and mingled with everyone else at the party. I knew it was hard for him to understand my point of view, but I was not ready to come back. Across the room, I saw him talking with Margaret and Spencer, and I could just imagine the scheming that was going on.

Let them scheme. If I had learned one thing while I was away, it was that money didn't solve everything.

I was about to get another drink when Audrey corralled me and pulled me on to the patio. People were clustered in small groups so she took me to a corner where we could talk.

"What is so important it couldn't wait?"

She looked over her shoulder at the living room, crammed with wall-to-wall people. "If you want to have any part of your inheritance, you need to come home soon. There's rumors that Margaret has Dad's ear, and she is angling for Spencer to take over if anything happens to Dad."

Her face was twisted into a grimace at the thought of what she described coming to pass. I blinked.

"So, let him. If they want it that bad, they can have it."

Her short, blonde bob swung against her chin as she shook her head. "Oh, no. If anyone should be the next CEO, it's you. Or me. Not him."

This. This is one of many reasons I was reluctant to visit, let alone return permanently. It wasn't enough they all had so much money their kid's kids couldn't spend it all. They had to get entangled in drama and strategies. I no longer cared. I could live without it.

"Look, Audrey, don't get yourself all worked up. I had a discussion with Dad, and he's not going to do anything, make any changes for now. He's agreed to give me some space, but I promise, this will all work out in the end."

I really couldn't promise anything to anyone, not even myself, but she relaxed at my words. It was worth a gamble. Besides, maybe things would work out in the end.

Anything was possible at this point.

Chapter Seven

Sacha

There was no one else in the office when I arrived Monday morning, which made my heart pound more furiously. Eight o'clock was well before the office staff arrived, and the sales reps tended to start even later. My boss, Dan Forber, was in the breakroom getting coffee.

"Sacha, good morning. I've got Vienna roast brewing here, if you'd like some."

"No, I'm good."

I'd never been one to turn down coffee, but my nerves couldn't take the caffeine.

He was older than me, by about ten years, but still physically fit. He'd come up through the ranks to obtain his position as district manager, so he understood what us reps had to handle in the field. We'd always gotten along pretty well, so I was counting on his support.

Once we were settled in his office with the door closed, his face turned from his usual jovial expression to serious. I waited patiently, hands in my lap, ignoring the rumble of my queasy stomach. I'd been so nervous that I puked in the parking lot, making it to the nearby bushes just in time. It was embarrassing to be so nervous. I was a grown-ass woman, for Pete's sake.

"So, Sacha… You know we're facing a big merger in the next few months."

"Yes."

"Well, I've recently gotten word it's going to result in some changes with our sales reps, but I think you're going to like it."

He sipped his coffee and avoided my eyes. His voice was cheery, but it was clear he was trying to put a spin on something he considered unpleasant. My gut was telling me to brace myself. I gripped the chair handles to give my jittery hands something to do.

When I said nothing, he continued.

"Long story short, they are reconfiguring the territories. What they want to do, long term, is to put our best people where they are most needed. Those reps with proven track records are going to be shifted so we can improve the sales in the regions that would benefit the most."

I stifled a groan. I could tell where this was going. All the years of hard work to build relationships with my clients was about to be handed to someone who knew nothing about them, who would reap the benefit of my sacrifice and hard work. For being a "great sales rep," I was about to be handed a territory that was a challenge. But I bit my tongue, hoping I was wrong. Then Dan launched into the meat of his speech.

"You've always been a solid performer. You have real potential. Your numbers have been great, and you seem to have a knack for finding clients who stick with us, year after year."

He paused. I was keeping a polite smile on my face but it took effort. "Thank you, Dan. I do my best."

Then he smiled, a too-bright smile for a few minutes after eight in the morning. "Yes, you do. So, we'd like you to take over the territory east of Birmingham."

I felt myself blink. "Alabama?"

"Yes, ma'am. Heart of Dixie."

What fresh hell was this? I'd pictured the outskirts of Atlanta or maybe even Macon. But certainly not...Alabama.

Not even Birmingham. "East of Birmingham."

He waited for my response. He sipped his coffee again. The silence dragged on, became uncomfortable.

"Um, I don't know what to say."

"Well, you have some time to think about it. This won't happen for another few weeks to a month."

Now my mouth dropped open. That wasn't much time, especially if I had to move. Dan rushed to assure me.

"Of course, you'll have more time than that to get settled. Start out slow. We'll increase your base pay for six months to give you time to build up your clientele."

"Can I let you know? This is a big change."

"Yes, of course. But you need to know something."

His voice had changed on the last sentence. I had always trusted this man, had never known him to be anything but a straight shooter.

"What is it?"

He hesitated then sighed. His normally pink cheeks took on a rosier hue.

"I'm not supposed to tell you this, but it looks like there won't be a place for you if you don't take the position in Alabama."

My gut clenched. This was so not happening. "But what about the management position that just opened up? I was honestly hoping I was on the short list."

"You were. But they're bringing in their own management. I'm sorry."

"So if I don't take it, I'm out of a job?"

His grimace showed me how he felt about the situation. But it didn't change the outcome.

"I'm sure they can find something for you, but you'd be better off taking the position, Sacha."

That was all I needed to hear. It was apparently their way or the highway. I stood because my stomach threatened to embarrass me if I didn't get some air.

"I'll give it some thought. Thanks for letting me know."

I walked out, barely making it to the ladies' room before my stomach demanded to be emptied again. Something was definitely wrong, and I had a feeling moving to Alabama was going to be the least of my problems.

~*~

Gibson

Monday morning, I left early for a job but stopped to check on Marvil. When I'd arrived home late Sunday night, I noticed the lights were still on at the old man's place. He was usually in bed early, so it seemed odd, but I figured he must have fallen asleep watching television. So I made a point of stopping at his cabin to be sure he was okay.

There was no answer when I banged on the door, but I could hear the television blaring. I peeked through the window and saw Marvil lying on the floor of the living room. He wasn't moving. Something was very wrong.

It took a few seconds to find the emergency key the old man had stashed near his rusty barbeque grill, but soon I had the door open. I rushed to his side, and he looked up, startled.

"Marvil. Are you okay?"

"Yeah. I always lay on the floor like this when I've broken my leg."

He had managed to put a pillow under the injured limb. I carefully pulled back Marvil's robe, revealing a bruised and swollen area just below the knee.

"I suppose it hurts. Don't move."

"What do you think, smart guy? It hurts like a son of a bitch. I couldn't get to the phone, so I've been here since last night. I even pissed myself this morning."

A stab of guilt twisted in my gut. I should have checked on him last night.

"I'm so sorry I wasn't here for you, buddy. Don't worry, help's coming."

I ignored his grumbles as I raced to the bedroom. I punched the buttons on the old landline phone and waited for the call to go through. When the dispatcher answered, I explained the situation, and she assured me an ambulance was on the way.

I returned to the living room, handed Marvil some clean underwear, and helped him change. I removed the soiled robe, and helped him into a sweatshirt, some loose shorts, and socks. If he was embarrassed, he hid it well. The pain was more of a challenge, and he cried out every time I touched his leg or jostled him. Once he was dressed, I placed some pillows from the sofa under him, taking care to not move the injured leg any more than was necessary.

"What were you doing, Marvil? Dancing in your underwear again?"

His smirk was quick, eclipsed by a grimace from the pain. "I fell asleep on the couch, and my leg was bent under me. It had gone numb. When I stood to go to bed, I tripped on the rug and down I went."

"Well, I'm sure you'll be fixed up in no time. Just stay still."

His dark eyes snapped open. "Where do ya think I'm gonna go, smart guy?"

Not So Broken

I ignored his question. It meant he wasn't feeling too bad if he could insult me in his normal fashion.

Soon the wail of the ambulance carried through the open front door, so I went outside to flag them. Two paramedics came in, and after examining Marvil, they determined it was best to get him to the hospital. He cursed and grumbled as they moved him to the ambulance.

It was almost an hour's drive to the nearest emergency room, but I followed them. I made some calls along the way so I wouldn't be expected on the job site. Marvil needed me, needed someone. There was no one else that I knew of in the old man's life. It was sad to think of him living alone all these years. What if I hadn't checked on Marvil? I didn't even want to think about what might have happened. I knew it wasn't my responsibility to keep watch on the old man, but it was simply the right thing to do.

Sitting in the hospital waiting room gave me time to think. I had come to Tilly to be alone, to find a way to survive on my own. I gave up a life of luxury so I would have no distractions. I needed to find out who I really was. Did I have enough grit to make it without everything being handed to me? Was I truly worthy of anyone's love?

I had vowed not to become involved with anyone while I was away from home. No friendships, no dating. Losing my wife and child had gutted me, and I had nothing left to give anyone. So it was best to stay to myself.

But a cranky old man whom no one could stand had worked his way under my carefully constructed shell. Now I couldn't imagine what living in Tilly would be like without him.

Maybe I'm not so broken, after all.

~*~

Sacha

I stood in my bathroom, naked, which wasn't all that unusual, except this time it was because I had to take a serious look at myself. I'd given myself a pep talk while I showered, but it hadn't helped. No matter how I tried to look at the bright side of my situation, I couldn't shake a sense of impending doom.

Which wasn't a good mind-set for someone about to take a pregnancy test.

Renee Regent

I hadn't eaten or slept well the day before, after my meeting with Dan. The uncertainty surrounding my job these past few weeks had totally stressed me out, so the physical symptoms I was feeling were probably directly related. My monthly cycles have always been irregular, and even Kevin couldn't get me pregnant after years of trying. So I hadn't even thought about missing my last period. But the possibility of a pregnancy, however remote, had festered in the back of my mind. Taking the pregnancy test was simply a way to prove my imagination was on overdrive, and thus remove that subject as another source of stress. Once the test was over, I could eliminate pregnancy from my long list of worries.

Besides, I'd received an email from the adoption agency last night, indicating I was being considered. I'd had a phone interview with them months before, and now they wanted even more information. I had stayed up late filling out their forms and obsessed about it for hours afterward. But at least I was moving forward with the adoption. It was the one bright spot in my life, something I could look forward to happening.

If I could afford to support the child.

Desperately wanting to feel normal again, I opened the packaging of the pregnancy test. I hadn't had anything to eat or drink yet, so I hoped to obtain an accurate reading. Following the directions, I peed on the stick and set it down on the sink. Then I grabbed a robe and headed to the kitchen.

I returned a few minutes later with a steaming mug of coffee and a clearer head. It would be nice to stop worrying. It was foolish, really. Although it was entirely possible my one encounter—with the mysterious mountain man—could have made me pregnant, it wasn't likely.

Setting the mug on the counter, I picked up the stick. It had two faint blue lines in the circle. *Two.*

Wait. What?

No. It can't be.

Something must be wrong. The test was faulty. I read the directions over, but it was correct. Two lines in the circle meant positive.

Pregnant.

I sank to the floor on my knees. The bathroom rug was still damp from my shower. The robe slid from my shoulder, and my still-wet locks hung down, chilling my back. Gooseflesh rose over my skin, though my face felt furnace-hot. The tiny stick was still in my hand, mocking me. Was this a dream? Or a nightmare?

No fucking way.

It had to be a cruel joke. I'd waited all my life for this moment, but never imagined it would be like this. If it wasn't a mistake, I had only a spotty recollection of how this had happened, and I didn't even know the father's full name.

Images of that night flashed in my mind, but they were still fuzzy. It had been a bad idea, but now it was too late for regret. In any case, what should have been the happiest moment of my life was now tangled up with guilt and shame.

But a tiny sprout of happiness grew in my heart. To finally be pregnant would be a blessing, no matter how it came about. If I dared to believe it was true.

A tear slipped down my cheek. I brushed it away. It couldn't be true. There had to be a mistake. I'd go to the drugstore and buy another test. Or two.

As I dressed, I looked in the mirror at my body. Turning sideways, I saw the slight pouf of my belly. But hadn't it been that way for a while? I was nearly forty. Maybe it was middle age spread creeping up on me. It couldn't be a baby.

Could it?

Chapter Eight

Sacha

"Three pregnancy tests can't all be wrong, Sacha. Congratulations."

Melanie was the only person I dared to tell about my situation. We were having lunch at a café near our apartment building. My stomach had changed from queasy to insatiable, and I was chomping on my second sandwich. I set it aside long enough to answer her.

"I know. What I don't know is how this happened in the first place." Melanie didn't answer, but made a rude gesture with her hands, forming a hole with two fingers and sliding another finger in and out of it, complete with what was supposed to be creaking bed noises. I gave her the evil eye. "That's not funny. Not in the least. And you know what I mean. It was the first time in my life I took a chance and did something crazy and look what happened."

"C'mon, does it really matter how it happened? It's what you wanted, right?"

I bit into my turkey panini to avoid answering, if only for a moment. I didn't really want to talk about this, but knew I had to tell someone or go crazy inside my own head. As it was, my imagination was working overtime with doomsday scenarios.

"Yes, of course, I'm thrilled. But this isn't exactly how I thought it would happen. I was prepared to raise my child my way. I had accepted the fact I would never give birth. I was ready to love a child who had no one, who needed a good home. If I'd thought I could have the baby myself, I'd have gone to the sperm bank or done in vitro. But now this complicates things because there's someone else involved."

"Mountain man? Do you even know how to get ahold of him?"

"Not really. We didn't part on the best of terms. But I'm sure I could find him in Tilly, somehow."

My appetite suddenly flagged at the thought of seeing Gibson. My feelings about him were mixed before, and now they were downright confusing.

Melanie was silent so I looked up. Her dark eyes were narrowed as she assessed me.

"But you really don't want to find him, do you?"

I sat back in my chair, pushing my plate away. I took a sip of water, wishing it was something stronger. "No, I don't. Is that horrible?"

"Not exactly. But I understand why you don't want to find him."

It was all I'd thought of from the moment I accepted being undeniably pregnant. Didn't the father have a right to know?

I sighed, unable to avoid the topic any longer. I had to face facts.

"It's not only that he was a bit of a jerk after we'd spent the night together. He was nice before that and sexy as hell. Good-looking and fit. But he's a handyman, working odd jobs. He's living in a remote cabin. He's got some kind of baggage, maybe because his wife died. I don't know. But if I'm being honest, he's not exactly the man of my dreams."

She was still giving me that look, like she was waiting for the rest of the story. Then she prompted me with "And?"

My stomach had settled with the food, but now it clenched as tension spiraled through me. "And my father left when I was a kid, and my husband dumped me for a baby-making machine. So no, I don't have much faith in men these days. There, I said it. Are you happy?"

Melanie sipped her wine, and I envied her for a moment. Wine was off my menu for the foreseeable future. Then she spoke, her voice firm. "It's about you being happy, not me. If you think you'll be happier doing this alone, then own it. And you don't have to marry him, you know. He lives far away, probably has no money, so what can he do? If he really is a jerk, he may not even want to be involved."

"Maybe."

"You don't have to do anything about him yet, so don't drive yourself crazy about it."

"You're right."

Melanie reached across the table to squeeze my arm. The tension was ebbing now, relief surfacing once again. Until she asked me the next question.

"Have you told your mom yet?"

"No, and please don't tell anyone about this until I figure out what I need to do."

"I won't. But be careful. I'm here if you need me, okay?"

"Yes, ma'am. I don't know what I'd do without you. And I'm paying for lunch, so don't even think about grabbing the check."

Later as we walked back to our apartment building, a sense of calm came over me. No matter what happened, this was *my* child. Part of me was growing into a whole other person. No one could ever take that away.

~*~

Gibson

A month had passed since Marvil's fall, and he was still using crutches but otherwise back to his ornery old self. I made it a habit now to check on him every time I passed on my way to town, to see if he needed anything and to bring in firewood. He insisted he didn't need me "hovering like a damned hen," but the smile that tugged at his lips when he didn't know I was watching told me he appreciated my efforts.

One morning I pulled up to Marvil's cabin just as Edna, the home health aid worker, arrived. She was about Marvil's age, perhaps a bit younger. The bags under her eyes that indicated many long workdays didn't detract from her shy smile, which she gave me in lieu of a greeting. Using the key she had been given, she opened the front door after a quick knock and preceded me into the cabin.

Marvil looked up from his spot on the sofa and frowned at Edna, but his eyes had a spark of interest. "You again? I keep telling them to send someone more attractive. If I have to look at you all day, my eyes will go crossed."

Edna rolled her eyes, ignoring the insult, so I answered.

"Hey, I've been working out. And you're not exactly a catch, old man."

Marvil simply snorted and tossed off the blanket, which had covered his lap. Edna's first order of business was to examine his leg, as per

64

her usual routine. She stood over him and motioned for him to move into place. Her voice had the same teasing tone as Marvil's.

"Stop complaining and assume the position. And you're not exactly Robert Redford, ya know."

They had been bantering like this for days. As gruff as he was, it was evident Marvil enjoyed being fussed over.

I watched as Edna's deft hands worked, unhooking the soft cast while taking care not to touch the still swollen and slightly discolored leg. Still, he flinched as she removed the cast and placed it aside.

"Ow! Take it easy, Sergeant."

A look passed between them, and I smiled. For all his fuss, it seemed Marvil actually liked this one. From her smile, I could tell she might like him too. As I worked to rebuild the fire in the fireplace, I couldn't help teasing.

"Careful, man. You've already run off two other caregivers. Three strikes and you're out."

"Hmmmpf" was all I heard in response.

The fire finally caught and was warming the place nicely. I'd taken out the trash and watered the few plants lining the kitchen windowsill. Edna was now replacing the soft cast, and she looked up as I approached.

"Sir, would you be able to refill his prescription today? It's already been called in. We'll be doing some therapy starting tomorrow, and he may need some pain relievers."

Marvil made a face. "May need? You can bet your ass I'll need them, if Sergeant Edna's in charge."

I saw the wink he gave Edna and knew my buddy was in good hands.

"Sure, I'll stop by the drugstore on my way home."

As I left, I couldn't help but laugh. It would be funny if Marvil and Edna actually got together. I hoped they would, not so I wouldn't have to take care of him, but because it would make him happy. Make them happy.

It was strange how fate worked sometimes. Who knew when something bad happening might actually lead to something good, which never would have happened otherwise?

~*~

My first stop that day was an old, run-down house at the end of a gravel road. A woman lived there, a single mother with four young kids.

Someone else I worked for had referred me, and I was happy to help. It was clear when I drove up to the house, she had no one to help her with the upkeep. Besides toys spread all over the yard, and the general disrepair of the place, it was her home. There was a time when I probably would have looked on in distaste and drove away. I was coming to learn there was more to people and their lives than the appearance of their possessions.

During a recent storm, a tree had fallen on her side deck and smashed the railing. I was here to clear it away and repair the deck.

I knocked on the door, and she opened it while holding a baby on her hip. She couldn't have been more than twenty-seven or so. Another child cried in the background, and she barked a sharp reprimand before turning back to address me. Gratitude showed on her face, and there was relief in her voice.

"Oh, thank the Lord. I was hoping you'd show today. I'm Tammie. These kids are 'bout to drive me crazy. They're used to playing on the deck all day."

I extended a hand, and she shook it. "I'm Gibson. Of course. I'll get started right away, if that's okay with you, ma'am."

"Help yourself."

It took a few hours to cut up the tree, drag it off into the nearby woods, and repair the deck railing. It was obvious where the wood was new, but the only way to hide that was to re-stain the whole deck. She had asked me to do the repair with minimal cost, so I doubted she was ready to take on that project now.

When I informed her the work was done, she came to inspect. All four kids looked it over, the youngest barely toddling along after his brother and sisters. My heart flipped over at the sight of them, so excited over having their play area restored.

I handed Tammie a receipt, and she looked at me in shock. "This is way less than you quoted."

I was packing up the tools in my truck. Over my shoulder, I smiled.

"It was no trouble, so I'm only charging you for the materials."

She stuck her hand out toward me, trying to give me back the receipt. "No. No way. A deal is a deal."

I faced her then looked at the kids playing on the deck, running back and forth. I looked back at her face, full of pride and determination.

"I tell you what. Next time I come to fix something, you can pay me a little extra to catch up."

Not So Broken

Her skeptical look turned into one of gratitude. "Well, okay. Next time. Thank you, Mr. Gibson."

I didn't bother to tell her that was my first name. She paid me, and I drove away, feeling better than I had in a long time.

Chapter Nine

Sacha

*I*t was just past noon when I rounded the last bend into Tilly. So much had happened since the last time I was there, it nearly made my head spin. Or perhaps it was motion sickness, something I'd never had before but seemed to come over me now when I drove on a winding road.

Which in Georgia, was pretty much all of them.

It was another weird side effect of being pregnant. I worried about every little flutter or ache, but my obstetrician had assured me that for my age, I was in good health. I was twelve weeks along, so chances were good I would carry to term with no problems. But that still didn't keep me from worrying over the future.

I almost hadn't made this trip. The temptation to simply go on with my life and never look back was strong. But I had been betrayed before and left in the dark. My father abandoned my mother and me when I was nine, never explaining why. And Kevin's transgressions had started long before I went on that fateful trip to Jersey years ago. If he had been honest with me about his dissatisfaction with our marriage, maybe things would have gone differently.

Maybe if my mother and my father had talked more about their marriage problems, he wouldn't have disappeared. Bile rose up in my throat at the memory of the day we discovered he was gone. I swallowed a sip of water from a bottle, willing the tragic images away. I had to focus on the task at hand, not the reasons that were causing my dread in the first place.

I let out a groan and gripped the steering wheel as I drove through town. Despite my strong desire to raise the baby my way, I couldn't escape my damned conscience, which told me the father-to-be had a right to know.

What he did with the information was his choice.

The entire three-hour trip, I'd rehearsed what I was going to say, and what he might say in return. If he wanted, I'd allow some involvement, but this was my show. If we actually had a chance at a relationship, things might be different. But as it was, we were from two separate worlds and would likely remain that way.

Especially if I moved to Alabama. Which still hadn't been decided. Just yesterday, I'd asked Dan for more time, stalling by saying my mother had taken ill. It was a lie, but I wasn't ready to disclose my pregnancy to anyone yet.

The company had taken over my life for years. They could wait a few more weeks.

Mom. I still hadn't told her about the baby. Somehow, keeping it to myself made it seem like it was just a dream. It wasn't real. Once everyone knew, there was no turning back, and then I'd have to accept the truth. For now, it was my secret, and I could fantasize about how I wanted the future to be.

I guess the decision to tell Gibson in person was my way of beginning to deal with the truth. Once that was over, the rest would be easier. I hoped.

If I could even find him. I was almost at the end of town, and the motel where I had stayed came in sight. *Knocked up by a one-night stand in a seedy motel after too many margaritas.* It was such a cliché, I almost laughed. Not exactly the picture of domestic bliss I'd envisioned when I first married Kevin.

"Oh, well. First stop, the Frisky Beaver."

I pulled into the parking lot of the bar, hoping Stuart, the owner, was in. He had been so nice and seemed like he knew everyone in town. I reached behind my seat for the bottle of flavored vodka I had brought as a gift.

"When you show up unannounced, always bring a gift," Mom once told me, and it never failed.

The bar was empty of customers, but music from a sound system competed with the sounds of someone banging pots and pans in the kitchen. A tall, skinny kid was mopping the floor, rearranging chairs as he went. I approached him since no one else was around.

"Excuse me? Do you know where I might find the owner?"

He nodded his head in the direction of the kitchen. "He's back there."

Stuart seemed genuinely glad to see me, though it meant abandoning his sink full of pots to be washed. Wiping his hands on a white apron, he escorted me to the bar where he set a pot of coffee to brew.

"So, what can I do for you, Miss Sacha?"

His conspiratorial wink made me worry he thought this might be a social call, so I got to the point.

"I'm looking for someone I met when I was here a few months ago. He…left something with me and I thought he might want to know."

"Let me guess. Was it the tall blond guy with the beard?"

My heart fluttered, an involuntary reaction. "Yes. That's him. Gibson was his name."

"Gibson? I have to admit, I don't know the guy. It was the first time I'd seen him in here. But he seemed to be smitten with you."

I blinked. "Smitten?"

Stuart laughed. "Yeah, I could tell he didn't want me hanging around, but I had to make sure you were having a good time here."

"I did. Thank you."

Stuart went on to talk about his regular customers, the strange things tourists would ask for, and a few other topics—nothing to do with why I was really here. But I listened politely, nodding and barely sipping the coffee. Twenty minutes had gone by before I could speak. When he stopped to take a breath, I jumped in.

"So, any idea where I might find this Gibson guy? Or is there anyone who might know?"

Stuart removed his ball cap and scratched his head. "I bet the guy who runs the drugstore would know. Everyone goes in there sooner or later, and he's been here forever. His name's Mitch."

"Is that the one near the post office?"

"Yep. Kitty-corner from it."

To be polite, I stayed another fifteen minutes listening to his stories. But he ended up placing an order for the flavored vodka, so my patience paid off.

My next stop was the drugstore, but I was told Mitch wouldn't be back until after three. Since I had a few hours, I made the rounds of the restaurants and bars in town, following up with some of the clients I had met before. My last stop took longer than anticipated, so it was after four p.m. by the time I made it back to the drugstore.

When I got there, Mitch was at the register, but there were five people in line ahead of me. As I waited, it seemed each person had to engage in a conversation with Mitch, increasing the time it took for each purchase. As customers began to line up behind me, I wondered if I should come back later. I really didn't want my conversation to be over-heard by half the people in town.

When I finally made it to the register, Mitch looked at my empty hands. "Can I help you with something, young lady?"

"Yes, I was told you might be able to help me find someone. I think he lives near here."

"I'll try. Do you have a name?"

I leaned forward, keeping my voice low. The woman behind me seemed to be hanging on my every word.

"Only his first name. Gibson."

Mitch's mouth opened to answer, but his eyes looked over my shoulder. I turned to find a man standing next to me. Tall, blond, and bearded, he said just one word.

"Sacha?"

~*~

Gibson

I couldn't believe my eyes.

The last person I expected to see in the drugstore on a Monday afternoon was Sacha. The woman who had taken over Bianca's place in my dreams and my fantasies. The fact I would never see her again had made those dreams and fantasies safe, but now that she was standing in front of me, I wasn't sure what the hell to do.

"Gibson? This is so weird. I was looking for you."

She looked back at Mitch and thanked him, then stepped away from the line of customers. Those haunting green eyes stared up at me, waiting, and I wondered why she had come looking for me.

"Yeah, I'm kind of in shock to see you. But glad."

She smiled then looked away. She was nervous about something. Well, we had parted on less than friendly terms. I looked down at the

71

vial of pills in my hand—Marvil's prescription—and joined the line of customers.

"I have to pay for this, but we can go somewhere to talk if you want."

"Yes, I'd like that. Somewhere private."

She pretended to browse the store while I waited in line. My mind began a systematic search for reasons why she would appear out of the blue like this.

She feels guilty about throwing me out.

She wants me.

She's madly in love with me.

She's buying a cabin and needs some work done.

She's figured out who I really am and wants to date a billionaire.

I discarded all of the possibilities but hoped at least the first three were close to the truth. My turn at the register finally came, and Mitch gave me a wink.

"Glad I could help you out, son. Hope it all goes well."

I gave him a thumbs-up sign and walked to where Sacha stood waiting by the door. I must have been nervous, because my voice warbled when I spoke, but I covered it with a cough. "I know where we can talk, if you don't mind sitting outside."

For mid-November, it was a warm day. The sun was out, and though it was getting near sunset, the breeze was slight. She didn't seem to mind my suggestion.

"Sure. Where?"

"Follow me."

I drove my truck the few blocks to the park along the river. There was no one in sight, so I pulled up next to a picnic area. She parked her car nearby and stepped out. I gestured to one of the wooden tables, where she sat on the bench across from me.

"So...um, how have you been, Gibson?"

Her petal-pink lips twitched. She was nervous, but I didn't press. Let her take her time with whatever it was. I was enjoying her company too much to rush. She was still gorgeous, but her face seemed rounder than I recalled, giving her a wholesome look.

"I've been fine. And you can call me Gib. How have you been?"

"I'm good. Well, Gib, I came here because there's something you should know."

My stomach dropped. The tone of her voice was serious, and I couldn't imagine what it had to do with me. "Are you in some kind of trouble?"

"I wouldn't say trouble, but..."

"Just say it."

"I'm pregnant. It's yours."

Her deep green gaze was locked on mine, as though daring me to react. The challenge on her face was unmistakable. My negotiation skills had been curated over many years of business experience, so I willed myself not to react. But inside I was a mass of emotions.

Shock.

Fear.

Disbelief.

Joy.

What? No way.

"Please don't take this the wrong way, but I have to ask. Are you absolutely sure?"

Her brows narrowed, lips tightened, and I saw the same expression she'd had right before she told me to leave her motel room. Her next words were muttered through clenched teeth, and the amber specks in her eyes became more visible, like tiny sparks.

"Absolutely, or else I wouldn't have driven three hours to search all over this godforsaken place for you."

Oops. I had to lighten the moment, so I gave her my most charming smile and touched her hand.

"What I meant was, you've taken tests, been seen by a doctor?"

Her expression hadn't changed, but she left her hand on the table, covered by mine. "I know what you mean. But yes, I've been tested. I'm almost twelve weeks along. That's how long it's been since I was here, with you. And I haven't been with anyone else."

"My memory of that night is a bit spotty."

I didn't want to upset her further by being graphic about what we had done. At this point, I wasn't even sure what we *had* done, at least not every detail. She withdrew her hand and covered her face with it.

"So is mine, but we actually did, you know...do it."

I wracked my mind, trying to conjure up images of that night. They were fragmented. I had a vague feeling of unease about it but didn't want to tell her.

"I don't know. I was pretty out of it. I do recall telling you about forgetting the condoms. I was trying to be a gentleman."

Her face softened. A breeze lifted a lock of her long, brown hair to caress her cheek. She brushed it away.

"You did. But we must have been drunker than we both realized. It was a mistake to sleep together. But does that really matter now?"

For some reason, I trusted her. It still made no sense, but my gut was telling me she was on the level. At least about this. Still, it bothered me she felt our night together was a "mistake." Her clinical attitude wasn't making this any easier to process. "Not at this moment. I mean, we can establish proof later if necessary."

She straightened her shoulders. Her eyes glistened with tears she was trying to hold back. But her words belied any emotion she might have been feeling.

"Personally, I don't really care. I don't expect anything from you, that's not why I'm here. I thought you had a right to know. I plan to raise the child on my own, in any case."

I wasn't sure how I felt about this. I barely knew her. But one thing I was certain of—she was having my child, and I wasn't about to let her cut me out of the picture.

~*~

Sacha

Relief washed over me like a cleansing rain the moment I told Gib about the baby, but something in his eyes made me wary. I had expected him to back off when I said I'd raise it alone, but now he was asking too many questions.

"So how do you plan to support the child? Where will you live?"

I didn't want to mention Alabama, since it wasn't set in stone. Yet. This was precisely what I feared—him wanting to take control of the situation and my life.

"I told you, I live in Kennesaw. It's north of Atlanta. I have an apartment, and I make decent money, because I'm damn good at my job."

"I'm sure you are. But I'm wondering how we're going to work this out."

"Work what out? I told you, you're off the hook. I'm raising the baby. Alone."

He placed both palms on the wooden table and leaned forward. His voice had lowered, but the tone was lethal. "You don't *get* to take me 'off the hook.' This is my child too."

We stared at each other for an intense moment. I had done some research, and in Georgia, all parental rights went to the unwed mother automatically. It would be up to him to establish paternity and legitimate the child, which might be difficult given his finances or lack thereof. Plus, the fact he lived in a remote area. I was counting on these factors to dissuade him from taking legal action. But to be safe, and fair, I offered a solution.

"Look. I'm not saying you will never see the child. We'll work something out. But let's be realistic. We aren't in a relationship. This was just a one-night thing, right?"

The skin above his beard reddened. He looked down at the table. "Right."

"We live hours away from each other. So logistically, it won't be easy. Bottom line, I think we have some time to figure things out. I'm not due until May. So, let's take it one step at a time."

I had no intention of giving him too much leeway. He was simply in shock and would probably calm down as time went on and the real responsibilities of parenthood began. Until I got to know him better, I wasn't going to commit to anything specific.

He could be a serial killer or some kind of nut. Only time would tell.

He sat back and sighed, his tension visibly easing. "You're right. This is all quite a shock. Not what I expected when you showed up in town."

I smiled for the first time that day. "What did you think I was here for? Round two?"

His grin was absolutely adorable, and I had to remind myself not to be influenced by his charm.

"You can't blame a guy for hoping. Especially since I don't recall much of round one."

"Fair enough. But I don't even know your full name."

The way he hesitated caused a prickle of fear up my spine. Was he hiding something?

"Gibson Cole—Colebank. And yours is?"

"Sacha Rowan."

I pulled my phone out of my purse to enter him as a contact. We exchanged numbers, and I promised to keep him updated on my progress. At least that put me back in control.

"I'm sorry I shocked you, Gib. I was shocked myself when I found out."

"Thank you for coming up here to tell me in person. That wasn't easy, I'm sure."

"No, it wasn't." I hesitated, as questions of my own began piling up. "So, you mentioned you weren't originally from Tilly. Do you have family here?"

Again, his gaze shifted away. When he looked back, his eyes were storm-cloud blue.

"No, they live near Atlanta. But I won't be telling them about this until we figure things out."

A sudden breeze made me shiver. It was getting late and I had a long drive home. "I haven't told my family yet, either. I'm still coming to grips with the idea myself, you know?"

He nodded and smiled. "Yeah, and you've had a head start on me."

We parted on what I thought were good terms, under the circumstances. We didn't hug, shake hands, or touch in any way. There was a distance between us, though we were forever connected now. All because we gave in to our reckless desires. In a perfect world, it wasn't supposed to happen this way, but it had.

As I drove away, I couldn't help but shudder with relief. The worst part was over. I hoped.

Chapter Ten

Gibson

*A*s I made my way back up the mountain, my mind was spinning with possibilities. *A child.* I was going to be a father. It seemed that fate had handed me this blessing once more, but in an unexpectedly ironic way. The woman who now carried my baby was a virtual stranger. An attractive, smart, maybe a little-bit-sassy one, but a stranger nonetheless. And judging from her attitude, she wanted to keep it that way.

We may not be together as a couple, but now our lives were forever entwined. I didn't regret spending the night with her, what I could recall of it. I hadn't anticipated the result of a complication like this, but the fact it happened despite our initial precautions told me it must be fate. How it came about was not important.

I'd already searched for her online after that night to see who she was. She had a few profiles but hadn't posted in months, with scant photos. It didn't tell me much about her. If I was going to get to know the mother of my child, it would have to be on her terms. I'd been careful not to give her much information about me. Everything online—that I knew of, anyway—referred to me as John Colebank, or J.G. Colebank, which were also Dad's initials. And there were no photos of me with a beard. She'd have to really dig to find out who I am, and she hadn't seemed suspicious.

Wary, maybe, but I couldn't blame her for that. I was wary about her too. She could be mentally unstable or a raving bitch. Who knows?

When I arrived at Marvil's place, Edna had already left. I opened the door with the extra key she had given me to find the patient lounging on the sofa, surrounded by pillows and blankets.

"Was beginning to think you drove to Florida to get my meds."

I placed the vial of pills on the coffee table. "No. Sorry I'm late. I ran into someone I know in town."

"A girl? Of course, why else would you be late?"

The old man's smirk told him me this was bait, but I didn't bite. "It was about a job. And besides, I was giving you more time alone with Edna."

"Hmmph. Couldn't get the dang woman to leave. I'm not help-less."

"No, but you sure look comfy, sitting there like a prince. You love the attention and don't mind having her around. Admit it."

His grimace was almost comical. Marvil was protesting a bit too much on this one.

"Well, it's better than hanging out with you, that's for sure."

I stayed a few minutes more to make sure Marvil was set for the evening. As I was about to leave, he pointed to an envelope lying on the coffee table. "That's for you."

I leaned over to pick it up. The words "Important Info" were scrawled on the face of the envelope.

"What is it?"

"I made you my emergency contact person. That's all my medical stuff, legal contacts, account numbers. You know, in case something happens."

I turned the envelope over in my hand. For an eighty-year-old man, Marvil seemed pretty spry. The accident must have worried him.

"I'll keep it in a safe place. But I'm sure I won't need it for quite a while. You're too damn stubborn to go anywhere."

The comment earned me a nasty look, which turned into a smile.

When I finally entered my cabin, it seemed empty.
Just like my life.

I had chosen this life of exile, but now it seemed to be changing whether I wanted it to or not. I had to admit, an unexpected pregnancy was not something I would have wished to happen. But now that I was beginning to accept the situation, I could see that it was a chance to redeem myself, to right the wrongs of the past. I'd lost Bianca and the baby, but perhaps I could give the child Sacha was carrying a good life. Not only with money, either, but by giving my time and attention.

If I told her now about my financial fortune, would that change her opinion of me? I wanted to be more than a bank account to my future son or daughter. I wanted to be more to Sacha than just a rich baby daddy.

And what if I never went back to my old life? Before I knew about this, I'd all but convinced myself I could stay in Tilly indefinitely. If I told Sacha I'm worth billions but gave it up, she'd think I was crazy. She'd likely expect me to go back to work at CB Resorts International and want to meet my family, and I'm not ready for all that.

So, I couldn't tell her the truth, at least not until we figured out how to make our situation work.

I didn't know how it was going to happen, but I wouldn't rest until Sacha accepted me as an equal partner in the life of our child.

~*~

Sacha

When I got home from Tilly, the first thing I did was look for Gibson Colebank online. I came up empty-handed, finding several listings and profiles for people with the last name "Colebank" but none that matched the man I had met. Melanie was over with her laptop, joining in the hunt, though she kept getting distracted by photos of hot-looking guys.

"You said he looks sort of like this?"

She pointed to a photo of a well-known Australian blond actor. There was an annoying tingle in my lady parts due to the sudden mental image of Gib, naked in my motel room. "Yes but more rugged. If that guy grew out his beard and dressed like Paul Bunyan."

Melanie licked her lips and kept clicking through the images on her screen. "Mmmm… Now I understand why you can't forget him."

"That's not why, and you know it. I have no choice, do I?"

My statement was true but seeing him again had triggered my sexual fantasies. I couldn't help it. He was even better-looking in person than I'd remembered.

"Well, if you had to get knocked up by someone, at least he has good genes."

"Yeah well, that's about all he has. That and a beat-up old truck."

"Well maybe he has other redeeming qualities. Is he nice? Smart?"

"I really don't know."

I didn't want to know. Getting to know Gibson Colebank meant letting him into my life, maybe my heart. I didn't have that to give to a man right now. My focus was on impending motherhood, not a romantic relationship.

"Well, you have some time, I guess. Are you sorry you told him?"

I put my laptop aside and leaned back on the sofa with a sigh. "Not sorry, really, because it was the right thing to do. But I'm just not sure about him. He seemed nice, but he's got an edge. And I think he's hiding something."

Melanie's dark eyes finally left her screen to look at me. "Like what?"

"I can't explain it. It's a feeling I have, like he doesn't really 'fit' in Tilly, you know? And he's been vague about anything I've asked, like where he was from originally. All he said was Atlanta."

The buzz of my cell phone interrupted. When I looked at the screen, I recognized the number and my heart almost stopped. "It's him."

Melanie stood. "I'll leave. But you better fill me in later."

As she reached the door, I called, "I will" and answered the phone.

"Hello?"

I tried to keep the nervous warble from my voice but failed. His tone was brisk and deeper than I recalled.

"Sacha? This is Gib."

I didn't bother to explain I'd known it was him, and simply said, "Yes?"

"I hope I didn't catch you at a bad time because we need to talk."

Closing the laptop, I settled back on the sofa. "No, I have time. What's up?"

There was only one thing he'd want to talk about, but I let him lead me along. I was still determined to remain in control of the situation but thought it best to let him have his say first. Then I'd know which way to proceed.

He cleared his throat then spoke, "I want to be an equal partner in the raising of my child. I won't settle for less. I'm just letting you know."

A stab of anger sliced through me. His tone was challenging, presumptuous, and infuriating. "What exactly do you mean by 'equal partner'? Are you planning on moving in with me?"

"If that's what it takes, yes. But I'm sure we can make some kind of living arrangements that are suitable for both of us."

"Whoa, wait a minute, Mr. Colebank. I'm the one who is carrying the child, not you. I have the final say, according to the state of Georgia. We're not married, so I am not obligated to you in any way. I told you what happened because I'm a nice person with a conscience. But don't think that gives you the right to tell me how to raise my child."

"*Our* child. I'm aware of the legalities, Ms. Rowan. I plan to assert my rights as a father, whatever it takes."

This had escalated quickly. My hands were shaking, and I almost dropped the phone. I knew the law was on my side, but if he wanted to, he could cause trouble in so many ways. Trouble I didn't have the time or energy to deal with. He didn't seem to have the money to wage a legal battle, but then I really didn't know much about him.

So far, I wasn't favorably impressed.

The blood in my veins ran ice cold at the thought of being pushed around by anyone, especially when it came to the fate of my child. I'd waited my whole life for this, and no one, not even the child's father, was going to interfere.

"Listen, Gib. I appreciate your wanting to step up and be a co-parent. What I don't appreciate is your confrontational attitude. I'm willing to work out a visitation schedule, and I prefer to do so without going to court. But if you insist on being a pig-headed ass about it, and think you can order me around, you'd better be prepared for a long battle."

~*~

Gibson

I held the phone to my ear but said nothing. I was standing on the back deck in order to get good reception. I did not want to lose this call, not while I had the nerve to tell Sacha Rowan she wasn't going to give me the brush off when it came to raising our child.

I let the silence drag on for a moment. I had come on too strong.

Maybe being businesslike was the wrong approach. I purposely lowered my voice now to a soothing tone. "Of course, I'm not trying to push you around. That would be stupid. But I am taking my responsibility in this situation seriously."

And you have no idea how much that means.

She huffed then gave a rueful laugh. "Good for you. What do you want, a trophy? There's no reason for you to start making demands when we haven't even discussed anything."

"Okay. I get it. I'm worried you'll disappear on me."

I hadn't meant for those last words to come out. My connection to this woman was tenuous, and I couldn't bear the thought of losing her and the child before I even had a chance to get involved. My fear was getting the best of me, so I took in a breath of the clean, bracing mountain air. My head cleared and I realized she hadn't spoken. "Sacha?"

"I'm here." She paused, causing another stab of fear to twist my gut. "So...maybe we need to start all over?"

Her voice was softer now too. Maybe another approach was what we both needed. "Okay. How do we do that?"

"Neutral ground. Let's meet somewhere, spend the day together, talk this through."

In the end, we decided to meet the following Saturday at a park near her apartment. There was a holiday festival going on, so we would have something to do in between having serious discussions about the future. It was a compromise, and we had to start somewhere.

Although talking things out hadn't gone so well yet. Would we ever be able to have a discussion without getting pissed off?

I wasn't sure about anything where Sacha was concerned.

Chapter Eleven

Sacha

*T*he following Saturday arrived too quickly. I was still suffering from morning sickness, and though my baby bump had not yet begun to show, some of my clothes were getting snug. I probably felt fatter than I looked, but it still made getting dressed a chore.

This morning was particularly irksome. I was nervous about spending the day with Gib and didn't know why. I wasn't afraid of him. I knew he could cause trouble for me, but my gut feeling said he wouldn't. So, my current anxiety over seeing him was a mystery.

After trying on five different outfits, I settled on a roomy, pink and green checked flannel over a long-sleeved white tee shirt and some stretchy jeans. My flat-heeled boots would be comfortable for walking and the layers would work in case it got warm. In Georgia, one could experience all kinds of weather in a single day.

I had rehearsed what I wanted to say to him, though now I was aware he had a knack for derailing me. I had to stay on my guard. The important thing to remember was to not let his good looks and masculine charm cause me to give in too easily. This meeting was not about dating him. It was about managing a future together as co-parents and nothing more.

I waited by the entrance to the park, looking for his truck. He hadn't confirmed and I had a fleeting hope he might have decided not to come.

"There you are."

His voice came from behind and I turned to find him at my elbow, all six feet something of him.

"Oh. You startled me."

"Sorry, darlin'."

Was he laying on the drawl or was it natural?

"Let's not get too familiar now, mister." I was only half-joking.

He leaned forward and placed a hand on my belly. "Darlin', that ship has sailed."

I removed his hand and stepped a few feet away. Then I turned and wagged a finger in his face. "Do not touch a pregnant woman's belly without permission."

He splayed his hands open, following me. "Well, that ship is long gone too. If you recall, I've already touched way—"

Now my finger was across his lips, silencing him. "Nope. Not going there. It happened, that's why we're here, but we don't need to rehash it. Let it go."

"Sorry."

He didn't know what to make of that, judging by his stunned expression. I knew he'd try to use memories of our night together to soften me up. Even though we both admitted to faulty memories of the night in question, I recalled enough to make parts of me tingle when they shouldn't. But I'd never let him know that.

As I turned to walk toward the festival, I heard him mutter under his breath.

"We're off to a roaring start."

I stifled a grin and started browsing the first booth. It was mostly hand-made jewelry, and an elderly woman stood beaming behind the cloth-covered table.

"Can I interest you in a bracelet, or a necklace maybe?" Then she winked at Gib, who trailed behind. "Maybe something pretty for your girl?"

He simply shrugged and looked at me.

"They are lovely," I assured the woman. "But we're just browsing."

We wandered past several booths, and I began to relax a bit. Now that he had backed off from his southern-charm routine, I thought we might accomplish something.

"So, Gib… Tell me something about you."

Not So Broken

I glanced behind me to see him scowling. "What do you want to know? My life story?"

"Not entirely. Let's start with where you were born, where you grew up. I was born in New Jersey, an only child. My mom moved us here to Atlanta for work when I was a teen. Your turn."

"Born and raised in Atlanta, one sister, younger. Parents still alive. Nothing much else to tell."

There was something in his tone that told me he was holding back. "Do you not get along with them?"

The sharp look he gave me all but confirmed my assumption. He pretended to browse the table in front of him, looking at handmade knives in a glass case, not meeting my eyes as he answered.

"Let's say we've had our ups and downs. It's a long story."

We walked on, and I spotted a row of food trucks at the edge of the park. My stomach rumbled, having been emptied three times that morning.

"Are you hungry? There's some tables over there, we can sit and eat."

"Sure."

Minutes later, we had plates of food and bottles of water laid out on a picnic table. I had been craving olives for some reason, so the Mediterranean food truck had been my choice. Gib had opted for Asian food, some kind of dumplings with a dipping sauce. When we finished most of the food, I tried to get the conversation going again.

"So, you told me you ended up in Tilly by accident. Do you plan to stay there forever?"

"I don't know. Maybe. I like it there."

"Do you have enough work? I mean, isn't it a seasonal town?"

"For tourists it is. Some of the businesses do shut down in winter, and my work slows down then, too. But not for long. There's always someone needing something fixed."

"So...You make enough income to live comfortably, then?"

His eyes flashed and I knew I'd crossed a line, but he probably wasn't going to give me a financial statement. I had to find out if he was responsible when it came to money.

"I'm not a deadbeat, if that's what you're asking."

"I'm not implying anything, so don't get all huffy. It sounds like you don't have a steady income, that's all."

He leaned forward, and his eyes bore into mine. "You said you wanted to raise the child without me, and now you're concerned about

85

my income?"

"No. I am concerned about you being a responsible adult. Working as a handyman, living in an old cabin on a remote mountain, avoiding my questions about your past… It all doesn't paint a picture of the ideal father for my child."

His voice was ice cold. "Lady, you don't know shit about me, if that's all you see."

He grabbed up his empty plate and left, throwing it in the nearby trash can with a little too much force. I got up to follow, throwing my half-eaten lunch in the can.

"Then enlighten me. Prove to me that you will be a responsible co-parent. Can you support yourself? Will you be flexible about schedules? What the hell do you want out of this?"

He turned on his heel to face me, and I stopped just before slamming into him. We were inches apart, so close I could smell the clean, citrus scent of his cologne.

"I want a second chance. That's all."

The pain in his expression took me by surprise. I wasn't sure what he meant, but before I could ask, he took my hands in his.

"Sacha, I can't tell you everything about my past, because it's still too painful. I lost my wife in an accident, and she was pregnant at the time. All I know is I don't want to miss out this time around. Not one second."

His eyes glistened with tears. It made my own eyes sting with moisture.

"Why didn't you tell me, then? I had no idea."

"I don't want your pity. I only want you and the baby to be safe. Whatever that takes."

For a moment, a breath caught in my throat. I squeezed his hand, and he drew me into a hug. We stood in the middle of the park like that for a minute, saying nothing. It seemed we had finally found our neutral ground.

~*~

Gibson

I had been pissed off by her assumptions, but when I held Sacha in my arms, all that melted away. She only saw what she saw—after all,

Not So Broken

I wasn't really being myself, was I? For a moment, I was tempted to tell her the whole truth. But I hadn't decided yet that I would go back to my old life, and it wouldn't be fair to dangle a life of luxury in front of her and then take it away. So, I kept silent. Soon she withdrew from my arms to look up at me with those deep green eyes, now full of compassion.

"I can't imagine what you've been through, Gib. That must have been awful."

I swallowed past the lump in my throat. "It was. But now I have hope. For the first time in a long while."

I gave her hand a squeeze as I released it, but she grasped it again and began walking. We wandered back to the festival tables, hand in hand. Entering a tent, she released my hand to point at a painting.

"Oh, that's beautiful. So real."

A man stepped forward, gray hair in tangles down to his shoulders. He had a huge smile on his wrinkled face. "Thank you. I'm the artist. It's a local scene. This park, in fact."

The painting was done in a somewhat impressionistic style, but the effect made it shimmer. A huge oak tree was the centerpiece of the scene, set in blazing autumn colors.

Sacha stepped forward to take a closer look. "Really? I thought it looked familiar."

The artist laughed. "Well, it doesn't look exactly like this. They had to put a fence around the Fortune Tree. That's what people call the oak in the center."

Sacha smiled in recognition. "I've heard of that tree. Do people really believe it tells fortunes?"

"Oh, yes. So much so, they had to block it off for fear the old tree would be damaged." He looked at me, and I'm sure I looked bewildered. He explained, "Legend says if you carve or draw a dollar sign on the tree, you'll come into money. If you draw or carve a heart, you'll find true love."

I said the first thing that came into my mind. "Better to draw both then."

Sacha chuckled then asked how much the painting cost.

The artist stroked his gray beard and looked over at the woman behind him. Her hair was also long and streaked with gray, her denim shirt splattered with paint. She was rearranging items on a table, unaware of our conversation. Then he nodded in her direction.

"This one's my wife's favorite, so I couldn't part with it for less than three hundred. I'll have to paint another one for her because we met under that very tree, years ago."

Sacha smiled, glancing at the woman. "Aww. That's so sweet. Maybe you should keep this one then."

The artist smiled back and winked at me. "Let me know if you change your mind. The painting might be good luck for you."

We continued on, and the mood was lighter than before. As Sacha browsed a clothing tent, I excused myself to find the restroom. When I returned a while later with the tree painting in hand, her shocked expression and the delighted smile that followed made my day.

"You bought it! I can't believe it."

"Maybe it will bring us luck. You take it home."

"Are you sure? You shouldn't have spent all that money."

I handed the painting to her. "Don't worry about it." She actually blushed.

"Thank you."

A moment passed between us, and I thought she was going to kiss me, but she held back. She took my hand and cocked her head.

"Come on. Let's go check out our tree."

Ours. Something is ours. It's a start...

Sacha saw the Fortune Tree from across the park and squealed. "There it is. Not as many leaves now as in the painting, though."

It was near where we had sat by the food trucks. She hadn't paid any attention to it then. As we walked, she told me of rumors she'd heard about a lucky tree in the local park but never had cause to check it out. Until now.

The fence that encircled the tree was a flimsy portable fence, and though signs were posted to warn people away, two kids had dared to trespass. With markers in hand, they were drawing on the tree and laughing. When she stood in front of the fence, I held up the painting.

"Yep. That's it. He even got some of the graffiti on the bark. Look."

She studied the painting and looked at the tree. The artist's rendition was not as riddled with scribbled marks as the real one but close. Sacha wrinkled her nose. "I'm not superstitious, but it's a sweet idea."

"Maybe this replica will work just as well."

I winked at her and was rewarded with a smile. Maybe Sacha Rowan was okay. I knew the painting was an impulsive gift, but she had shown me some empathy. Still, she continued to protest.

"I hope so, but you shouldn't have wasted money on that. I love it, but still…"

I frowned. She really was stubborn as an ox. "Consider it a peace offering. A sign of good faith in our future."

She looked at me, giving in. "I will. So, what happens now?"

"We hang the painting."

~*~

Sacha

We walked through the parking lot and stopped when we reached my car. Gib set the painting down by his knee and crossed his arms over his chest. "Before we go, I have some questions."

"What would you like to know?"

"Do you live near here? Do you plan to stay?"

He was throwing my own questions back at me. I almost told him about Alabama but the words wouldn't come. I still hoped to get out of it somehow, and if I told him, then it would seem inevitable.

"Yes, I have a nice apartment. It's close to everything I need."

"Can I see it today? Or is it too soon?"

It was silly to worry about letting him into my life now. My earlier fears had dissipated in light of our conversations. He didn't seem to be a freak or anything, so why not?

Just to be safe, I'd text Melanie when I got in the car. "Sure, you can follow me. It's not far."

He took the painting with him, promising to hang it for me. When we arrived at my apartment, I had a strange sense of déjà vu, fumbling for my key with him escorting me to my door. I had desperately wanted him to come into my room that night, drunk as I was from tequila and desire. This time I was sober, but the desire had returned with a vengeance.

He entered behind me, carrying the painting. I wished I had tidied up more—I hadn't expected him to come back to my place.

"Sorry for the mess."

He shrugged. "I live alone too."

I put on a pot to boil for tea and set out a box of cookies. Gib was standing near the fireplace with the painting, holding it up.

"How about here?"

He held it in front of the mantle, which was covered in photos and mementoes. The painting would fit, but I'd have to move the clutter somewhere else.

"Maybe. But I think the colors would match the décor in my bedroom better." The thought of Gib in my bedroom made my heart thump. Why did I say that? He must have felt something too, judging from his silent stare. I cleared my suddenly dry throat. "Please, set it down and we'll figure it out after the tea is ready."

He set the painting against the wall. He gestured at the framed photos on the nearby shelf and smiled. "Is that you?"

He nodded toward the one on the end, of me at graduation from high school. Mom was at my side, beaming with pride.

"Yes, and that's my mom. She was over the moon because she'd never finished high school."

"Because she had you?"

I wasn't sure if he was being impertinent or just curious. "What makes you think that?"

"She looks so young there, your mom. You two look more like sisters."

That made me laugh. "We get that a lot. She was eighteen when I was born. My dad was a few years older." I paused, weighing whether to tell him the rest of that story. I settled for the abridged version. "He skipped out on us when I was nine. On my birthday, in fact."

The teakettle was whistling, so I went to the kitchen to make the tea. Over my shoulder, I heard his response.

"That's not cool. How could anyone do that?"

When I returned with the mugs of steaming herbal tea, I answered, "I have no idea. You'd have to ask him. But Mom's remarried now, living in Jersey again. That's where her friends and family are, so she's happy."

His eyes met mine. "Have you told her about the baby yet?"

"No. I'm waiting for the right time. But I have to soon."

We chatted about random topics and sipped tea. He told me about his grouchy neighbor, an old man no one else could stand but who seemed to have adopted Gib as a surrogate son. He described the view from his cabin, and how it changed throughout the seasons.

"You should see it. Plus, there's plenty of wildlife—deer, raccoons, 'possums…"

I wrinkled my nose. "Eww. No thank you to 'possums."

He grinned. "Aww, c'mon. They're mean but they are cute. Well, ugly-cute."

Not So Broken

I felt much more relaxed now but wondered how long he would stay. I couldn't keep my eyes off his forearms since he'd rolled up the sleeves of his denim shirt. In the past few days, I had spikes of horniness for no apparent reason. Well, except for my hormones going wild.

But sleeping with him again was definitely not a good idea. It could seriously complicate things. I was wondering how to get him to leave when he stood up.

"So, should we hang that painting? May as well while I'm here. I can reach places you can't."

There was something about the way he said the last few words that made my stomach drop. It sounded like innuendo, but maybe my hormones really were affecting my judgment. It was safer to get the task done so he could leave.

"Sure. This way."

I walked to the bedroom, hoping I hadn't left bras laying anywhere. A quick look around relieved my fear—only an errant towel lay across the bed. My bedroom furniture was cream colored, and the comforter and pillows were various shades of burgundy, green, and gold.

"Yeah, this will go great with your colors in here," Gib observed as he held the painting up over the bed.

An old black and white artsy photo hung there, totally out of place. It had been a gift from Melanie, and though it wasn't my style, I hadn't wanted to hurt her feelings. I'd have to hang Mel's photo in the living room or maybe the hall.

"Yes, that'll be awesome."

I watched as he pulled off his boots and stepped up onto the bed. He took the old photo down from the wall and handed it to me. I gave him the tree painting, and he quickly had it resting on the same hooks as the photo had been. It was larger but not much heavier since it had no frame.

"How does it look?"

He stood balancing on the bed, with one hand against the wall. I stepped back to admire the view, and the painting too.

"Beautiful. I'll have to get a frame, but it looks perfect there."

He smiled and hopped down, ending up next to me. One hand came up to caress my cheek, and I froze.

"It's nice, but not the most beautiful thing in this room. That would be you."

The panicky thought that kissing him was not a good idea flew through my mind and out the window as his lips touched mine. It was an infinitely gentle kiss, barely a brushing of lips. The effect was electric, igniting sparks all up and down my body. I stood still, not daring to breathe, not trusting myself to move.

He pulled away slightly, still so close my breath mingled with his. I wanted to stop him, to cling to my defenses, to remain in control. But my hormones were ramping up so fiercely I could almost feel my blood heating.

"We...we shouldn't."

It was a whisper, or maybe a whimper. He didn't answer me with words, but his hands slid up my arms then across my back to pull me close. His head tilted and he placed the same feather-light kiss on my neck.

"Maybe not, darlin'. But I can't help but want you. You drive me wild."

His words described how I felt about him too—a little wild. He had been my wild wanton moment, my last fling, but now I couldn't get him out of my life or my mind. Or my blood. It was easy to dismiss him when he was hours away, but in close proximity, something primitive took over and I found myself craving him with every cell in my body.

It was crazy.

Or maybe I was going crazy. The hormones had messed with my mind.

It didn't matter. I was powerless to control it at the moment, so I threw my arms around his neck and went full on into his embrace. The kiss that followed was mind-blowing, fierce. His mouth claimed mine, no longer gentle. His beard tickled my skin then scratched it as he deepened the kiss. I didn't care.

He twisted and took me with him, so we landed on the bed. I lay alongside him, still locked in the kiss. When I pulled back for air, he laughed.

"For two people who think they shouldn't be together, we're not doing so well."

I rested my head on his chest, lacing my fingers with his. "No, we're not." The joke broke the mood, and I felt my head clearing. "I think...I just think we should take it slow, you know?"

"I know."

His other arm was under me, his hand stroking my hair. I lay next to him like that for a few minutes, until my breathing returned to normal. I had to do better at keeping control of myself.

"I didn't mean to lead you on or anything. But I'm afraid if we hook up again, things could get complicated."

"I know. I started it, not you. I guess sometimes I forget the effect I have over women."

I groaned at his sarcasm and smacked his hand. I looked up at him, only to see his smart-ass grin. "Don't kid yourself, sir. I'm at the mercy of my hormones."

"Ouch. And all this time I thought it was my charm."

I sat up and willed myself to leave the warmth of his side. It would be too easy to start kissing him again and that might escalate quickly to a place I wasn't ready to go.

"Thanks again for the painting. I love it."

He hauled himself off the bed with a sigh. "And that's my cue to leave. But you're welcome."

I should have protested out of politeness, but it was past time for him to leave. I'd never intended for him to even see my place this soon. I wondered how it compared to his cabin in the woods.

As he neared the door, he stopped. "Hey, I've seen your place. You should come and see my cabin. Maybe it'll ease your mind. It's not a hovel, and I'm not one step away from being homeless."

Now he was reading my mind? "I never said that. You're the one who said it was remote and small. But maybe that is a good idea."

"Then we'll both have a better understanding of who we are, and how we can make things work. When do you think can you can come back up to Tilly?"

"How about next weekend?" The words were out of my mouth before I'd had a chance to think it through. Damn, was he getting under my skin?

"That'll work. I'll call you later in the week to confirm."

I nodded, holding the front door open. He hesitated a moment, then gave me a quick hug. I thanked him, and he left without another word.

Chapter Twelve

Gibson

I spent all of Sunday cleaning up around the cabin. I had jobs to finish during the week and would have little time for housework in the evenings, since it was getting dark earlier. I hoped Sacha would make good on her promise to come for a visit, so I had to make the place presentable. In my old life, I'd simply inform the housekeeper and the cook of a visitor coming, and they'd handle the rest. But now I wore those titles alone.

Leaves, cobwebs, and clutter all had to go. The cabin was not brand new, but when it was cleaned up, it was homey and inviting. I pulled the comforter from the bed to have it dry-cleaned, and even used the ladder and a long-handled duster to clean the ceiling fans. By evening, I was worn out, but my rustic little cabin looked better than it had since I'd moved in.

Earlier, I had put a pot of chili on the stove, so around five I took some down to Marvil. I was greeted with a terse "It's about time" as I ascended the steps to the porch, where Marvil sat in a rocking chair. He was bundled up in a blanket, which was fleece and covered with cartoon characters. The old man's penchant for whimsical clothes and household items was so not in keeping with his gruff personality.

As usual, I ignored his complaint and countered with a cheery comeback. "Hungry, are we? I'll get you a spoon so you can eat out here.

If you like."

I took the old man's grunt in response as a "yes" and went inside the cabin. Returning with a fold-out tray and utensils, I placed the bowl of chili in front of Marvil, who proceeded to eat like it was his last meal.

In between bites, he asked, "What ya been doing up there all day? You were gone yesterday too."

I sat on a swing at the end of the porch and zipped my leather jacket against the chill evening air. "Cleaning. I may have a visitor next weekend."

Oops. I didn't know what possessed me to divulge that information. Now Marvil would never leave it alone. I cringed as the old man's bushy eyebrows shot up.

"A visitor, huh? Would this be a lady friend?"

Now the brows wiggled comically, and I almost laughed. "Yes, but she's just a friend. Don't go making up stories about my so-called love life."

"A friend. Hmmm…What do they call that these days? Friends with extras?"

Now I did laugh. "Benefits. Friends with benefits. But it's not that kind of friend."

Except for the fact I knocked her up.

"Well good luck, and keep the noise down, please. I have to get my beauty rest, you know."

Smiling at his own joke, Marvil finished his chili.

It was going to be a long week.

~*~

Sacha

The paper-thin gown was no match for the air conditioning in the examination room at my obstetrician's office. Shivering, I crossed my arms over my chest, to shield my taut nipples as much as to warm myself. How long was I going to have to wait like this? Practically naked and totally aggravated.

The aggravation had started that morning. I woke up in a pissy mood, which might be the fault of hormones but who knew? It seemed the closer it got to the weekend and my latest jaunt to Tilly, the worse was my outlook. I couldn't figure out exactly what was making me apprehensive. It was only Wednesday, so there was still time to back out. But my curiosity about Gib was winning out over my good sense, which meant I really should stay the hell away from him.

The doctor's entrance into the room broke me out of my thoughts. Martha Kapoor, M.D. was small in stature but had a large personality, warming the room instantly with her bright smile and loud voice.

"So how are we today? Are you chilled to the bone yet?"

The joke about the room temperature should have made me more upset, but I chuckled. Something about Dr. Kapoor's smile was infectious. I had only seen her twice so far but had immediately felt comfortable with her. Which was extremely important when the woman was going to examine my most intimate parts.

"Okay, young lady. Lay back and spread 'em."

The slight accent made Dr. Kapoor's brusque joke funnier. She sounded like she should be giving a lecture to academics, not telling a naked woman to bare her nether parts.

The humor eased the tension I had been feeling. Today was my first ultrasound, and that had to be part of why I was so worked up. We would be listening to the baby's heartbeat if all went well.

Dr. Kapoor was thorough in her examination but gentle. When she finished, a nurse came in to prepare me for the ultrasound. A gel was applied to my stomach at several locations, and the sensors were attached. The nurse stood by while Dr. Kapoor adjusted the machine.

My heart was beating so fiercely in my chest, I thought it would drown out the baby's. *I've waited all my life for this moment. Please be healthy...*

Dr. Kapoor held the stethoscope to my belly, which was only slightly pouched. I was thirteen and a half weeks along, and only beginning to show.

"Shouldn't I be bigger by now, doctor? It's over three months."

"Some women's bellies are bigger at this point, but some also take a bit longer to grow. Everything feels right, so far." I held my breath as she continued to listen, feeling my belly in sections. It seemed to be taking forever. Then Dr. Kapoor gasped. "Wait. I found it. Listen."

She nodded to the nurse, who turned up the volume on the machine. *Thump-thump. Thump-thump.*

It was faint, but it was obviously a heartbeat. A really fast heartbeat. Tears came, followed by a joyful laugh. "Oh, wow. I can't believe it."

Not So Broken

"Believe it, honey. You're going to be a mother."

My baby was alive and well. This was really happening. I felt nothing but gratitude in that moment, for the miracle of life growing within me. I even felt like thanking Gib for giving me this priceless gift.

Would he feel the same joy as I was now? After what he went through, losing his wife and child, would he be able to love this baby? He said he wanted to care for us, and he seemed sincere. But what was he really capable of giving?

The procedure was over, and I wiped my eyes on the thin gown. Only time would tell how it was going to work out with Gibson Cole-bank. All I knew was, no one was ever going to hurt me again or harm this child in any way.

~*~

Gibson

Wednesday afternoon I was at a client's house cutting a piece of wood with a power saw when I felt my phone vibrating in my shirt pocket. When I finished the cut, I turned off the saw and reached for it, catching the call before it went to voicemail.

"Hello?"

The female voice on the line made my heart skip a beat. It was Sacha.

"I heard it."

"Heard what?"

"I heard the baby's heartbeat today. At the doctor's office."

"Wow. That's awesome." Suddenly hot, I removed my wool cap and wiped my brow. I walked to the edge of the deck to ensure good reception. I didn't want to drop this call.

"I'm sorry if you're at work. I had to let you know."

"It's okay. I'm glad you called."

I wasn't glad, I was freaking thrilled but didn't want to scare her off. Sacha seemed to like feeling in control, and I was content to leave her in charge, if that meant she was safe.

She went on to describe her experience, and the joy in her voice warmed me. Maybe there was a chance she'd let me into her life after all. I planned to win her over completely this weekend, whatever that took.

"Doctor Kapoor said we can find out the gender at eighteen

weeks, if we want. What do you think? Do you want to know or be surprised?"

Her question brought me out of my mental preparations for her visit, and I knew the answer immediately. "I want to know. I never found out, um, the last time."

My voice faltered on the last words. Would I ever be able to just talk about it?

"I agree. It will make it easier to prepare, I think."

"Yes, it will." I paused, still reeling from the news. "Thank you for calling me. I have to admit, I'm surprised."

"Why?"

I should have said thank you and let it go…

"You haven't been exactly welcoming about my involvement, you know."

She was quiet for a moment. I'd wanted to tell her how it bothered me, but maybe this wasn't the time. When she answered, I heard a touch of regret. "I know. And I'm sorry. This has all been overwhelming."

"I understand. But I'm not your enemy, okay?"

"Okay."

There was a slight hesitation in her tone that spoke volumes. She still wasn't sure about me. Another reason to get her up here as soon as possible.

"So, you'll be here in Tilly by noon this Saturday, right?"

"That's the plan. Can we meet at the motel parking lot, and I'll follow you?"

"That's probably best. GPS doesn't always work up here."

We chatted a few minutes more, and I came away with a vague feeling of apprehension. I should have been overjoyed by the news of the baby's heartbeat, and I was. It meant the baby was healthy. But Sacha's hesitant attitude toward me was a cold splash of water on the warmth that was growing in my heart.

She was only coming to see my place and then leave. I hoped to talk her into much more. It was time we really got to know one another. Time for me to take back control of the situation. She would come to realize it was best for all three of us.

How could I protect them both if she kept pushing me away?

~*~

Sacha

My phone call with Gib went well. Telling him about the baby had been nice—it was a warm, sharing moment. So, why was I still apprehensive? I knew logically he had a right to be included, but how to do that without giving up control of my life was the tricky part. If we were a romantically involved couple, it would be a different story.

There was one more hurdle to face—telling my mother. Attempting to control the conversation would be futile. She had pushed the idea of me giving her grandchildren even before I married Kevin, so I knew she was going to be ecstatic.

At first. Then she was going to let me know exactly how things should be done. Never mind she was a day's drive away. Steeling myself, I pushed the button on my phone and waited for the show to begin.

"Mom?"

"Hey, sweetie! We were just talking about you. I was telling Roger about Atlanta. He wants to come and see the zombies. I mean, you know, where they film them."

"Okay. That'd be fun. Listen, Mom, I need to let you know something, though."

"What's the matter? You sound ill."

"No, I'm not ill. But I am…"

I froze. The words wouldn't come. Mom should have been the first to know, and I had chickened out about telling her. Now it was going to hurt the poor woman to find her daughter was over thirteen weeks pregnant.

"What is it? Tell me."

An undercurrent of panic laced her voice, so I blurted out the news. "I'm pregnant."

The silence was almost deafening. Then she let out a shriek, causing me to hold the phone away from my ear.

"Ohhhh, my gawd, pregnant! Are you freaking serious?"

"Yes, I am. I'm just past the first trimester."

Squeals and giggles erupted on the line, followed by her shouting the good news to my stepbrother, Roger, and her husband, Frank. Then there was an abrupt silence.

"Wait. That's like, three months, and you're telling me now?"

"I wanted to be sure it was viable. I didn't want to upset you if something went wrong."

Her voice softened. "Oh honey, that's what a mother's for. To be there when things go wrong. You'll see."

With the initial shock over, the rest of the conversation went smoothly. We talked about my doctor appointments, when I was due, and other pregnancy related details. But the elephant was still sitting in the room, or on the line, and I knew it had to be addressed.

Should I lie and say I got a donor?

I was tempted to lie, but when Gib showed up to claim his son or daughter, Julia would be even more upset if she had no idea who he was.

"So, Mom... I never meant for it to happen this way. I thought it never would. You know how long Kevin and I tried."

"I know. Then it was particularly devastating for you the way he went about...what he did."

Discussing Kevin or the divorce was still painful, so I shifted the focus back on to me.

"Even though I've been alone, I still desperately wanted a child. So, I began the process for single-parent adoption several months ago. But before I could be approved, this happened. I guess the universe had other plans for me."

She clucked her tongue. "And you didn't tell me about that either. Sacha, we talk every day. What am I, a monster?"

"No, Mom. But that process could take years, and I didn't want to say anything until I was approved. If I hadn't been, I'd have been devastated all over again."

She sighed and said, "I know. Well, it's moot now, anyway. So... Do you know who the father is?"

I knew why she asked, but it still stung. "Of course, I know him. I'm not...I wouldn't..."

"Good. I thought maybe you went to the sperm bank or something. So, who is he?"

"His name is Gibson. The pregnancy was not planned, of course, but he's happy about it." A judgmental-sounding 'hmmm' was all I heard on the line. At least he wasn't a stranger. Well, not any longer. "He's a nice guy, Mom. And he understands I'm raising the baby alone, though he says he wants to be involved. We are working all that out, one step at a time."

Another silence followed, and I held my breath, waiting for the barrage of advice. Instead, she asked me one question.

"Are you happy, Sacha?"

It was so like Julia to cut to the heart of things. My mother's frankness had always irritated me, especially when it was an uncomfortable subject. But I knew it would be brought up again and again until I answered.

"About the baby, yes. I'm thrilled. About co-parenting with Gib? I'm not sure. We'll see."

Chapter Thirteen

Sacha

I waited until Friday afternoon to call Dan at the office. It was kind of chicken shit, I know. I should have told him about the pregnancy before now, and it was possible he wouldn't even get the message until Monday. But I'd wanted to wait until all my orders were in for the week. Every order helped my case, so I could negotiate a better situation than moving to Alabama.

At least that was my plan. I'd been procrastinating all day and called Melanie to come over for moral support. She watched as I pushed the button for Dan's number. When he didn't pick up, I sighed in relief and waited for the beep.

"Hey Dan, it's Sacha. I wanted to tell you this in person but wasn't able to get into the office when you were there. Anyway, I'm not sure if this changes anything, but I need to let you know I'm pregnant. I'm not due until May. We can talk about it on Monday if you want, just let me know. Thanks."

I hung up the phone and looked over at Melanie, who looked back at me with raised brows.

"Don't you feel better now? Everyone knows."

"Not really. I feel sick to my stomach, actually. And it's not morning sickness."

"What can they do? You probably have more leverage now.

Not So Broken

There's no sense getting upset until you hear a response. You have enough on your mind already."

"I know. You're right, but I wish I could predict what was going to happen. With this merger going on, I have no idea how they'll react."

"I hear ya. Just today, our bass player quit. Right before a gig. We'll have to go on without one if we can't find someone else. I know it sounds like no big deal, but if we don't do a fantastic job, we won't be asked back."

"That sucks."

"Tell me about it."

"I wish I could help, but you're the only musician I know."

I went to the kitchen and put water on for herbal tea, a brand Mom had recommended to soothe my stomach troubles. It was an obscure brand, but she knew someone who swore it worked. I'd been to three natural food shops before I found it. I opened the fridge looking for milk and spotted my last bottle of wine. Still feeling bad about her troubles, I handed it to Melanie.

"You can have it. It'll be awhile before I can drink again."

"Thanks. I'll probably need some tonight after the gig. So, back to Tilly and your Mountain Man tomorrow, eh?"

I felt heat creep onto my cheeks for no apparent reason. "Yes, just to see where he lives. I plan on being home before dark."

The sly look she gave me didn't help my nerves one bit. I was apprehensive about this visit, and it pissed me off to feel that way. I was a grown-ass woman, not some inexperienced kid. This wasn't my first time seeing a man's home.

"Well, don't forget to call or text me when you're on the way home. I want to hear all about it."

"I will."

With the bottle of wine in her hand, Melanie walked to the door. "If I don't hear from you by dark, either he's kidnapped you or you decided to stay. Maybe you better take a toothbrush, in case...you know."

Now I was the one giving her a sly look. "This is not a date, it's a business meeting. We are in the planning stages of co-parenting. That's all. There will be no juicy details to divulge, so forget about me and go get ready for your gig. Good luck, and I'll see you when I get back."

Melanie's smile was more of a smirk. She said not a word, but I knew what she was thinking as she closed the door behind her.

Why doesn't she believe me?

To prove a point to myself, I left home the next morning with only my coat and purse. I didn't pack anything "just in case." There was no need. There would be no hanky-panky like there was in my bedroom during the hanging of the tree painting. I would look around, maybe have lunch with him, and that was it.

We needed to start handling our relationship in a more business-like fashion. That way, there would be no drama, no power struggle, and it certainly wouldn't escalate into any legal issues. Gib seemed like a reasonable man, if a little arrogant at times. He would see the wisdom of leaving me in control of the situation, since I was the mother and main caregiver.

As I headed north on GA 400, I realized my nerves had settled. I was sure we would work things out. I felt a sudden flutter in my lower stomach, and I couldn't help but imagine it was the little one telling me he or she approved. It was a good sign.

~*~

Gibson

I parked my truck on the street in front of the motel, the one where Sacha and I spent our only night together. Fragmented memories bounced around my mind, leaving irritation in their wake. I knew better than to get that drunk. I was an idiot. But in my defense, I'd been pent up for way too long and got carried away, plain and simple.

It wouldn't happen again.

My heart thumped suddenly as Sacha's car came into view. My involuntary physical reactions were another source of irritation. I had to remain in control of my mind and my body. She had made it clear that her pregnancy was the only thing tying us together. This was more of a business arrangement than a personal relationship. I would show her my home, and we would make a plan to handle things going forward.

Thinking of it that way helped. She pulled up to the curb behind me, and I went to greet her. As I leaned in her open window, she was so close I could smell her clean, floral scent. For a moment, I forgot what I was going to say. She blinked, and I regained my composure.

"Are you sure you want to follow me? The road up to my place is all gravel and kind of rough. Maybe I should drive."

She hesitated for a moment, biting her bottom lip. I wasn't sure whether it was the thought of driving on a rough road or being alone with me that made her pause. Then she reached into the back seat to grab her purse, asking, "Do you think my car will be safe here?"

"For a few hours, sure."

She turned off her engine, and we walked to my truck. I helped her climb inside, grateful I'd thought to clean it up the day before. It was the first time a woman had seen the inside of this truck, and it felt strange. I glanced at Sacha as I started the engine and pulled onto the road. Was she really more beautiful each time I saw her, or was my mind playing tricks on me?

Her chestnut hair had golden highlights and fell in waves to her shoulders. Her make-up was minimal, and she really did seem to have a glow about her. She didn't look pregnant, that I could tell, had I not known. She seemed healthy, and for that I was grateful.

"How are you feeling, Sacha?"

Her smile was quick but warm. "Pretty good, except for tummy troubles now and then."

"That's good. I was worried."

"Don't be. My doctor is wonderful. Plus, my good friend Melanie lives next door. She checks in on me all the time."

As we traveled the winding road out of town, I played tour guide, describing the local sites as we passed. First, it was the giant bear statue in the middle of town, then the diner, then the waterfall just outside the town park. As the more natural scenery began, the narrow road hugged a rock wall on one side with the tumbling, shallow river on the other. It was one of my favorite parts of the drive.

"There's the Chattahoochee River next to us. Or as the locals call it, 'The 'Hooch.'"

She craned her neck to see. "They call it that in Atlanta, too. It's a lot wider and muddier down south."

"That's true. My parent's place overlooks the river. It is definitely wider there but much deeper, better for kayaking and such. Here, they mostly use inner tubes in the summer."

I'd slipped and mentioned my parent's house, but she wouldn't be able to tell much from the comment. Still, I'd planned to keep my former life private, for now at least.

Some kids on the riverbank had poles in the water, despite the chill of the day. Sacha spotted them and asked, "The fishing is pretty good up here, right? That's what some of my clients said."

"Yes, and I know of some of the best spots to fish, if you ever want to try it."

An image flashed in my mind, of Sacha, a little boy, and me. We were walking to the spot Marvil had taken me, poles and gear in hand, ready for a family outing. It was foolish, but I entertained the unbidden fantasy for a moment before pushing it from my mind.

"Maybe someday."

She was lying, but I appreciated her effort.

The road grew steeper as we neared the turnoff. Being Saturday, I had to endure traveling at a snail's pace behind tourists, but it gave me the opportunity to watch Sacha. She stared out the window at the passing landscape, spiky bare trees interspersed with clumps of tall pines. As we turned onto the gravel road that led to my cabin, she gasped at the sight of the narrow wooden bridge up ahead.

"You didn't say anything about that."

I couldn't suppress my smirk as I maneuvered the truck onto the one-lane, rickety bridge. "You didn't ask."

Suspended over a wide creek, the bridge was sturdier than it looked. A waterfall tumbled over two huge boulders on one side, and the creek pooled at the bottom then ran under the bridge. Sacha glanced from side to side, taking it all in.

"It is pretty. But scary."

She held onto the door handle as we bumped over the rocks protruding from the graveled surface of the road. I was practiced enough to avoid the worst ruts, but it still wasn't a smooth ride. "See why I insisted on driving?"

She merely nodded and appeared to be holding her breath. I stifled a laugh, recalling how nerve-wracking it had been for me the first time I'd gone up this road. When I had seen the cabin and the view from the back deck, it had been worth every mile.

Soon we rounded a curve and Marvil's cabin came into view. It was larger than the one I lived in but a few years older. It didn't have the views mine had, but was nestled among the pines.

"Is that it?"

"No. That's where my landlord lives. The older gentleman I told you about."

"Oh."

Disappointment had laced her tone when she saw the old cabin. I wondered what she was going to say about my place. We kept climbing, the truck's gears grinding, bouncing along the next half mile. As the green metal roof of my little cabin came into view, partially obscured by trees, Sacha let out a sigh of relief.

Not So Broken

"The drive wasn't that bad, was it?"

She huffed. "Only for my stomach."

I pulled up in front of the porch so she wouldn't have far to walk. Helping her from the truck, I stood by while she took in her surroundings.

"It's quiet here."

"Except at night. Wildlife sometimes makes its presence known."

Her eyes went wide, but she said nothing. She walked up to the covered front porch and touched the logs that made up the structure. "Pine?"

"Yep. Georgia white pine. Only the floors are different, made of oak."

I unlocked the front door and let her precede me. I'd placed bowls of pine cones and scented candles out to enhance the room. I figured some aromatherapy couldn't hurt. Sometimes the cabin had a musty smell, especially when it was closed up for a time. I wanted her to be comfortable in my home.

She looked around at the living room, the floor-to-ceiling rock fireplace, the cheery kitchen off to one side. Sunlight filtered in from the upper windows and the panorama of rolling mountains, still flecked with fall colors, was showcased through the sliding glass doors.

"Not bad."

"That's what I said the first time I saw this place. Then I moved in. Can I take your coat?"

She slipped off her coat, and I instinctively looked at her stomach. She wore a peach-colored sweater, and though it was loose-fitting, it still flattered her figure. There was no baby bump yet, but her breasts seemed larger than I recalled.

I chastised myself for the rush of desire that immediately flooded my veins. This wasn't going to be easy.

I took her coat and hung it on a hook near the front door. "Would you like something to drink?"

She was still looking around at the furnishings, the walls, and out the windows. The place had come furnished, so the decor was plain, but I had added a few touches to make it my own. Like the Georgia Bulldogs throw on the sofa, the Tiffany lamp, and the leather ottoman in front of the recliner. It made the place feel a bit homier, albeit much less fancy than what I'd been used to.

"Do you have any ginger ale?"

"I might. I have some sandwiches made, too. We can eat outside." I opened the sliding glass door so she could step onto the deck. I pointed to the nearest rocking chair. "Make yourself at home. I'll be right back."

When I returned a few minutes later with two cans of soda and a tray, she seemed quite content. She was rocking slowly, her head back, taking photos of the view with her phone. "This is actually pretty nice. I apologize for doubting you about your cabin."

I placed the soda in her hand and put the tray on a small table between us. "No harm done. It's plain but comfortable. Plus, you can't beat the view."

"No, you can't. I'm impressed."

We chatted about the mountains, about Tilly, and how different it was from Atlanta. Soon the sandwiches were gone, and the conversation lagged. I knew it was time to get to the real conversation, now that she was relaxed.

"I'm glad you feel comfortable here, Sacha. I love this place, and if I'm still living here when the baby comes, I'm sure we could work something out. I'm certainly willing to go to your place most of the time, but I would want our child to know what's it's like, living closer to nature. When he's older, of course."

She was staring at me with a blank expression. Then her cheeks went pink and her mouth tightened. "You're *willing*?"

Her tone held a warning. Where was this going?

"Yes."

"Honey, you don't have a choice. The child will be living with me. I'm not keen on dragging a newborn or a toddler up here for the weekend, and who says it's a 'he'?"

Damn, she was quick to argue. Pushing her buttons was so easy, I didn't realize I was doing it until it was too late. But now she was pissing *me* off.

"It's just a figure of speech. I don't care if it's a boy, girl, whatever, as long as it's healthy and safe. Don't get your panties in a wad."

She stood and hefted her purse onto her shoulder. "You know, I came up here wanting to work with you. But your attitude makes it impossible."

"My attitude?" What the hell?

Leaning back in the rocking chair, I placed my booted foot against the deck railing, effectively blocking her from entering the house. "Sit down, Sacha. Let me explain myself."

Her chin jutted out, in a cute pout I didn't dare acknowledge with a smile. Instead, I gestured to her rocking chair with a hand, but she crossed her arms over her bosom and leaned against the railing. "Start talking."

"What I meant was, of course you will have the baby most of the time, especially in the beginning. But I plan to visit every chance I get and would like you to bring him or her up here, when it is suitable. Deal?"

"And who decides when it's 'suitable'?"

"We do. Together."

The turn of her lips indicated she still wasn't satisfied. "Well, you can't show up at my place unannounced. I'll need notice. And I'll text or call you on a regular basis."

Now I stood and took a step closer to her. "That's doable. I wouldn't want to show up unexpectedly and interrupt your love life."

Her eyes went wide at the implication. She dropped her arms, and the chin went out again. "Well, I don't want you bringing your dates on a visit, either. Let's agree to keep our private lives private."

I could smell her scent again and inched closer. "Right. I'd hate to make you jealous by bringing someone else around with me."

Now I was taunting her, but I couldn't help myself. I meant it as a joke, but her narrowed eyes indicated she wasn't amused. I thought maybe some humor might make her see she was being ridiculous. She waved a hand at me in dismissal.

"Jealous? Now you're really fooling yourself."

She wasn't backing away, though she could easily walk around me. There was a challenge in her eyes, and it sent a thrill up my spine. She was daring me to come closer, so I did, until we were inches apart. "I guess I am a fool when it comes to you."

I tentatively touched her cheek. She placed a delicate hand over mine, so I paused, but she didn't push me away. There was a split second of doubt, when my conscience told me to pull back. But the chemicals flooding my veins, and heading straight for my groin, won. Holding back was futile when I wanted to touch her so badly my body ached. Even when she pissed me off, I found her irresistible.

I slid my hand behind her neck and looked at her lips. They were trembling, so I bent down to kiss her.

Her grip on my hand tightened as I deepened the kiss, sliding my tongue across her mouth. When her lips parted to allow me in, I lost control. I wrapped my arm around her, pulling her softness against me.

Her taste was sweet from the ginger ale. Her tongue briefly

explored mine, backed by a soft moan. I was carried away on a river of lust, focused on feeling every inch of her, and hoping it was going to be as good as I'd imagined.

That's when Sasha pulled away, pushing against me with both her hands on my chest.

"Wait. We can't do this."

~*~

Sacha

"Why not?"

Damn him. No, damn me for letting Gib get to me, with his logical arguments and soft kisses.

I walked into the cabin without a word. I didn't mean to be rude but was trying to formulate a logical answer, and logic on my part was difficult when he was only inches away. I could sense he was right behind me, so I turned to face him, hoping the right words would come.

Gib stood looming over me. Was the hurt I saw in his eyes simply unrequited lust, or something else?

I hadn't meant to let it get this far. Probably why I reacted so strongly to his words, when he really was being reasonable. But we shouldn't be kissing, let alone groping each other like this. Sex might lead to feelings, and feelings would get in the way of my plans. Plus, having feelings eventually got you hurt.

No way was I going down that road again.

"Gib, you're great guy for stepping up like you have been. But us having sex again is a very slippery slope." From his grin, "slippery" probably wasn't the best choice of words. He took a step then another, walking toward me. I kept backing up, not sure where I was headed but hoping it was near the front door. "What I mean is, I don't want to be friends with benefits. Especially with the father of my child."

His lips twitched, barely noticeable under the moustache and beard. His eyes had a feral look, and his husky tone reflected the hunger I saw there.

"Maybe we could be more. Maybe we can't. But can you deny this attraction between us? It's not going away."

I couldn't deny it, when every inch of me was at war with my brain. The smart thing to do was to leave, and only see this man when I

110

absolutely had to. But what my traitorous body wanted right now was to wrap itself around him and never go home.

It would pass, but I had to get out of here before he touched me again.

Too late.

My back was against the wall. My purse slid from my shoulder to land on the floor near my feet. Gib was inches away, so close I could feel the heat radiating from his skin. One of his hands had settled on my hip, the other was brushing my jaw. His deep blue eyes, the color of a stormy sea, bore into mine. I had to look away. He was waiting for an answer. When I found my voice, it was thick, foreign-sounding.

"I don't want you. It was just a one-time thing."

"I don't believe you, Sacha. You're trembling with desire for me. Aren't you?"

His hand was caressing my collarbone and moving lower. Why was I still standing here?

I laughed, but it wasn't the confident, sarcastic sound I had been going for. It was more of a shaky, nervous warble. I had to push him away, to stop this madness. But his hands were leaving a trail of heat across my skin, and his now-obvious arousal was pressing against my thigh. My mental defenses were weakening as hormones raged out of control, stoked by the primal male now holding me in place. I moved my hands to his chest again, intending to push him away, but instead I gripped the front of his shirt and pulled him closer.

"Frenzied" is too tame a word for the feverish way we clung to each other. Months of pent-up desire and longing surfaced, and I smashed my mouth against his so hard I felt his teeth. It stung a bit, but I didn't care. Overcome with the desire to devour him, I used my tongue to explore his mouth, as though I'd never tasted him before.

I hadn't, really, since I was drunk the first time and nervous as hell the second. But now I couldn't get enough of him, and he was generously plundering my mouth as well. When he finally pulled away, I was gasping for breath. Reason returned and in a flash was gone.

"Damn you, Gib. This is so wrong."

His frantic movements stopped, and he leaned his forehead against mine. "Then tell me to stop. If you really don't want me to make love to you, I won't."

Damn him again for leaving it entirely up to me. I stood there, panting, my back against the wall, his cheek resting on mine. Once again, he was being the gentleman, which made him even harder to resist. The thought occurred to me that maybe, once we satisfied this crazy itch, we could go back to being simply partners. He was right, the desire had not gone away, and it seemed the harder we tried to fight it, the stronger the pull became. I closed my eyes while the urge to leave sparred with the heady intoxication of having him so near.

I opened my eyes and looked at him, all beard and hair and muscle and male. There was only one thing I could say.

"Take me to your bed. Right now."

In one swift movement, he picked me up. I clung to his neck as he took a few steps and kicked open his bedroom door.

Chapter Fourteen

Gibson

figured I was dreaming, because having Sacha in my bed seemed surreal. Time had slowed, and every touch, every movement became precious. It had been so long since I made love to a woman. I didn't even count the night we had spent together at the motel. That wasn't lovemaking. That was drunken fumbling. I'd never had a woman kick me out the way Sacha had that next morning, and I planned to make her regret it, by showing her what she'd missed since then.

I laid her down on my quilt-covered, queen-sized bed without breaking the kiss. Her soft hands were surprisingly strong, gripping my biceps as though she hated to let go. I slowed the kiss, finally pulling away.

"You look gorgeous in that sweater, honey, but I need to see you naked."

Her coral-pink lips parted in a gasp, but she promptly unbuttoned her sweater and tossed it on the floor. Her breasts were encased in a cream-colored lace bra, which hooked in the front. Unable to stop myself, I reached out to run a finger along one breast as slowly as I could. I was purposely teasing, and her shivers were my reward. I stopped when my finger reached the clasp, and I paused to admire the view before snapping it open.

Through trembling lips, she commanded me.

"Do it."

With a twist of my fingers, the bra fell open, revealing perfectly formed breasts. Cupping one, I kneaded, feeling the weight of it. Sacha laid her head back on the pillow and moaned. When I withdrew my hand, her eyes opened. She looked embarrassed, and crossed her arms over her chest.

"No, don't cover yourself. You're beautiful. Now take off those pants."

Her brow furrowed and the haughty expression she'd had on the deck returned. "Well, you better get naked too. Before I change my mind."

I lifted her face up with a hand under her chin. "Don't worry, I will. And for once, lie back and enjoy yourself. I'm in charge now."

She didn't try to hide her smirk. She must have thought I was joking, but I could sense she needed this. Needed to lose control, let go, and let herself be worshipped.

She began to unzip her jeans, and I bent to remove her low leather boots, and socks, and then the jeans. I tossed them all in the growing pile on the wood floor. She added her lacy panties to the pile and lay before me, naked, her nipples taut from the cold. Or maybe it was desire. I stood next to the bed looking at her, taking in her raw beauty. I had missed this on our first night together.

She rolled onto her side, leaning her head on one hand. "Okay, you might be in charge, but I have a request."

"Yes?"

"Strip."

Now it was I who couldn't hide a smirk. Just to be a smart ass, I didn't rush, undoing my denim shirt one button at a time. With a flourish, I twirled it around and threw it across the room, making her giggle. I kicked off my gym shoes, then socks, and turned my back to her to remove my jeans.

I'd worn my best briefs underneath, the silky ones that made my junk look even bigger. At least I thought so, and I figured she might get a kick out of my striptease, so I kept them on. Easing the jeans down my hips, I stepped out of them and turned to face her. Those coral lips were open in surprise, as were her eyes.

Running a finger along the waistband while I swayed my hips had caught her attention. She appeared to be fascinated by my erection, which now strained against the silky fabric. To tease her, I moved both hands into a "V" formation around the area she was looking and began touching myself. Sacha's eyes grew even wider, and a pink tongue came out to lick her lips. I felt a surge of desire but kept going, touching myself slowly, drawing out the show. If it turned her on, it was worth doing something I'd never done before. For anyone.

Her hand reached out, beckoning me. "Come here."

I shed the briefs. The show was over. It was time to put my other skills to use.

I sat on the bed, resting a hand on her hip before sliding it back to cup her bottom. "Lie on your stomach." At the curious look she gave me, I sighed. "I want to give you a massage, so I can feel every inch of you. And, so you can relax."

She lay on her stomach, hugging the pillow. I kneeled over her, my erection brushing against the smoothness of her thigh and aching because of it. But I ignored it. I really did want her to relax before I took her to the pinnacle of pleasure.

Starting with her neck, I began with feather-light touches. My fingers danced across her skin, eliciting muffled sighs from her lips buried in the pillow. My fingertips trailed up and down her back, over her buttocks, along her thighs. Then I moved back up again, kneading with more pressure. I kept repeating the process, with a firmer touch, until she was groaning from the release of tension. I finished with light pressure then started all over again, this time with my tongue.

Her skin was sweet and slightly tangy, reminding me of salted caramel. Her fresh, clean scent was tinged with musk, and I knew if I touched her feminine folds, she'd be wet. I was leaving that for last, before turning her over to devour her anew.

My tongue licked a trail down her body. I was enjoying this as much as she was. Sacha *oohed, ahhed*, and giggled when I licked the back of her knees. I gnawed gently on her calves and placed delicate kisses on her toes. I'm not a foot guy, but even her feet were pretty. Her entire body said, "delicate female" which contrasted with her strong, independent personality.

I knew right then what turned me on so much about her. It was the contrast. She was a beautiful, strong woman who didn't need a man. Yet here she was, leaving me in control of her pleasure. I wasn't about to let her down.

~*~

Sacha

If heaven was reachable by mortals, I was convinced this was it. Gib was working me over good, and we hadn't even had sex yet. He was performing magic with his hands and tongue, stimulating every last nerve ending I had. In a deliciously good way.

When he turned me onto my back, I felt woozy with pleasure. Almost drunk with lust, I couldn't wait to take him inside me. What he had done so far had really relaxed me, though I felt energized at the same time. I'd even forgotten about the baby, for the moment. All that mattered now was the delicious way this man was making me feel. He was taking such care, being so patient and concerned for my pleasure. No one had ever made love to me like this, certainly not Kevin.

I pushed away all thoughts of anyone else and focused on the muscular man now looming over me. He hadn't stopped his ministrations, using his hands to touch nearly every part of me. His fingers were feather-soft one minute, strong and manly the next. The only place he hadn't touched was between my legs, and I was suppressing the urge to beg him to do just that.

When I moved my hands to caress his back, he gripped my wrists. "No. Lay back and let me take care of you."

I nearly melted into the mattress. He placed my hands back on the quilt and continued his movement down the front of my body with his tongue, nipping my neck as he went. When he flicked a nipple with his tongue, I almost rose off the bed. The tension was building up inside me and about to explode. Gib merely smiled and continued, swirling his tongue around then sucking gently. Then without warning, he bit the side of my breast, a quick nip that didn't hurt but had me crying out in surprise.

His wicked smile made me even wetter.

This was exquisite torture, not being able to touch him and having no control over what he did to me. I'd never admit it, but I was loving every damned second of it.

Gib sat back on his knees next to me and continued his exploration. Alternating between his hands and his mouth, he evoked sensations I'd never felt before. Like how sensitive my lower abdomen was. No one had ever caressed me like this. I wanted it to go on forever but also knew if I didn't have release soon I was going to scream. But it wasn't up to me, so I kept my eyes closed and allowed myself to drown in sensation.

Not So Broken

My eyes flew open when Gib parted my legs. His blond head was hovering over my most intimate spot. If he was half as attentive down there as he had been with the rest of me, it wouldn't take long to come.

His warm breath preceded his tongue, which gently licked the inside of my thigh. I couldn't help but quiver, anticipating the immense pleasure to come. But he took his time again, licking and nipping at my thighs and the outer folds of my sex. Everything but my pleasure button. He even sucked at the outer lips before dipping his tongue into my opening. Electric-like shocks jolted through me, and I moaned uncontrollably while his hot tongue darted in and out.

With a hand across my belly, he held me down. Which was a good thing, because I was squirming and thrashing. When he finally swirled his tongue across my clit, I exploded, shaking and letting out a high- pitched squeal. So unlady-like, but I had absolutely no control left.

He kept lapping, licking up my juices, as I bucked and spasmed beneath him. It seemed to go on forever, aftershocks of pleasure wracking my entire being. I finally found the strength to push him away, trying to stop the intensity of it. He moved from me, and through my semi-coma, I heard him laugh.

When I opened my eyes, he was resting next to me, his blue eyes heavy-lidded. The room had darkened with late afternoon shadows. A chill crept over my skin, and my limbs were like bags of sand.

"Did I fall asleep?"

"Yes. For a few minutes."

He must have noticed the chill bumps on my arms because he reached for a blanket at the bottom of the bed and pulled it over us. Taking me into his arms, he pulled me close. I was mortified that I'd fallen asleep, when he had been so obviously aroused.

"I'm sorry. I guess I really needed that."

"Apparently. I'm glad you enjoyed it. One of the many services I can provide."

"I'll write my review later. Five stars, by the way."

He kissed my forehead in response, and I snuggled into his shoulder. *Looks like I will be staying, after all.*

~*~

Gibson

117

I'd never imagined taking a nap after having such a raging hard-on, but when Sacha snuggled up to me, all sated and warm, I had no choice but to relax. The sounds she'd made, her uncontrolled responses, told me I'd done a good job at getting her off. It was a satisfying first round, and I still had some things to show her.

When we awoke from our short nap, around four, I suddenly felt hungry again. While she used the bathroom, I pulled on a robe and went to the kitchen. The fridge was nearly empty, except for eggs and the leftovers from a previous dinner. Within minutes, I had an omelet going and a pot of coffee on to brew.

Sacha returned to the kitchen, partially dressed in her long sweater and some socks, looking like she didn't know what to say. I set down the spatula and pulled her up into a bear hug, complete with a passionate kiss, just to let her know that fun time wasn't over.

"Don't even think of leaving, Missy. I'm making us an early dinner here. Refueling, as it were."

I gave her what I hoped was my sexiest grin, but the apprehension had returned to her face. *She thinks too much. Gotta work on that.*

When I released her, she sat on a chair next to the kitchen table. "I am hungry again. But I better not have coffee. Do you have any herbal tea?"

I did, and brewed her a cup. Minutes later, we were eating in companionable silence, or so I thought. I was mentally working on a way to seduce her again, with some clever line or move that might impress her, when she sat her fork down and looked at me expectantly.

"Everything okay, Sacha?"

"That was awesome, what you did to me in there."

"My pleasure. But?"

"But we shouldn't have."

"Really? You're still clinging to that. Do you get more excited by pretending this is wrong? Because it's not."

Her green eyes flashed with indignation. She was about to get defensive again. But I meant what I said, so I held my ground, waiting for her to lash out.

"How is it not? We agreed to remain just partners, co-parents only."

"You keep saying that, but you're still here. My guess is that you don't hate the thought of being more than co-parents."

Maybe calling out her confusing behavior would piss her off

again, but it had to be said.

She stared at the wall for a moment then fixed me with a serious look. "I don't hate the idea, no. But that doesn't mean I think it's the best course of action, given our situation."

I thought about her words for a minute, sipping my coffee. It seemed she was playing a game with herself called, "push him away before something bad happens." If all we had going here was sex, she wouldn't care so much. She would just enjoy it and then hit the road. Her protest meant she was having some feelings for me, feelings she didn't want to deal with.

I couldn't force her to face her feelings, but if I could get her to stay, the chances of this thing between us being about more than sex would increase.

"Well, let's enjoy ourselves then. If it's just sex, and us getting it out of our systems, we can forget about it after you go home, right? We've already been intimate, so why don't you stay tonight and we'll see what happens?"

Her skeptical look wasn't the reaction I'd hoped for, but she didn't get up to leave. She sipped her tea, and I watched a parade of emotions cross her pretty face. Then a smile crept back onto her lips, and it was like the sun coming out again.

"Maybe you're right. I'm probably overthinking it. Let's get all this out of our systems, so we can get on with the business of co-parenting."

Challenge accepted.

"Agreed. Now, let's clean up these dishes and get back into bed. I'm not done with you yet."

Chapter Fifteen

Sacha

*T*he sun setting over the mountain range was magnificent, so we sat on the deck to watch it before going back to the bedroom. Gib insisted I sit next to him on the wooden bench, and he wrapped a soft, fuzzy blanket around us. I snapped photos of the sunset with my phone, but the results didn't do justice to the multi-colored panorama. Over the silhouette of mountain peaks, the sky was varying shades of pink, from magenta to pale peach and everything in between. Clouds and jet trails dotted the sky, adding silvery-white accents. The solitude of the place and the gorgeous scenery had an addictive quality that was making it harder for me to think of leaving.

Which I definitely would come morning.

I had texted Melanie while using the bathroom. To her credit, she didn't say, "I told you so" when I admitted I was staying over, but she did include a snarky wink emoji in her response. Now I regretted not taking Mel's advice to pack some essentials.

We had been sitting in quiet awe for a few minutes. Heat from Gib's body and the blanket had warmed me nicely. I was almost sad to see the sun fading from view over the hills. "The sunsets in Kennesaw are never this pretty. Too many city lights, I guess."

"Personally, I love the peace and quiet. And the changing of the seasons."

Not So Broken

His arm was around me, holding me as I leaned against him. *He's more affectionate than I thought he'd be. I wish he'd stop.*

When the first star made its appearance on the horizon, Gib pulled me onto his lap. I was still under the blanket with my back to him, wearing only my panties and the long sweater. I'd left my bra laying on the bedroom floor along with my jeans, thinking I'd get fully dressed after dinner. But now Gib's hands had other plans for me.

With one hand, he was unbuttoning the sweater. My nipples stood at attention, whether in anticipation or from the chill night air, I wasn't sure. His hand was warm, and he cupped one breast before tweaking the nipple into a taut peak. He gave it a slight pinch, causing me to cry out.

Warmth flooded the area between my legs. My breasts had become ultra-sensitive lately, so the line between pleasure and pain was blurred. I squirmed, seeking relief from the tension that was building up again.

"Sit still," he commanded, so I gripped his legs with my hands. He was still naked beneath the robe, and the evidence of his arousal was a spear of heat against my bottom. Involuntarily, I pressed against it, causing a soft groan and a warning from him.

"Keep that up and you will find yourself flung onto my bed again." I responded, not with words but deeds, grinding my bottom against him and leaning back to kiss his cheek. He gave a soft chuckle. "So that's how she wants to play it?"

Now it was I who groaned as his hand settled between my legs. Rubbing and caressing through the silk of my panties, he almost brought me to a peak again. No one had ever had such an effect on me. The man just touched me and I was ready to explode.

Must be my crazy hormones again. He can't be that talented.

I was arching my back, leaning against him with my eyes closed and legs parted. If anyone saw me this way, I would die from embarrassment. I was so out of my element here but had lost the will to do anything but respond.

Without warning, Gib removed his hand and stood, wrapping the blanket around both of us. He propelled me forward step by step, until we reached the glass door. He opened it, and led me into the living room, tossing the blanket onto the sofa. I followed in a daze of desire, heart pounding. When we reached the bedroom, he removed the robe, letting it drop to the floor. My breath caught in my throat. He was magnificent, with his blond hair a messy wave of tangles, his broad shoulders, and

121

tight abdomen. I wanted to taste and feel every inch of him, as he had done with me.

But he moved first, reaching out to finish unbuttoning my sweater, and pulling my panties down at the same time. Then he pulled me close, and the shock of skin to skin was an almost unbearable pleasure.

"Lie down."

I needed no further encouragement. Once I settled back on the pillows, he moved to lie on top of me. He started slowly again, kissing my face, my jaw, my earlobe. I couldn't take another prolonged foreplay session, not this time. I grabbed his head and smashed my lips against his in a ferocious kiss.

Gib responded with equal passion, thrusting his tongue into my mouth with a quiet fury. One hand grabbed a handful of my hair and the other slipped under the small of my back, tilting me up to him. His erection was pressed against my opening, demanding entry. As slick as I was, he slipped in without effort, but I still gasped in surprise as he filled me to the hilt.

A sweet burn of pleasure in my core made me clench, causing him to moan my name. As he began to move in and out, he whispered in my ear.

"We are going to fully remember this night, I promise you."

His thrusts were vigorous, but not enough to make me uncomfortable. He varied his pace, stopping every now and then to hold himself immobile. That was almost maddening, especially when he looked down at me with that wicked grin.

Once he even pulled out, causing me to curse at the sudden emptiness.

"Damn it. Don't stop now."

"Why not?"

"I was so close," I gasped.

He began again, moving his hips in ways I never knew a man could move. When he finally pressed forward and held himself in place, I bit his shoulder as my climax rumbled through me. Moments later he stiffened, groaned, and released his seed into me once again.

This time I felt it, savored it.

As he lay limp across me, I enjoyed the weight of him. His back was slick with sweat, right above his butt. I gave his butt a squeeze, and he sighed in my ear. When he moved away to lie next to me, I snuggled against his shoulder.

Yes. This was worth staying for.

Not So Broken

"You were right, Gib. That was much better than the night we met."

He turned to face me. In the dim light, his blue eyes were almost indigo. He placed a finger under my chin and kissed me, a sweet brush of his lips.

"Darlin', we've just begun."

~*~

Gibson

I woke to the savory scent of frying bacon. For a split second I panicked, thinking I'd left something on the stove. Then I recalled I hadn't slept alone.

Throwing on my robe, I went to the kitchen. Sacha was there, cooking breakfast. I could get used to seeing her like this, being domestic. She was fully dressed and turned to look at me when I reached for a mug in the cabinet.

"Good morning. I hope you don't mind me cooking. I was starving."

I responded by leaning down to kiss her cheek. "Not at all, and no wonder. We had quite a workout last night."

Her grin spoke volumes, as did her pink cheeks. She enjoyed it. *Good. I've still got it.* We had made love twice, not counting the episode before dinner. She'd come each time, I was proud to admit.

"Yes, we did. It was wonderful."

Something in her tone made me stiffen, and not in a good way. "But?"

She was placing the cooked bacon on a plate covered in paper towels. She shrugged and kept working without looking at me. "We did it. It was fantastic. And now we get on with our lives."

I wanted to continue being polite, to extend the warm glow I'd felt for her earlier. Holding her while we slept had given me such peace. It was the best night's sleep I'd had in a long while. But her emotional shields were back up, and it was pissing me off.

"Sounds like a plan, Ms. Rowan. Except for one thing. Like it or not, now you are my life."

Her mouth dropped open, but she said nothing. Then she threw the tongs she'd been holding into the sink with a clang. She turned to me,

123

her mouth now a thin line.

"Listen, Mr. Colebank. Don't think you're going to woo me into some kind of romance here. We had sex, and yes, it was hot. But it won't happen again. We scratched the itch, now we can move on. End of story."

Her words were calm, her tone business-like. But her lower lip trembled as she stood there, watching me for a response. I purposely let my robe fall open and was rewarded with her furtive glance at my junk.

Then she turned to get plates from the cabinet. Her movements were jerky, her hands trembling. But her facial expression was ice cold.

"Sacha. Look at me."

I moved next to her, placing a hand on her shoulder. She froze, staring at the wall, refusing to look at me. I didn't budge but prompted her with a light squeeze. When she turned her eyes to me, they glistened with moisture, but her face remained placid. The woman had tremendous self-control. When it suited her.

"Sacha, maybe you can pretend this is nothing, but I can't. You're carrying my child. No one in the world is more important to me right now. No one."

She pulled away, removing my hand from her shoulder as she did so. "Be honest with me, and with yourself, Gib. It's not *me* you want. You feel responsible, and I admire that. But don't imagine this into some domestic bliss situation. We come from different worlds, we have different goals in life, and we'll both end up disappointed."

I'd closed my robe again, suddenly feeling vulnerable. Her ability to shut herself off so soon after the searing passion we'd shared left me bewildered. Most men would have been happy to say "hasta la vista, baby" after such a night. But I just couldn't let her go, not like this, and I wasn't even sure why.

"You know, Sacha, I get it. I'm not going to push you into anything you don't want. It's your call, all the way. But I'd appreciate you including me whenever you can, and to be honest, I'm concerned you'll get busy and forget about me. Can you promise me that you won't?"

Her face softened. If she didn't agree, she'd come off looking like a bitch, which I knew she wasn't. She was a bundle full of control issues, with a tender, sweet center. Getting past her ice queen routine would be the tricky part, but I had plenty of time to learn.

"Well, of course. I just want to be clear on where this is going. Or, should I say, *not* going."

I moved forward again and placed my hands on her shoulders.

"How about we have some breakfast, then I'll take you to your car? We'll take the rest one day at a time. Okay?"

"Okay."

I pulled her into a hug, and she held on but didn't throw herself into it. She was still holding back. So, I set about getting breakfast on the table, pretending everything was normal.

The food smelled delicious, and tasted even better, but for some reason I had lost my appetite.

~*~

Sacha

After breakfast, I took a quick shower but really wanted to get home as soon as possible. I'd already stayed longer than I ever intended. As great as last night was, this morning felt awkward as hell. I was still wearing yesterday's clothes, not looking forward to the walk of shame past Melanie's door to get to my apartment. The only saving grace was she would probably sleep until after noon, since her band had a gig last night.

Gib was giving me some space after our discussion, but he kept looking at me with those puppy-dog eyes. As he helped me into his truck, he checked the time on his phone.

"You know, if you can spare a few minutes, there's something I'd like to show you. It's sort of on the way to town."

I wasn't in the mood for sightseeing, but I knew I had been a bit cold toward him this morning. A touch of guilt had seeped in, so I didn't have the heart to refuse. "How long will it take? I really need to get home."

"About fifteen minutes or so. It's a special place, and I think you'll like it."

"Well, okay."

We traveled down the bumpy gravel road in silence. There was still a chill in the air, but the rising sun promised a pretty day. We passed the other little cabin on the road, the one he'd told me belonged to his landlord. Nice as it was, I still couldn't imagine living in such a remote location.

When we reached the main highway that led to Tilly, Gib turned in the other direction away from town. He easily handled the truck on the steep, winding road. Soon he turned onto a gravel road that was partially hidden by overgrowth. It was fairly flat and soon turned into dirt. It was then he pulled over and parked.

"C'mon. We have a short walk."

I stifled a groan and swung down from the truck. My flat suede boots were not designed for walking on dirt. Gib led the way, carefully navigating around ruts in the path. The property was overgrown with bushes and trees, bare of leaves because it was almost winter. I could only imagine how thick it would be in the height of summer.

A far-off rushing sound reached my ears, and I realized he was leading me toward the river. When we came to a clearing, my breath caught in my throat. Large boulders formed a stepladder of sorts, with the Chattahoochee River cascading over them. It looked as though the hand of a giant had placed them just so, to form the perfect waterfall.

He was watching for my reaction. I couldn't help but smile, the scenery was so gorgeous.

"It's beautiful. How did you find this place?"

"From Marvil. He knows the owner, apparently."

I walked closer and peered over the edge of the riverbank. Farther downstream, the river widened and a large, shallow pool formed. "That would be perfect for swimming in the summer."

Gib's face lit up. "Yes. And there's a flat area over here that would be great for some picnic tables, and maybe a pavilion over there…"

He went on for a few minutes, describing an upscale lodge, with an infinity pool and a hot tub overlooking the river. Apparently, he'd given the idea some thought, down to the detail of how many restaurants the place would have, and how the rooms would be decorated.

"That sounds awesome, Gib. This place is ideal for that type of resort."

I was humoring him. He had no money to fund such a project, of that I was certain. But it was nice to see his enthusiasm—and his creativity.

He stared out at the water, suddenly contemplative. His hands were in his pockets, and he shrugged. "Well, apparently the owners have been approached before, and they refuse to sell it. They want to keep it natural, I guess. I can respect that, and my plan would be to limit the footprint of the resort as much as possible. Make it blend in with the natural surroundings so people can enjoy nature without destroying it."

"People would pay good money to stay in a place like that. I worked at a resort once, in Tennessee. It was only for the summer, but I was made manager of food services after only a month. I loved it."

I realized we had not even discussed much about our past jobs. I'd assumed he'd always been a handyman.

"You managed a restaurant? Cool. I guess that makes sense, with your present job."

"I have a background in catering too. It does help. I'm good at what I do now, but someday I'd like to not travel so much."

He laughed. "You can manage my resort here."

I chuckled at the thought. "It's a nice dream, to build a resort in this place."

The conversation lagged, and we stood for a minute, listening to the song of the 'Hooch. It was a peaceful place, and my urgent desire to go home had waned.

Gib picked up a rock and tossed it into the river where it disappeared with a plop. "I wanted to show you why I fell in love with it here. Tilly is a tourist town, but there is so much more to these mountains, this area."

"I can see why you like it."

The rest of my thoughts remained unsaid. I had plans for the baby and me—and they didn't include living in a backwater, as beautiful as this one was. But there was no reason to spoil the peace of the moment, or Gib's enthusiasm, especially since I would be on my way soon.

He must have sensed my unspoken thoughts and turned toward the path. "Let's go. I've kept you long enough."

He took my hand and led me back to the truck. I took one last look at the idyllic scenery then dismissed it from my mind.

I had no future here.

Chapter Sixteen

Gibson

*T*he skies had clouded up by the time we made it back to Tilly. A distant rumble of thunder threatened, and I began to worry about the road conditions.

"You'll be all right driving home if it starts to pour?"

Sacha gave me an exasperated look. "I drive all over the state four days a week. I think I can handle a little rain."

"Just checking. You're carrying precious cargo now, darlin'." I threw in the endearment to be sarcastic, but she smiled. As I pulled up alongside her car, she touched my arm.

"Don't worry about me, I mean…us. We'll be fine."

"Will you let me know when you get home, then?"

"Yes, dear."

Now she was being sarcastic, but I liked it. Better than her ice queen routine.

She unlocked her car and turned to face me. Right there in the street, I kissed her, a long, slow, sensuous, final claiming of her mouth. I wanted her to think about it all the way home.

She didn't resist this time, despite her earlier protests. I didn't care who saw us—I was going to hold her for as long as she let me. When I looked down at her, I saw longing and desire, and maybe a touch of regret in those cat-green eyes. Did she regret our hooking up or the fact she now had to leave?

She pulled away and I released her. Her voice also had a touch of regret. "I better go."

"I know."

I stood on the sidewalk and watched her car disappear down the street. I had my own regrets, but I'd spent the night making love to her, and that I would always remember.

Rain splattered the windshield as I made my way back up the mountain. The gravel road would soon be muddy, and I wanted to get home before the downpour. As I drove, I replayed in my mind every minute with Sacha. I wanted to savor it in case it never happened again.

Despite that possibility, I was in a pretty good mood. Even the gloomy turn of the weather didn't bother me. The image of Sacha beneath me, crying out, was enough to make me smile through any storm.

Better check on the old man...

I'd ignored Marvil the past few days since I'd been entertaining. As I rounded the last curve before Marvil's cabin, I saw a flash of light. I glanced at the sky, but the lightning had abated. The rain was coming down in buckets now, so it was hard to see. But there was no mistaking the bright red glare from the ambulance parked at Marvil's place.

"Holy hell," I cursed, pulling up near the porch. The front door of the cabin was open and Edna was standing on the porch, wringing her hands. The paramedics must be inside.

I parked, and as I ran through the rain to the porch, I could hear a police siren in the distance. I reached Edna, whose face was red and puffy from crying. "What happened?"

Tears spilled from her eyes, and she wiped them with her sleeve. "Oh, Mr. Gib. He's gone."

~*~

Two hours later, I opened the door to my empty, dark cabin. The sky was still heavy with rain clouds, though the downpour had eased. A sad, steady rain beat a tattoo on the tin roof, echoing the drumming in my ears. I had a hell of a headache, so I put on some coffee and went in search of an aspirin.

Marvil's death was caused by a myocardial infarction, the medics said. A heart attack. Edna had found him on the sofa, wrapped in a blanket with the television blaring. He'd been wearing pajamas with cartoon characters on them and the slippers that looked like bear paws. It would have been comical if he were still alive. The man everyone called "The Grouch" had a sense of humor, after all.

When the coffee was made, I sat on the back deck, staring at the rain. I couldn't imagine life in Tilly without my cranky friend. I knew it wasn't my fault, the heart attack would have happened anyway, but I couldn't help feeling guilty for not checking on the guy earlier. Surely Sacha wouldn't have minded.

Still, it didn't ease the lump in my throat or the twisting in my gut. It was beginning to feel like death was following me. Maybe if I had checked on Marvil, I'd have been able to help him, to save his life. Who knew how long he'd been sitting there?

First thing in the morning, I was going to call Marvil's attorney to discuss what needed to be done. I had no idea if Marvil had a will or who the executor was, but Marvil had given me the man's name and contact information, so I would do what I could to help.

The coffee tasted bland, or maybe it was me. I sat on the bench where I had been with Sacha just the night before. But instead of her warm body, in my mind I saw another woman, one who was cold and lifeless. Images of Bianca's funeral flashed unbidden in my mind, no doubt triggered by Marvil's passing.

I allowed a tear to slide down my cheek before getting up and going to the kitchen. In a cabinet, way up high, was a bottle of Scotch. I pulled it down and poured a hefty dose into my half-empty coffee cup. I downed the hot liquid in one gulp then poured another shot. This time I sipped as I walked back onto the deck, bottle in one hand and the mug in the other.

It was going to be a long night.

~*~

Sacha

I turned over in bed and picked up my phone from the nightstand to check the time. It was a few minutes after one. I couldn't sleep, and reading hadn't helped. My legs were jittery, my mind restless. It didn't help that my boss had texted me about meeting first thing in the morning, but that wasn't the source of my insomnia. I was anxious about it but not enough to keep me from sleep. I had pretty much resigned myself to the fact that I would soon be moving to Alabama, unless a miracle occurred.

Not So Broken

My mind kept going back to Gib. I thoroughly enjoyed our love-making—he was a skilled, generous lover. But his intensity scared me. It was flattering the way he insisted on caring for me, but I wasn't used to it. When Kevin and I were married, we each had our own interests. We gave each other space. We were together, but separate.

Maybe that wasn't so great, after all.

We had drifted apart and lost interest in each other. I knew now, in my heart, that my ex wasn't the only one guilty of neglecting their partner. I had become obsessed about having a child in order to fill the void left by a disintegrating relationship, instead of working with my partner to build a family.

The irony of my situation now was not lost on me. My dream had come true—a baby was on the way. But now I had a partner who insisted on being part of my family, whether I wanted him or not. I hadn't called Gib when I got home as I had promised, but texted instead. He'd simply replied, "great."

The sudden buzz of my cell phone interrupted my thoughts. My heart lurched at the sound, and I switched on a lamp. I saw Gib's number and my heart leapt. *Why is he calling me now?*

"Hello?"

"Sacha. It's me. Gib."

His over pronunciation of the words told me he was hammered. *Speak of the devil...*

"What is it? Are you okay?"

Silence filled the line for an awkward pause, and I worried he might be hurt. Then he cleared his throat, speaking so softly I almost didn't hear him.

"Yeah. But Marvil died today."

"Who?"

"You know, my landlord. The guy that lived in the cabin below me."

I was fully awake now, the last vestiges of fatigue clearing from my mind. I sat up in bed, rearranging my pillows while I spoke. "Oh, I'm so sorry to hear that."

"Thanks. It was a shock, even though he was old."

There was another long pause as I searched for something else to say. I wanted to be of comfort. I felt guilty for being irritated at him for being drunk and assuming the worst. He probably just needed to talk about it. "So, what happened?"

"Heart attack. His home health aide found him. When I came

back after dropping you off, the medics were already there."

"Wow. That's horrible."

"I'm sorry to wake you, but I had to talk to someone."

That struck me as odd. He'd called *me* first. Not friends or family? I was happy to comfort him in his time of need, but it made me wonder once again why he had latched onto me. I sensed it was more than just the fact of the pregnancy.

"That's okay. I was awake anyway."

"Well, I won't keep you. I'm sure you have to work in the morning."

His voice had sobered a bit. Maybe it had been more suppressed emotion than booze. I couldn't really blame him for either, under the circumstances. Perhaps the high and mighty attitude he sometimes had was a cover for how deeply he really felt. Caring for his elderly neighbor the way he had, showed he did have a heart.

"I do." I paused as an idea hit me. "Hey, Gib… I have a doctor appointment next Friday. Would you like to go with me? That way you can meet my ob-gyn, and you'll know we're in good hands."

"Of course. I'll be there."

"Great. I'll text you the address."

We hung up. I turned over and hugged my pillow. I had a sense of resolution. I still wasn't one hundred percent certain about Gibson Colebank, but at least I didn't have to go through this pregnancy alone. Maybe he could be a friend as well as a co-parent.

~*~

Gibson

Passing by Marvil's cabin everyday was hard. I kept expecting to see him standing on the porch, coffee in hand, waving at me. Or yelling at me to slow down. I still had a key, so I'd gone in once to water the few plants that had been sitting on the windowsill, shriveling with neglect. I put them out on the porch so they could get some sun then later took them up to my cabin when I couldn't bear to go back into Marvil's empty house.

The rest of the week I threw myself into my work, finishing two projects in record time, much to the delight of the homeowners. The only thing getting me through each day was focusing on the upcoming doctor visit with Sacha. Our last phone conversation had actually been pleasant. She seemed to be looking forward to it, too.

By Friday morning, I hadn't heard back from Marvil's attorney, so I called his office. I wasn't sure how long I'd be welcome to stay in the cabin now that my landlord was gone. When the assistant finally put me through to Michael Stazky, the attorney handling Marvil's will, the guy wasn't much help.

"It will probably be a few weeks before the necessary paperwork is complete, but the county probate judge will be out of town starting Tuesday."

Small town life was sometimes frustrating, and I couldn't even play the wealth card to get my way. Not this time. Even if I wanted to buy the cabin outright, it wouldn't speed things up, especially as we were getting into the holiday season.

"I wanted to be sure I was doing the right thing. Will you please call me when you find out?"

"Will do. I wouldn't worry if I were you. I haven't had any relatives of Mr. Crouch coming forward yet to make any claims. You're not in imminent danger of being evicted. But I'll let you know what's going on as soon as I know."

I'd almost forgotten about the holidays coming up. I had no idea what Sacha's holiday plans were, but a fantasy spooled in my mind about taking her home to meet my family.

Wouldn't that shake them up?

I could imagine my mother's face when she got the news. Not only had her son finally returned home, but with a pregnant girlfriend on his arm.

Well, I hoped she would someday be more than a girlfriend. I could definitely imagine Sacha Rowan as my wife. She was the mother of my child, and therefore tied to my legacy. More than that, she had a body I longed to hold, and the fierce heart of a warrior woman. She'd been through some tough times, from what she'd told me. It was why she held me at arm's length, why she kept insisting there was nothing more than casual sex between us, denying the searing passionate connection whenever we touched. She was in denial, trying to protect her heart and our child.

But I was strong enough to protect them both, and I planned to prove it to her as soon as possible. Which also meant I had to pull myself out of denial and admit that I was falling in love with her.

133

Chapter Seventeen

Sacha

*D*r. Kapoor's waiting room was packed on Friday afternoon. I guess everyone was trying to get an appointment in before the holidays. I had no plans to celebrate, since I usually ended up working extra hours anyway. It was always just another week for me.

I checked my phone again. Gib had called to say he was close, but unexpected traffic had made him late. People were on their way out of town, making Atlanta's usual Friday afternoon rush hour even worse. Something I was used to, but he probably wasn't.

It had been a hell of a week. Several of my accounts had called in huge orders for the holidays, waiting until the last minute but still expecting quick service. I'd done my part, but some of the orders wouldn't be fulfilled and had to be backordered. The supply chain didn't always cooperate, and I was the one who took the flak from the customers. Meanwhile, in my meeting with Dan, he'd thrown me a curveball—the pregnancy wouldn't prevent me from being transferred to Alabama, but there was another option.

The regional manager based in Birmingham had announced he was retiring. The new company, in all its wisdom, had decided to split the position in two, and they had already hired the new regional manager from their own ranks. But the position of Regional Training Coordinator was a new position, which would not require as much field time as the sales rep or other management positions. If I was chosen and accepted the job, I would be responsible for recruiting new reps, training them, and following up on their progress.

I liked the idea of not being on the road as much but still wasn't excited about relocating. When I asked Dan how much time I had, his answer wasn't reassuring.

"Well, I've recommended you for the position, but it's not set in stone yet. The new manager needs to meet you and give his blessing."

"When can I meet him?"

"There's a party this weekend at an art gallery downtown. Apparently, his daughter is an artist and has some pieces in a show. I was given two tickets, but you can have them if you'd like. It might get you on his good side right away."

I'd accepted the tickets, of course. What else could I do? This might save having to drive to Birmingham for an interview. Perhaps my potential new boss would be in a good mood at his daughter's event, and the meeting would go well.

Add to that my nervousness about being with Gib again, and it was a wonder I hadn't curled up in a ball on the floor of my closet and not come out.

As the front desk called my name, Gib walked through the door. His face was flushed, but his hair was slicked back. With his beard, he still looked like a lumberjack, but an upscale one if such a thing was possible. The brown leather jacket over a white button-down shirt and dressy jeans gave him an air of the suburban dad-to-be I suspected he was trying to portray. I smiled and stood, not minding when he kissed my cheek.

"Sorry I'm late."

"No problem, I just got called."

A nurse led the way through a door near the front desk and down a long hallway. When we reached the room, she handed me a small plastic cup and pointed to the adjacent restroom.

"There's a collection box for this behind a small door. Once you've filled the cup, place it in the box. Then come back to this room."

I glanced at Gib, who shrugged and entered the examination room to wait for me. Once my task had been completed, I joined him. A nurse came in and did all the pre-exam paperwork, drew a blood sample, and took my pulse. Then it was time to disrobe and wait for the doctor.

"Turn around, Gib."

He smirked, as I knew he would. "Nothing I haven't seen, darlin'."

"I know. But this is different."

He was a gentleman and faced the door while I disrobed and donned a thin cloth gown. Then I sat back on the table, willing myself to relax.

He heard the movement and looked over his shoulder, coming to stand next to me. He took my hand and lifted it to his lips.

"I know it's too soon for them to tell us the gender, but I want to be with you when you find out. That is, if you're sure you want to know?"

I was sure. The suspense would kill me otherwise. "Yes. It will make it more real, I think."

His face changed, going dark. I hated that we couldn't talk about the baby and avoid his past pain at the same time. It stole a bit of my own happiness to see him grieve.

Dr. Kapoor burst into the room, saving us from another awkward conversation. "Are you ready? It's baby time."

I'd forgotten to warn him about the doctor's sense of humor, but his slow smile told me he got it. "Ready as we'll ever be, I guess."

"Dr. Kapoor, this is my... This is Gib. He's the father."

"Welcome, sir. Now you sit over there for a minute or in the waiting room. Ladies choice."

She looked at me questioningly. "He can stay." There was nothing he hadn't seen before. Plus, I wanted him to see how thorough Dr. Kapoor was.

When I looked back at Gib, he had retreated to a chair in the corner, looking like he didn't know what to do with himself.

Dr. Kapoor bustled about the room, pushing buttons and moving equipment into place. When the examination began, she kept us distracted by talking about the baby and the stages of development.

"He or she should be about four inches long and weigh around 2 ounces. He's becoming developed, and you may feel some movement soon."

I smiled. Hearing her talk about the baby's growth made me less nervous. "I'm looking forward to that."

Once the exam was complete, Dr. Kapoor stood up. She turned to Gib, asking, "Would you like to hear the heartbeat?"

His face lit up like she had offered him a fortune. "Yes, I would."

With my stomach exposed, she felt around with her hands then applied the stethoscope. A few moments passed, and then she nodded, beckoning him to come close. When he did, she placed the stethoscope to his ear.

His mouth dropped open, followed by a wide grin. "I hear it! Wow, that's awesome."

He looked at me, and as Dr. Kapoor withdrew, he moved to my side. He held my hand and gave it a squeeze. I used my other hand to wipe away an errant teardrop that had formed.

"See? I told you we're in good hands. I've heard the heartbeat a few times now, but it never gets old."

"I'll still worry. But I see what you mean." He turned to the doctor, who was preparing to leave. "Thank you, Doctor Kapoor."

It was just another day for her. "You're welcome. And make sure she gets plenty of rest." She wagged a finger at me. "Due to your age, we'll need to monitor your progress closely. Your bloodwork and the urine test will tell us if everything is as it should be. If not, you'll get a call."

I had no problem with that. "Yes, ma'am."

As the doctor left, Gib didn't even wait for me to get off the table before he pulled me into his arms for a long kiss.

~*~

Gibson

I walked Sacha to her car, reluctant to let go of her. I hadn't expected to react so strongly to hearing the baby's heartbeat, but I was practically floating. Now shit was getting real. I didn't want this feeling to end, and Sacha was holding onto my arm like she wanted to extend the glow too. I had to think of something to keep her with me.

"Sacha, have you had lunch? Or I guess it's closer to dinner, huh?"

A shadow of a frown crossed her face, and she pulled out her phone to check the time. I figured it was close to five because the sun was sinking behind the buildings. My own stomach rumbled in response to the question—I hadn't eaten since breakfast.

"Well, I guess we could grab something near here, and let the traffic die down. My place is a few miles up the freeway."

"Great. Looks like there's a restaurant across the street. You in the mood for Chinese?"

She agreed, so I clasped her hand and led her to the crosswalk.

When we reached the restaurant, I held open one of the heavy, bright red doors for her. Inside, the scent of ginger and soy sauce perfumed the air, making my mouth water. We were led to a cloth-covered table, positioned near a huge fish tank that spanned the length of one wall. Sacha smiled and pointed to a yellow and blue tang swimming idly through the water.

"Cool. I used to have a fish tank when I was a kid."

"Me too. Not as big as this one, though."

We were interrupted by a server who took our drink orders and frowned when we both said, "water." When the server left, Sacha's green eyes met mine. She steepled her fingers, a smile creeping onto her lips. "So, I guess we should start thinking about names."

A sudden mental image of my father intruded. *Holy crap. If it's a boy, we can't name him "the fourth." That's ludicrous.* My father was still upset I never liked being "the third." Surely my parents wouldn't insist?

"It's up to you, darlin'. Well, as long as it's not something goofy."

Her eyes narrowed, but before she could respond, the server returned with two glasses of water and a basket of wonton chips. Once our food order was taken, I braced myself for Sacha's retort. I didn't have to wait long.

"If you leave it up to me, you'll have to accept it, even if it is goofy."

"Really? And what about a last name?"

The flash of her eyes told me this was the wrong question to ask, but I'd be damned if I was going to let it go undiscussed. I had railed against the numerical designation of "fourth," but the child would still be a Colebank, and an heir. Of course, I hadn't yet divulged that piece of information to her.

Sacha's voice wavered, an indication of her discomfort with the subject. "Well, I had planned on giving him or her my last name. Rowan."

"That doesn't change the child's parentage. He'll be a Colebank too."

She arched a brow. "Yes, but unless we are married, I can't see having him use your name. I can have you listed on the birth certificate, if that's what you're worried about."

I gripped the edge of the table to keep my hands still. Heat flared up my spine in response to her comment. The Ice Queen was back, turning an otherwise happy moment into a business transaction.

"I want him to know who he is, what family he comes from. To have pride in his name. Or hers."

"And what's so great about the Colebanks? You haven't told me much about them, you know. Only that they live in Atlanta somewhere. What does your father do? Will your mother like me?"

I released the table to run a hand across my head. This conversation was becoming more uncomfortable by the second. I mentally kicked myself for bringing it up. "You'll get to meet them soon enough. I didn't want them involved until you and I had…worked things out."

"I see."

The server suddenly appeared with food, sparing me from further questions about my parents. I changed the subject to her weekend plans, since I was hoping to spend the night with her. I'd packed a bag, in case she agreed.

"We have plenty of time to discuss our families once we figure things out. Until then, I was hoping we could spend some more time together while I'm down here. I know it's short notice, but I can always help you out around the apartment, get things ready for the baby and all that."

She didn't look at me but kept twirling noodles around on her fork. I knew it was kind of rude to invite myself, but I couldn't leave without trying. She didn't seem upset, though, just hesitant.

"Thanks, but there's not much to do. I'm not going to worry about a crib and all that until later."

It wasn't a flat-out no. There was still hope. "Well, at least let me see you to your door. I insist."

She agreed, and the rest of the meal passed without argument. I only half-listened to her conversation because my mind was filled with images of the passionate kiss I was going to give her when we reached her door. The one that would have her begging me to stay the night.

~*~

Sacha

I didn't know whether to be flattered or annoyed by Gib's insistence on following me to my apartment. He was in turns charming and exasperating. We couldn't seem to agree on anything, and the effect his penetrating gaze and smooth, deep voice had on me was infuriating. I wasn't supposed to be getting all hot and bothered by him. The warmth between my legs that flared every time he touched me was most inconvenient.

Having him stay the night was a totally awful idea, especially after what happened the last time. Yes, he was probably the best lover I'd ever had, but he'd already complicated my life more than I'd ever imagined. I had to get a handle on the situation and stop this lustful infatuation we had going before someone got hurt. Because once my belly started to get really big, and the reality of impending parenthood set in, he wouldn't be so eager to stay with me. And by then, I will have fallen for him.

Am I falling for him?

I parked in my usual spot, and Gib pulled his truck to the curb in front of the building. He bounded across the lawn in time to help me out of the car. He even carried my briefcase, walking with his arm around me, as though we were a couple.

I didn't hate it.

Frantically searching my mind for a way to get him to leave without starting a fight, I didn't notice the man standing in front of my door. When I did, I felt Gib stiffen next to me. I stopped walking and stared at the tall, gray-haired stranger as he emerged from the shadows. I wondered for a moment why this man seemed familiar. Then my heart gave a thump and the ground turned to water beneath my feet. My words came out in a croak of surprise.

"*You.* What are you doing here?"

He was dressed in a long, black trench coat, and his silvery hair was new, but there was no mistaking the smile. It was one I'd seen in so many photographs. The crooked smile that masked a crooked heart. I saw his prominent eyeteeth, almost fang-like, as he spoke.

"That's all you have to say? Don't talk to me like that, Pumpkin. I've come a long way."

He held out his hand and took a step forward, but Gib blocked him in one swift move. "I don't think the lady is glad to see you, pal. What's this about?"

The man didn't answer but looked at me.

My head was swimming. Nausea was dancing in my stomach. It wasn't the baby causing the sick feeling. The cause was standing in front of me, a man I thought I'd never see again. The man Gib was about to chase off my doorstep.

Not So Broken

"It's okay, Gib. I know him. He's my father."

Chapter Eighteen

Sacha

"**I**'m Garth Rowan. And you are?"

He extended a bony hand to Gib, who glanced at me before moving a muscle.

"It's okay to shake his hand if you want to. He won't be staying."

I held out my hands to take my briefcase from Gib, who handed it to me, still looking bewildered. I then moved past both men to unlock the door, tossed my briefcase and purse inside, and stood in the doorway like a sentinel guarding a besieged castle. I felt rather besieged, with the both of them staring at me. Gib shook Garth's hand briefly, said his own name, and now stood rigidly awaiting a cue from me.

I ignored him and addressed my unwanted visitor. "How did you find out where I live? And why are you here?"

Never one to give a straight answer, Garth smiled and pulled a photo from his pocket. Moving next to Gib, he showed him, pointing. "She was a cute little imp, wasn't she? But now she's become a beautiful woman."

Gib nodded, but before he could speak, I lost what little restraint I had left. "Oh, cut the crap. I don't care how many old photos you have of me, you haven't been around for most of my life. So, tell me why you're here right now before I call the cops to report that I'm being harassed."

Not So Broken

The charming smile faded from Garth's face. His gray eyes were sunken, and his cheekbones prominent, lending him a ghoulish look. I recalled he'd always been thin, but he didn't look well. He snatched the photo from Gib's hand and shoved it back into his coat.

"I heard through the online grapevine that I'm going to be a grandfather. I contacted Kevin again, and he told me where you live."

My cheeks heated instantly. *Goddamn him.* "Kevin had no right to... What do you mean, again?"

"I guess he never told you. I contacted him at the catering place a few years ago. He said you were out of town, well, back in Jersey, actually...and he'd give you my number when you got back. I wondered why I never heard from you, but I figured it was because you were pissed at me."

"Son of a bitch." Either Kevin purposely didn't tell me or had forgotten during our fight and subsequent breakup. "I'll deal with him later. And 'pissed' is not the word for it, Garth."

I had purposely used his given name. He hadn't earned the title of "Dad."

Gib stood aside, not saying a word. His eyes had darkened to a storm-cloud blue, and a muscle in his jaw flinched. I sensed he was ready to pick my father up by the collar and toss him into the street, if I asked. When I looked back at Garth, he had moved closer.

"So, is it true, Sacha? Are you expecting?"

"Yes. I am. What about it?"

"Well, I...congratulations, Pumpkin. That's all I wanted to say."

"Thank you. Now get the hell out of here."

~*~

Gibson

I was torn between the instinct to protect Sacha at all cost and my personal motto of never getting involved in other families' squabbles. The venom in her voice and white-hot fire in her eyes told me she had a ton of unresolved business with this man, her father. It was not my place to intervene, but I couldn't walk away, not when she was so upset.

There was a tense moment when both father and daughter had a staring contest. Then the elder man caved, hanging his head.

"Fine. I wanted to say I'm proud of you, that's all. I know I

143

screwed up. No one knows that better than me."

Her blazing eyes softened—a touch. "Good to know you realize it. But it makes no difference now."

Garth looked at me then with a curious eye. It didn't take a genius to figure out what he was thinking. Should I disclose my status or leave it to Sacha?

She answered the question before I could decide. "It's none of your business who the father is. None of this concerns you in any way, so crawl back to wherever it is you came from."

Making a mental note to never piss her off, I moved in Sacha's direction. Garth took the hint and shuffled down the walkway. He stopped a few feet away and turned.

"I'm staying at the Marriott near the airport if you decide you want to talk. Just ask for me at the front desk."

Then he disappeared into the darkness.

Sacha stood in the doorway, stone-faced. Waves of anger, confusion, and a jumble of other emotions surrounded her. I didn't know how I could sense all that, but I did. I took her arm gently, prompting her to go inside. "Come on, let's get you out of the cold and make some tea."

She didn't resist, walking stiffly ahead of me like a doll. She sat in one of the dining table chairs, and I searched the kitchen for a teabag. While I prepared the tea, she sat with her head in her hands. Then she began to crumble.

A sob escaped her lips, followed by silent crying. The kind that had her shoulders shaking. I rushed to her side, but she waved me off.

"I'll…I'll be okay. I was not ready for this. Not now."

I handed her a napkin, and she wiped her eyes. "I don't blame you. That was pretty intense."

Her green eyes had a golden cast and were rimmed in red. She took a few deep breaths, regaining calm. "I'm sorry you had to witness that. I haven't seen that bastard since I was nine."

"That's a long time. Do you think the baby's the only reason he showed up now?"

"Who knows? It could be anything. He's a con man. Always has been."

I leaned over her, my arms around her shoulders. I planted a kiss on the top of her head. "Well, don't worry. No one is going to take advantage of you while I'm around."

That may have been overstepping my bounds, but I couldn't help it. She needed someone to back her up right now, whether she admitted it or not. But she didn't flinch nor pull away. Instead, she patted my arm. "Thank you."

The squeal of the teakettle interrupted, and I went to the kitchen. When I returned, she appeared to have recovered. I sat down opposite her.

"You want to talk about it?"

Sacha stared into her cup, stirring the brown liquid idly with a spoon. When she looked up, it wasn't at me but over my shoulder toward the door. Then she made a "tch" sound and shook her head.

"I should have kept my cool, but it was a shock seeing him. Now I'm wondering why he tried to contact me before. If Kevin had told me when Garth first tried to contact me, I would have dealt with it then. But we had problems of our own back then, I guess."

I raised a brow. She had mentioned her divorce a few times, but not any details. "I'm sure. No divorce is easy."

She sat back in her chair and closed her eyes. She shook her head before opening them, and placed her hands on the table, balled into fists at the recollection that must have been playing in her mind.

"You really want to hear how it went down? I came home from visiting my mother in New Jersey with the intent of rekindling the romance in our marriage. We'd tried for years to conceive with no luck, and it sort of drove a wedge between us. When he met me at the door, he informed me he was in love with someone else, and *she* was pregnant."

"Wow."

Now her strong reactions made some sense. Who could trust anyone after that?

"Yeah, it wasn't fun. But I survived."

"Yes, you did. Hell, I'm impressed with how you handle things. I mean that. You're a strong woman."

Her skeptical gaze amused me. Would she ever let her guard down enough to trust me? Could I trust her with the truth?

Now is not the time to lay another bomb on her. Maybe later.

When she finished her tea, we moved to the sofa. She didn't ask me to leave, and I didn't mention it. When she snuggled into my side and turned the television on with the remote, I relaxed for the first time that day.

After flipping several channels, she settled on a mindless sitcom. It was more background noise than entertainment because she continued to talk about her past.

"So after my ninth birthday party, which was at a local pizza

145

place, Mom and I came home to find out why Garth hadn't been there. A farewell note was on the table, along with five one hundred-dollar bills, like that was supposed to excuse what he did."

"Wow. That must've been confusing for you at that age."

"Not really. He and Mom had separated before, and like a fool, she always took him back. But this time he was gone for good. The note simply said, 'I can't. I'm sorry.' Like it was a job he was quitting, not his family."

"No explanation?"

"None needed. He was a drinker, a gambler, always in and out of jobs. He was likely in some kind of big trouble. We were probably better off without him."

I was glad she felt she could talk to me and get it out. The feel of her soft, warm body next to mine was comforting. And arousing, but I controlled my reaction. Pushing her was the last thing I wanted to do.

Later, she dozed, her head against my shoulder. It was getting late, and I had to go to the bathroom. I moved a bit to rouse her.

"Sacha. You need to go to bed."

She sat up, drowsy-eyed. Stretching, she yawned and looked up at me. "Don't go."

I held out a hand and helped her to her feet. "I won't unless you want me to."

She answered with her lips against mine. "Mmmhmm."

The sweetness of her mouth was all the confirmation I needed. I held her tight, relief shaking loose my bones. I was staying the night. When she pulled away, I released her with a sigh.

"Let me go get my bag out of the car."

"You came prepared, huh?"

The snark of her tone indicated I was busted.

"Yes, ma'am. I sure did."

~*~

Sacha

I slept better that night than I had in weeks. The warm male body sharing my bed must have had something to do with it, but I was also exhausted from the events of the day before. We hadn't had sex, but Gib held me close all night. I was beginning to enjoy having him around, as much as that went against my instincts. He was still snoring lightly when I slipped out of bed and tiptoed to the kitchen on bare feet. After making a pot of tea, I pulled out my cell phone to tell Mom the news.

We chatted for a bit about my doctor visit and the baby's progress, but I didn't mention Gib. I wasn't sure why. She would find out eventually if we continued seeing each other like this. Would we? In any case, I didn't want to complicate matters just yet. Once the initial excitement began to wane from her voice, I dropped the bombshell.

"I had an unexpected visitor at my door last night when I got home from the doctor's office."

"Who was it?"

"Dad. Garth."

The stunned silence on the line didn't surprise me, but my mother's choice of curse words did. It began with the word, "mother" and ended with another word I wouldn't repeat out loud. This was followed by a barrage of questions.

"What the hell did he want? How did he even find you? What did you say?"

"Apparently he's been in contact with Kevin for years. The asshole gave him my address without even asking me. I was livid, to say the least. Anyway, he was all, 'I'm so proud of you', and gushing about my pregnancy, calling me 'Pumpkin.' I almost threw up on him."

"He did always call you that. You used to like it."

"Yeah, when I was a kid, but now it only pisses me off. I know it was because my birthday is near Halloween, and every year I'm reminded of how he dumped us with no explanation."

"So, you sent him off? How did he look?"

I sipped at my tea to ward off the chill brought on by the mental image of Garth. He resembled a walking cadaver. If I hadn't known who he was, he'd just be a creepy-looking stranger.

"Not well. Maybe he's ill, I didn't ask. I was kind of in shock. I told him to leave before I called the cops."

Julia chuckled at that. A tinge of guilt seeped in. Maybe I had been too harsh on the guy. But then, it was what he deserved for showing up out of the blue.

"That's my girl. But now you don't know what he really wanted. You know he's not going to simply fade away. Not if he's finally had the guts to show his face. He must be in big trouble to contact you like that."

"Yeah, that's what I thought. He said he found out about my pregnancy from someone online. Do you know anything about that,

Mom?"

I could almost see her squirming in her seat. Julia's penchant for gossip was one of her most endearing qualities but also a bad habit. I knew she wouldn't keep news of the baby a secret, but this turn of events was ridiculous.

"Mmmm... Well, I did tell some of my old classmates, and some friends, and well...pretty much anyone who would listen. It may be that someone contacted him somehow."

"I guess it doesn't really matter at this point. Garth told me he is staying in town for a while, but I have no intention of contacting him."

A voice behind me was the only warning I had before Gib slipped his arms around me. "There you are."

I pressed the phone tighter to my ear, but Mom had heard. "Who was that?"

"I have to go, Mom. It was the TV. Love you bunches. I'll keep you posted."

Her voice was skeptical, but she concluded the call. I set the phone down and stood to return Gib's hug.

"The TV, huh? Guess you haven't told your mother about me, either."

"I mentioned you once before but that's all. She insisted on hearing every detail of my visit to the obstetrician, and then I told her about Garth showing up. I figured all that was enough to drop on her right now."

He released me, moving toward the kitchen. "Point taken. How did she react about your father showing up?"

I shrugged. "Shock, anger, suspicion. Pretty much like I did."

In the kitchen, he began making himself at home. "You hungry? How about an omelet?"

"Sounds wonderful."

Soon he had a spread on the table—toast, fruit, juice, and a veggie and cheese omelet that was superb, better than any I had ever made. "Where'd you learn to cook?"

His smile seemed to hide an inside joke. "I taught myself. You can find any recipe online these days, with videos showing exactly what to do."

After breakfast, I looked at the calendar on my phone. "Oh, crap. That's tonight."

Gib looked up from his own phone. "What's tonight?"

"I have this party to attend. At an art gallery downtown."

"Oh. Well, I'll be out of your hair soon."

His face was placid, but the disappointment in his voice was unmistakable. I really should let him be on his way, so I could attend the party without distraction. My career depended on this meeting tonight. But going it alone wasn't exactly appealing. Perhaps having an escort would make me look more respectable, more reliable. It was a shame I had to think that way, but I had no idea how my new boss would view a single, pregnant woman. He could be a Neanderthal. What would it hurt to have Gib along?

"You can come with me if you like."

"I'd love to, but I'm not dressed for a party. Especially a downtown Atlanta party."

It struck me as odd he would care how he dressed, but I knew so little about him. After last night, he certainly knew more about my personal life and background. Maybe this was a chance to even the score.

"So, let's go shopping."

~*~

Gibson

I hadn't really expected to find decent clothes at the bargain close-out store where Sacha took us to shop. I'd never ventured into one, at least not since I was really young. My father's finances had improved tremendously by the time I was twelve, and before that, my mom and my sister bought my clothes. Once I was an adult, I wore fine clothes because it served a purpose and projected a certain image. An image I had rejected recently, only to discover I rather enjoyed wearing comfortable clothes again. I no longer cared what I wore, much like when I was a boy.

But Sacha had led us to the racks of designer clothes, in the basement of an old department store. They were a few seasons old, but there were some gems among the rubble if one had the time to search.

She had an eye for detail and found the perfect wool sports jacket for me in a rusty shade, shot through with specks of emerald green. I selected a cream-colored button-down shirt with interesting wood buttons. I was already wearing my best pair of jeans, but my work boots wouldn't suit. After trying on several pairs, I found faux leather boots in my size. They didn't look like real leather, but the color was right. Sacha assured me they were the right pick.

149

"No one will notice. This crowd will likely be vegan, anyway, so they'll applaud your choice."

"Where is this gallery?"

The likelihood of running into someone I knew on a Saturday night in Midtown was pretty good. I knew it was a risk, but worth it, because it also gave me the chance to spend more time with Sacha.

It was good that I'd not shaved off the beard or cut my hair.

"Near Midtown. It's a private gallery. Very exclusive, but I hear it's not tiny. Big enough to hold a party, anyway."

Some of the shops and galleries in Midtown, or nearby Little Five Points, were tiny. Rent was expensive, but more than that, it added to the chic atmosphere of the villages surrounding Atlanta.

"We'd better find a belt that isn't leather to go with. Or I'll have to wear the shirttail out."

In the end, she decided I looked more "artsy" with the shirt out, but what really pulled the outfit together was the dark green vest Sacha discovered on a clearance rack. It was a bit snug in the shoulders, but no one would notice under the jacket. I had to admit, I looked good. Sacha agreed, her eyes roaming over me as she looked at my reflection in the full-length mirror.

"Pretty hot. For a mountain man."

"Yeah, I clean up nice, eh? But I'm not wearing a scarf, so don't even think about it."

"Awww."

She had picked one up during our foray through the clothes racks. I wanted to look like I fit in, but a guy could only go so far. She tossed the scarf on a nearby table with a shrug.

Sacha had picked a colorful blouse for her outfit, one roomy enough that her growing belly bump wouldn't show. The cream and blush tones, accented with teal, would bring out her eyes. The pattern was artistic but minimal.

We paid for our purchases separately. I tried to pay for hers, but she wouldn't allow it, leaving the line we were in for another cashier. The woman could be infuriatingly stubborn. I had enough room on my prepaid credit card to cover both of our purchases. Maybe I'd gone a bit too far with this low-key persona. I didn't want her thinking I was a charity case.

On the car ride back to her place, I decided that it was time to tell Sacha the truth about my life. Her actions the past few days had proven she was not the type of person to take advantage of a situation. She was fiercely independent, perhaps to a fault. It was no wonder, with what she'd been through in her life.

If she knew the truth about me, perhaps it would ease her mind. I couldn't have her thinking I didn't have the ability to take care of her and our child financially. Maybe then she'd be open to being more than just co-parents.

Yes, I'd tell her tonight after the party. When we were alone, and she was relaxed.

Chapter Nineteen

Sacha

*B*etween lunch and shopping, the day had disappeared. I had just enough time to shower and get dressed before we had to leave. When I emerged from the bathroom in a robe, Gib was standing in my bedroom in nothing but his tighty-whities.

"My turn, now? I only need a quick rinse."

He demonstrated what he meant by running a hand down the length of his torso, causing heat to skitter up my spine. The flat, muscled expanse of his abdomen was dusted with fine golden hair. My fingers twitched, an involuntary response to the mental image I had of what I'd like to do to him—but I managed to stifle the urge.

"Sure, I'll get dressed while you're at it."

He stopped on his way to the bathroom to kiss me, his hand tilting my chin up. He followed that with a sultry look then a glance down at my robe. The collar had fallen open and one breast was partially exposed. I moved aside, closing the robe, but gave him a smile.

Maybe later...

He disappeared to take his shower, and I used his absence to regain my composure. Tonight was not about him or anyone else. It was about my career. If I had to move to Alabama, at least this was a chance to secure a better position for my child and myself.

Our child.

The time had come to tell Gib the truth. It wasn't fair to keep him in the dark about my plans, but I didn't want anything to disrupt my confidence level this evening. I would tell him after the party, once I'd assessed my new boss. Maybe I didn't even want to work for the man, and it would be a moot point.

Yep. Once I knew for sure, I'd tell Gib about my plan to leave the state.

By the time he emerged from the bathroom clad in only a towel, I had dressed, curled my hair, and put on makeup. He strutted across the room, the olive-green cloth slung low on his hips. As he bent to pick up his jeans from the floor, I cleared my throat, which had suddenly gone dry. Gib turned, his wet locks flinging droplets everywhere.

"You're dripping on my floor."

"Sorry."

He ran a hand through the tangle of blond, slicking it back behind his ears. He gave me a grin and went back to the bathroom to dress. It took a moment for the flush of desire to leave my cheeks, making me look presentable again. It took a bit longer for the image of us in the shower together to leave my imagination.

When we were finally ready to leave, I had to admit Gibson Colebank was one handsome man. His now-dried hair was tousled, giving him a beachy surfer-dude look. His beard was neatly trimmed and combed. The suit fit him well, and though the pieces were mismatched, they coordinated in a way that looked creative. His jeans fit well, were tight in all the right places.

Yes, this was more my style. He no longer resembled the rough-hewn mountain man I'd come to know but was now a cosmopolitan man of the city. Who knew he had a sophisticated side?

He seemed to be impressed with me, too, if the way his lusty blue gaze traveled over me was any indication. My navy pencil skirt seemed made to go with my new blouse, and the pumps I wore showed off my calves nicely. I wouldn't be able to wear high heels much longer, so I figured this was a good night to get some use from them.

"You look gorgeous. No one would guess you're...you know."

His cheeks turned pink as he stumbled over the right way to indicate my condition. I wasn't exactly trying to hide my pregnancy, but for tonight, there was no reason to flaunt it. I wanted to be judged on my ability to do the job and nothing else.

"Thank you. I know what you mean. And just for tonight, let's forget about everything else, okay?"

"Got it."

He held the front door open for me and walked me to my car. I had already explained the party was more of a work function, and I would be networking. Gib promised to be an unobtrusive escort, without me prompting him. Except for his joke about him being "arm candy," I was grateful for his support.

When we arrived at the Vertex Art Gallery, the place was already buzzing. My potential new boss, Colin Redfield, was speaking to the crowd, which was gathered in a circle at the back of the gallery. A young woman stood next to him.

"Since she was a child, Ella was extremely creative. She's dabbled in music and art throughout her life, and though I am most definitely biased"—he paused with a grin, prompting polite chuckles from the crowd—"she is quite talented. Her eye for detail in the photographs and watercolors you see here tonight will astound you. And she's only twenty-one."

Applause broke out, and the young woman nodded to the crowd. She seemed at once proud and embarrassed. Her father went on to announce she was soon to graduate from the Savannah College of Art, prompting another round of applause. Then he gestured to his daughter to speak.

"Please, everyone, enjoy yourselves. If you have any questions, please ask. It is my honor to be here, and I am so glad to share my work with you."

Though her words must have been rehearsed, she seemed sincere. Watching her proud papa, I decided he might be an approachable man after all.

I handed my club soda to Gib. "I need to go introduce myself. Would you wait here?"

"Yes, ma'am. Good luck."

He winked at me as I turned to make my way across the room. He had no idea that this introduction could mean I was moving farther away from him. The thought made my gut clench, and it wasn't just the guilt over keeping my plan a secret.

I was going to miss him.

~*~

Gibson

I looked around me at the gallery—the crowd, the funky holiday décor, the ambient lighting. I couldn't recall ever attending a party where I wasn't the reluctant center of attention. Those parties had been more for business and networking, anyway. I found I rather liked being anonymous. It gave me a chance to observe people. No one was fawning over me, pretending to be a friend, or flirting in hopes of spending some of my money. I walked among the crowd, unnoticed.

There were several small cliques, all dressed either elegantly or funky-chic. Not the Frisky Beaver crowd, to be sure. I sipped at a glass of prosecco and wandered the gallery, admiring the artwork. Every few minutes, I glanced back at Sacha to see her engaged in conversation with the artist and her father. She seemed to be holding her own, and I felt a surge of pride at the way she handled herself. Aside from Bianca, I'd never been involved with such a strong, independent woman.

A black and white photograph caught my attention. Moving closer to observe, I studied the image. The subject was a woman, viewed from behind, leaning over a railing on the side of a bridge. Her long hair blew in the breeze, and her hands gripped the railing. Was she contemplating jumping or admiring the view?

As I pondered the photo, a woman stood next to me. She sipped from her glass of red wine then leaned over, her voice low and curious.

"Would you say she's ready to jump or watching someone else who already has?"

An involuntary huff escaped my lips, and I looked down at the woman. My heart began to pound so loudly that I barely heard my response.

"I wouldn't know."

I moved to leave, but she caught my arm, gripping it tight.

"Not so fast, mister. We need to talk."

~*~

Of all the people in the world to run into, Bettina McCord was the worst. The nightmare scenario I had feared happening at this party was unraveling fast. Not only had she recognized me but she had a score to settle, and she didn't hesitate to make clear her intentions. As I moved quickly to a darkened corner of the room, she was holding her cell phone up and snapping away.

"Oh, this is so going viral. I can't believe it. An elusive John G. Colebank sighting."

With my back to the corner, I turned and faced her. My hands were up, trying to block her view of my face. "Bettina, listen. I can explain."

Her dark eyes widened in mock excitement. "And I can't wait to hear it. How you disappeared from my bed without a word and refused to return my calls or texts? Yes, let's hear what a coward really sounds like."

She held a pretend microphone in front of my mouth, feigning interest in my response.

It was shortly before I left on that fateful motorcycle trip and ended up in Tilly that we met. A drunken night at a club had led to a weekend in bed with Bettina, who had quickly showed her crazy side. A side which served her well as a journalist and blogger, writing shock pieces and gossip for several local magazines and websites. She had been interested in exploiting my family and me as fodder for her posts. It wasn't me she wanted but the status that came with dating a billionaire. I didn't normally ghost a woman like that, but at the time, I saw no other way to discourage her.

She was the kind of woman I most wanted to avoid. Now she was up in my face, demanding my full attention.

"I was going through some shit. You knew I was recently widowed. I had to disappear from everyone, not just you."

"Mmm-hmmm. So now you're finally back among the living?"

Her callous disregard for my feelings shouldn't have bothered me, but it did. "Sort of. Look, I'm sorry I never called. I didn't think you cared to hear from me, anyway."

Much as I wanted to get away from this woman, I couldn't afford to be rude to her. She'd likely make good on her promise to "go viral" with the photos and whatever else she felt like spewing about me. Now that she had found me, she wouldn't rest until she had uncovered every aspect of my new life, and I could not let that happen.

I had to diffuse her ire, and the only way to do that was to flirt and make her feel like she had a chance again. I couldn't let Sacha, or my family, find out the truth by seeing it online. I had to take control of this situation, fast.

I looked around to be sure Sacha wasn't nearby, and then put an arm around Bettina's shoulders. "Let's find a place to discuss what an idiot I've been."

~*~

Sacha

"So, what would you say is your greatest strength, Sacha?" My conversation with Mr. Redfield had evolved into a mini-interview. His daughter had moved on to talk with some friends, and now his attention was focused on me, his prospective employee. He seemed impressed that I came for the showing, and I wanted to take advantage of the moment.

"I have built excellent relationships with my clients. That's crucial because they need to have trust in their rep. Even though the client's managers and staff may come and go, once a relationship is established, they tend to keep ordering from us."

"And you think you can teach newbies the secrets of your success? Some can't teach, they can only do."

"Yes, sir, I can. I have several ideas on how to accomplish that objective. And how to tailor it to the various needs of the reps. Not everyone learns in the same way."

His face was placid but for the turn of his lips into a shadow of a smile. He was trying not to show how interested he was. I could sense he was favorably impressed.

I was about to elaborate when his daughter appeared at his side.

"Daddy, I need you to meet someone," she cooed, looking over her shoulder at a young man standing a few feet away. Mr. Redfield nodded to me and apologized, then promised to be in touch.

It was the best I could hope for, given the crowd and the distractions. He seemed like a reasonable man, if a little snooty. But I could definitely work for him, if I got the position.

I looked around for Gib, who was nowhere in sight. *He must be using the restroom.*

Deciding I needed to use the restroom myself, I strolled in that direction, browsing the photos and paintings as I passed. Ella Redfield was indeed talented, for one so young. Envy stabbed at me. Why had it taken me until almost forty to realize what I truly wanted from life?

I was about to enter the restroom when I caught sight of Gib's blond hair. He was standing near the front door of the gallery with his back to me, and the expanse of his broad shoulders in the tweed jacket made me almost melt with desire. As I walked toward him, it appeared he was in a conversation with someone. I couldn't see who it was, until he leaned forward and a woman's arms came around his neck, pulling him close to her.

I stopped cold. My lungs seized up as his head moved downward, indicating he was kissing the woman. It was over quickly, and the brown-haired woman left, blowing him a kiss. He stood still, watching her leave.

Nausea rose up in my throat. I made it to the bathroom in time, but barely. My insides turned, but only water came out. Thank God I hadn't eaten in several hours.

I leaned against the wall, trying to breathe.

Damn him. I knew I couldn't trust him. Why do I even try?

Chapter Twenty

Gibson

*R*elief cascaded over me like a spring waterfall. I'd talked Bettina into holding off on her posts for a week. She demanded in return that I take her to dinner, and I'd agreed, but it would never be arranged. I hated lying, but it was the only tactic I could think of. Once I came clean to Sacha and my family, it didn't matter what she did.

I hadn't meant to go so far as kissing her, but she'd grabbed me and planted one on my lips before I knew what was happening. But now she was gone and I had dodged one hell of a bullet.

Well, maybe. I still had to talk to Sacha.

As I went to get another drink, I saw her disappear into the ladies' room. I used the time to mentally prepare my speech. She'd probably be upset that I'd been hiding things from her, so I had to say the right words to make her understand why.

Telling Sacha that I assumed at first that she might only want me for my money would sound horribly shallow, but for me it was a real concern. Bettina was a prime example of that, but I couldn't mention her.

"I'm ready to go now." Sacha had appeared at my elbow. Her face was blotchy, and her eyes were wet.

"Are you okay? You don't look well." Her response was a glare. Maybe the networking she said she was here to do hadn't gone so well. I

159

knew better than to pry. "I'll get your coat."

As we walked to her car, the cool night air seemed to calm her. I saw her taking in deep breaths, and I began to worry about the baby. She still hadn't said a word, so as I helped her into the driver's seat, I asked again.

"Are you feeling ill, Sacha?"

"No. I'm fine."

She slammed the door and flipped on the engine. I walked to my side and climbed in.

Her focus was on the road. She barely looked in my direction. Something had clearly upset her, and I had a sinking feeling in my stomach. Thank God Bettina had another party to attend, or else I'd have been in a tough spot. But now I was more worried about Sacha than my own problems.

"Want to talk about it?"

"No."

She turned on the radio and cranked the volume. I got the hint— she wasn't going to tell me what the hell was wrong. At least not now.

My stomach rumbled. The bites of food at the gallery had been miniscule, not enough to even consider an appetizer. I needed food, especially if I was going to have a tough night ahead.

"You hungry?"

"No."

Sitting at a restaurant while she fumed sure wasn't appealing. Maybe there was something in her fridge I could nibble on. I'd rather be nibbling on her, too, but sex certainly didn't seem to be on the menu tonight.

It wasn't until we entered her apartment that she spoke. Throwing her coat and scarf on the back of the sofa, she whirled to face me.

"Who was she?"

I blinked, knowing I looked like the proverbial deer in the headlights but unable to stop it. "What are you talking about?"

Her finger came up to jab me in the chest. "I leave you alone for a few minutes and you're kissing someone. I mean, you couldn't stop yourself and at least pretend to be with me?"

"I was with you. I mean, I am."

I went to place my hands on her arms but she moved away.

"You certainly didn't act like it. We had an agreement that we wouldn't bring other people around in front of our child. But you couldn't even control yourself for just one evening, so how can I trust you?"

"It wasn't how it looked. She was...I knew her from a long time ago. And I didn't kiss her. She kissed me. Caught me by surprise, if you want the truth."

The skeptical look she gave me had a softer edge to it than the anger I'd seen a few moments earlier. Then she crossed her arms over her chest and leaned against the back of the sofa.

"So, is she still interested in you? Were you making plans for a date?"

If I said no, it would be a lie. If I said yes, but I had no intention of seeing the woman, I'd look like a dick. This interrogation was not how I had hoped to spend the evening. "No. She wanted to, but I'm not interested in her. That's all there is to it."

"Really?"

"Absolutely."

She paused, thinking it over. "Why didn't you tell me, then?"

"Because you were acting like a she-bear and I was afraid."

Her angry face began to crumble, and she looked away. I reached out to touch her, and this time she let me. Then she began to laugh, falling into my arms.

One hurdle down. One to go.

~*~

Sacha

I didn't want to laugh and forgive him. I had felt like a fool thinking Gib might be someone I could trust, but now I wasn't so sure. His explanation of what happened with that woman was plausible, but it still made me uncomfortable.

But when he was so near, his breath warm on my cheek, the citrus scent of his cologne invading my nose... It was hard to be mad at him. Not to mention his denim-blue eyes pleading for understanding.

Besides, I had no claim on him. Wasn't I the one saying I needed space? That we should keep it platonic and businesslike?

I had to respond, and the heat had gone out of my ire. "I'm not sure I believe your story, but... I didn't mean to scare you."

I knew he was joking about my temper. But what happened wasn't the end of the world, now that my anger was fading away. He was

161

an attractive man, who probably had a string of women in his past.

"It's all right. Are we good now?"

"Yes. Please be honest with me from now on, okay? I won't tolerate dishonesty."

His face fell from a sexy grin back to the guilty-surprised look he'd had a few moments ago. My gut twisted again, for the second time that night. What now?

He pulled back but held onto my hand. "Sacha, there's some things I need to tell you."

I desperately needed a glass of water. The events of the evening had my head spinning, and my lower abdomen was tight. It ached like I was having a period—that sensation of nausea in the lower belly. I excused myself to the bathroom while he got me some water.

There was no cause for alarm, no bleeding, but now my lower back had begun to ache. It must have been the stress. I needed to relax before listening to whatever it was Gib was about to confess. I put on comfy pajamas and splashed my face with water. Then I joined him on the sofa, drinking an entire glass of water before settling back onto the cushions.

He'd changed into sweats and a tee shirt, and was holding a throw pillow on his lap, kneading the corner of it. His cheeks had gone slightly pink above his tawny beard, and I almost smiled at his nervousness.

Maybe I really had scared him. Good.

He took a breath and began, his voice solemn. "When I told you about how I ended up in Tilly, I left some things out. You never know when you first meet someone whether or not you can trust them, right?"

I nodded, because it was true, and gestured for him to continue. He did.

"I was distraught over the loss of my wife and unborn child. I've already told you that. But how it happened is why I ran away from my life in Atlanta. The bottom line—which I will never forgive myself for—is it was my fault they died."

The pain in his eyes was unbearable. I could sense he wasn't embellishing this. He'd choked on the words, and I reached out to squeeze his hand. "Go on."

He took a deep breath, and his eyes had darkened to the blue of a sea at dusk.

"Bianca was roughly eight to ten weeks pregnant and not having an easy time of it. She often felt tired and had morning sickness. Well, I

Not So Broken

was on a trip to the Bahamas on business. She insisted on coming, on the agreement that if she felt bad, she would return home without me to see her doctor right away.

"Everything was fine until the last day of our trip. I had a meeting that was supposed to close the deal. The client had been changing his mind, and I had spent a lot of time with him, trying to get a commitment. It was clear I was going to need a few more days to accomplish that. Well, Bianca was in some pain that morning, only minor, so she stayed in bed. There was a doctor on the island, a midwife of sorts, but she didn't want to be examined by anyone but her own doctor back in the states. She insisted she would be fine and wait until we could return. But by afternoon she wasn't feeling better, so I made the decision to put her on a helicopter which would take her to the airport in Nassau right away."

He ran a shaky hand through his hair. The other hand was balled into a fist. "She begged me to go with her, despite our earlier agreement. She wasn't in such pain that she couldn't walk, and she wasn't bleeding or anything severe. She just felt off. She had an almost irrational fear of going alone, but I felt she needed to be seen by her doctor as soon as possible."

He paused to put his head in his hands. My heart wrenched. I didn't want to hear what happened next but I had to. Maybe he had to tell it, to gain closure.

"It sounds like a tough decision."

When he looked up at me, his eyes were rimmed in scarlet, and glistened with tears. "It was a mistake to bring her with me. Anyway, I calmed her down and assured her the helicopter service was the best in the islands. She finally agreed to go, and I drove her to the small airfield where the helicopter service operated. We kissed, we hugged, and she waved at me from the window as they took off. It was the last time I saw her."

"Gib, you don't have to—"

"No, I do. I need to tell someone. I want you to understand."

"Okay. What happened to her?"

"The helicopter never made it to the airport, crashing on the shoreline after takeoff. It was a malfunction of some sort. They never were able to verify the cause from the wreckage. There were no survivors."

"Oh my God. That's horrible."

What else could I say? Guilt wound its way through my heart, for thinking the worst of him earlier. The poor guy had been through hell.

163

"Yeah. If I had let her stay, she'd still be alive today. As would our child. Or if I had gone with her, we'd all still be together."

The import of his words chilled me to the bone. He'd rather be dead and with his wife and child than to live without them. Suddenly it all made sense. He'd latched onto the baby and me to redeem himself.

"Oh, no. Don't think like that. You didn't know what would happen."

"Yes, but I made the decision to send her off. She wanted to stay, or for me to go with her. I chose business over my family, and believe me, that will never happen again."

Silent sobs wracked his shoulders as tears fell from his eyes. He brushed them away and sat with his head in his hands. It killed me to see a man so broken. It occurred to me he hadn't explained what business he was on in the Bahamas, but it didn't matter. Whatever he had done in his life before this horrible incident, he had left behind. He was a man who cared deeply, and for now, that was all I needed to know.

~*~

Gibson

My insides felt like they'd been stirred with a white-hot poker. Emotions I had repressed for nearly two years surfaced as I told Sacha about the crash. I hadn't meant to go into such detail, but once I'd started, the words tumbled out like a landslide. Maybe it was a good thing, because she seemed much more sympathetic now. She was holding me close, whispering words of comfort. It helped tremendously. Somewhere deep inside, a glimmer of hope flickered. Perhaps healing was possible.

I meant what I said—that I would never again put business first. It was why I'd rejected a high paying, world-traveling, corporate position. If I ever returned to the family business again, it would be on my own terms.

There was still so much to tell her, but now she was brushing my neck with her warm, soft lips. When she took my face in her hands and looked into my eyes, I saw not pity but concern. And maybe something close to love?

I pulled her onto my lap and crushed her mouth with mine. Every cell in my body needed her, needed to be as close as humanly possible. We had already created a miracle, a life. To me, the fact she was carrying

Not So Broken

my child made her all the more beautiful, and the only way I could convey what I felt was by giving myself to her. Words were not enough.
Her plush white terry robe fell away to reveal a pale-yellow nightgown. Her breasts had grown in recent weeks, and the taut points showed through the silky material. My fingers did a slow exploration of one nipple while my other hand cupped her bottom. Sacha squirmed and whimpered, the sound making a small vibration against my lips.
She broke the kiss, just long enough to breathe, "Take me to bed."
"Yes, ma'am."
I stood, lifting her up with me. I was several inches taller than she was, and even at roughly four months pregnant, she didn't weigh much. I picked her up and carried her, and her head fell against my shoulder with a sigh.
When we reached the bed, I set her down on the mattress. She knelt, removing her nightgown. She hadn't worn panties, a fact that made my excitement all the more evident. My own clothes took seconds to hit the floor, and she fell back on the bed as I covered her body with mine.
"This is crazy," she murmured in between kisses.
"Don't think, just feel. This is right. This is us."
I rolled onto my back, pulling her into a sitting position on top of me. I didn't want to crush her. The position would let her set the pace. Besides, the view was awesome.
She eased down onto my shaft, the slick heat making me gasp. In the dim light from the living room, I could see the flare of her hips, her full breasts. As I ran a hand over her, from her neck down to her thigh, she shuddered. Her eyes were closed, but when she opened them and saw me admiring her, she frowned.
"Don't look at me. My belly is getting big."
Placing both hands on her belly, I caressed it. "It's beautiful, because it's you."
She responded by leaning over to kiss me, and then began to move her hips in a rhythm. I grabbed hold of her hands so that she sat straight up, supported by me. This gave her the leverage to move however she wanted. I was just along for the ride, and oh, what a ride it was.
It took some effort to control my reaction. I didn't want this to be over anytime soon, so I closed my eyes to concentrate. Sacha was now rocking back and forth, moaning as the friction increased her excitement. She slowed down then sped up, experimenting. I countered her every movement, pushing my hips up as she came down. The result was an

165

escalation of mind-bending pleasure.

I was close to losing control when she quickened the pace of her movements, rubbing her mound against me while her insides clenched. I felt the rush thunder through me as she cried out her own release. It seemed to last forever, though it was only seconds. Soon her frantic pace slowed, and she fell limp on top of me. My arms came around her to hold her close.

Sacha slid off to lay beside me, with her head on my chest. "Oh my God. That was the best orgasm I've ever had."

I kissed her forehead. "My pleasure. You can ride me anytime."

Her soft sound of agreement was music to my ears.

Soon her shallow breathing told me she was asleep. I lay staring at the ceiling, enjoying the pleasant drowsiness. A turning point had occurred, not only with Sacha but in my life. I could sense it.

Starting tomorrow, our new life would begin.

Chapter Twenty-One

Sacha

*T*he next morning, I woke up ravenous and craving French toast. No wonder, since we ended up in bed before making it to the kitchen. And so far, pregnancy sex had been intense. After last night's session, I'd slept like the dead. Wrapping myself in a robe, I walked to the kitchen to make breakfast while Gib took a shower.

As I busied myself with the preparations, I couldn't help but laugh. All I'd done the past few months was try to convince myself to stay away from Gib, but the man was like sexual quicksand. The harder I tried to get away, the stronger his pull. Learning about what he'd been through with his wife's death had made my final resistance melt away. He was a good guy who'd been through hell. So, what if he wasn't a rock star or a billionaire? He had a good heart and a hot body I couldn't seem to refuse.

I'd always pictured motherhood as my own pursuit, but having someone around to help out now and then would be nice. He seemed sincere in his efforts to prove he'd make a good father and companion. I was honestly running out of reasons to reject him.

I was setting the table when I heard Melanie's signature knock on the door. Gib was still in the bedroom getting dressed so I went to answer it.

"Hey girl. I brought you some muffins and juice. Want to have

167

brunch?"

She didn't wait for an answer but walked in as she normally did, headed for the kitchen. I closed the door with a grin, thankful Gib hadn't wandered out naked.

"Sure, there's room for one more."

The look on Melanie's face as she spun around was comical. Her dark hair was a mess, and she still had on leather pants and a ripped tee, presumably from last night's gig.

"Wait, what? You have company?"

"Yep. Gib stayed the weekend. He went to the gallery thing with me."

"Oooh. Somebody got laid."

I didn't deny it, but didn't agree. My wicked smile spoke for me, confirming Melanie's guess. "Shh. He'll hear you."

"Hear what?"

My heart thumped as Gib's deep voice announced his presence. "Gib, this is my friend Melanie. She lives next door."

He extended a hand. "Nice to meet you, Melanie."

She placed the paper bag she was carrying on the counter and shook his hand. "Likewise. I've heard so much about you."

"Well, I hope it wasn't all bad."

"Not all of it."

I was plating the French toast. "Stop, you two. Time to eat."

We spent the meal mostly talking. Melanie was quite chatty for someone who'd been up all night, but she'd told me before that playing a gig always wound her up. She couldn't sleep until at least noon, which it would be by the time we finished brunch. She stopped in the middle of devouring her second helping of French toast to pull an envelope from her jacket pocket.

"Oh, I almost forgot. Some guy was here last night, looking for you. I was leaving for work and he was hanging around your door."

"Looking for me? What did he look like?"

"Tall, thin. Older guy. He gave me this note 'cause you were still out. He wanted to leave it on your door, but he had no tape. He asked me for some, and I told him I'd see you got it."

Gib's brows rose as I shot him a look. He knew as well as I who it was. "Must have been my father again."

Melanie's dark eyes widened. "Again? Cripes, I don't see you for a day or two and miss all kinds of drama."

I rolled my eyes. "It wasn't as much drama as you think. I told him to go away. You can't pop up after almost thirty years and pick up where you left off."

"Well, he didn't take the hint, apparently."

"No surprise."

The envelope sat on the table now, and both Gib and Melanie were eyeing it then looking at me. I simply shrugged and kept eating.

"I want to enjoy my brunch first, if you two don't mind."

Soon the suspense was too much, and I picked up the envelope. My name was written on it in that familiar, messy scrawl Garth had always used. I ripped the seal and extracted the folded paper. My throat was parched despite the large glass of juice I'd just finished. With shaking hands, I held the note up and read.

Pumpkin (I know you hate that, but there was a time you didn't),
There are no words to tell you how sorry I am. I know it won't make a difference now, but I want you to know I do love you. And your mother. I never stopped loving either of you.

I did some bad things in my life, and God has seen fit to make me pay. I had cancer years ago. I finally beat it, after a long struggle. But I guess the joke's on me because it has shown up again. I'm not sure if I'll beat it this time around, so I knew I had to make amends. That's why I had to see you again, if only to beg your forgiveness, so I can die with a peaceful heart.

Someday if you're willing to sit down with me, I'll explain more about why I left. Until then, just know how happy I was to see you healthy and living a great life. I wish I could be around to see my grandson or granddaughter, but who knows.

I'll be here for a few days more. Call me if you want to talk or get together.

Take care of yourself, Pumpkin.

Love, Dad

His phone number was scrawled on the bottom of the note, along with three x's and o's. Was he trying to be cute?

I let the paper slip from my fingers onto the table. I blinked twice, but the tears welled up anyway. I looked up at Melanie, and then at Gib. I must have looked like I was about to crumble, because in a split second, both had their arms around me. They held on, hugging me as I cried.

My shoulders shook as the sobs came. I hadn't meant to react, not in front of anyone. But Mel and Gib weren't just anyone, and my guard fell. I took in a big breath then put into words what I felt in my heart.

"He's still an ass. And he's right, it doesn't make a difference."
I let them read the letter, and after handing it back, they both looked at me, not saying a word. This was my decision to make, and making it was breaking my heart. No, Garth Rowan was breaking my heart, all over again. My friends were still silent, so I let my anger out.

"Well, it doesn't. I'm sorry he's sick, but that's the only reason he's trying to make peace, so he can die with a clean conscience. He doesn't really care about us, no more than he ever has."
I tossed the note back on the table and walked to my bedroom to have a good cry. The sound of the door slamming behind me wasn't as satisfying as I had hoped. Throwing pillows across the room helped, as did kicking over the wastepaper can in the bathroom.

I turned on the shower. Maybe the hot water would rinse away the disgust I felt holding that note. Once the water was cascading over me, I slid down the wall into a crouching position and let the tears flow.

~*~

By the time I emerged from the bedroom, Gib had cleaned the kitchen and Melanie had gone home. He stood staring out the window, holding a mug. As he took a sip, his eyes watched me cautiously. It was the same look he'd had last night before calling me a "she-bear."

The recollection made me smile, and his face relaxed. For the first time, I noticed a few wrinkles at the corners of his eyes, and a few stray white hairs in his blond beard. We both weren't getting any younger, were we?

"Gib, I'm sorry for my outburst. I guess I have a lot of baggage where he's concerned."

He set down the mug to fold me into his arms. "It's okay. I understand. We all have baggage, you know."

"I know."

He held onto me, rocking us slowly back and forth. I'd decided in the shower the time had come to tell Gib about my job situation. I hated my father for never being honest, and I didn't want to be like him in any way. I hadn't lied exactly, but there comes a point when keeping the truth from someone can be as harmful.

Sometimes the truth isn't what we want to hear, but it's exactly what we need.

Plus, I had to admit, I was no longer as excited about the new training position. It would take me further away from Gib. He must have sensed my discomfort because he looked down at me with a question in his eyes.

He released me from the hug. "Is something wrong?"

"Let's sit down. We need to talk."

As I sat on the sofa, I winced. That dull ache in my lower back had returned, and my abdomen felt heavy. Maybe the sex had stirred something up. If it continued, I would call Dr. Kapoor in the morning.

Gib sat facing me. I placed a throw pillow on my stomach, which helped ease the ache a bit.

"So last night was more of an interview than a networking event. Mr. Redfield, the artist's father, may be hiring me soon. I think it went well."

"That's great, darlin'. No wonder you were nervous."

"I was, a little. Anyway, the thing is, if he hires me, I'll be moving to Birmingham."

"Alabama? Oh. Will you still have to travel so much?"

He didn't seem upset. I wasn't sure if that was good or bad.

"Some, but not like I do now. I'll be training reps in the region."

"Is this what you really want? I mean, is it your dream job?"

His question caught me by surprise. *Dream job? Where did that come from?*

"Well, no. Liquor sales has never been a dream job, but it pays the bills nicely. This new position would pay better and will involve less travel. If I could choose my work situation, I'd really love something I can do at home so I can be with the baby. But that's not likely to happen."

He smiled then winked at me. "So, being a stay-at-home mom is your dream job?"

Damn him, it kind of was. Would staying at home mean I was selling myself short?

It really didn't feel that way. I loved my independence and my career. But my child would always come first, no matter what.

"I never thought of it that way, but yes. I'd love to be able to afford to spend time with the baby, especially the first few years. But that's not likely to happen anytime soon, so I'll do whatever it takes to give him or her a good life. I'll always do my best at whatever job I happen to have."

He looked thoughtful, holding his chin in his hand. Something about his eyes told me he was formulating a plan. "Hmmm. Well, you know I'll support your decision, whichever way you choose to go. And I agree, the baby's needs should come first. Work will always be there."

I nodded. I was glad the Alabama thing didn't upset him, but it made me wonder why. "So, you know this means we'll be even farther apart if you're still living in Tilly."

He took my hand in his. His touch was warm, sending a tingle through me, but the dull ache in my back overrode my desire.

"That's true. But I have an alternative that might work for both of us. Before I explain, I'd like to show you something."

His smile was that of a child who peeked downstairs at Christmas before dawn. He was hiding something.

"What is it? You know I don't like surprises. Just ask my father."

His brows rose, but he took my hand and kissed the back of it. "It's better if I show you. Can we take a short drive?"

~*~

Gibson

The flip of my stomach as we entered the freeway brought to mind the roller coaster I'd ridden at Disney World when I was a teen. I could almost hear the tension-building, clackety-clack of the coaster car inching its way to the peak before plummeting. Was I really about to do this?

I was taking a huge gamble, but nothing had ever felt more right. Sacha would no doubt be impressed with my family's estate. Simply telling her "I'm rich" wouldn't have the same impact as seeing firsthand the way my family lived. It was the only way to convince her that I could provide the life of her dreams, if she'd give me the chance.

My parents wouldn't dare make a scene in front of her, so this was the best way to inform them about their new grandchild. Perhaps this would help prevent the drama I'd been dreading.

Sacha kept giving me questioning looks as she drove. "How much further?"

"A few more miles. I'll let you know before the exit comes up."

"You sure you don't want to tell me where we're going?"

"You'll see. Don't worry, it's something you'll like."

Not So Broken

I hope. What woman wouldn't want to live in a mansion, or a penthouse suite, jet around the world at whim, and be able to buy anything her heart desires?

I ignored my racing pulse and took a deep breath. My self-imposed exile was about to come to an end. Was I really about to throw away my carefully guarded secret identity?

The answer was a resounding "yes." I couldn't wait to see the impressed look on Sacha's face. To find out her scruffy baby daddy was really Prince Charming.

Well, sort of. I didn't believe in fairy tales, but little girls loved that stuff, and they grew up to be big girls who still dreamed of marrying a rich man.

And then Sacha and our child would never want for anything. I would see to it.

I told her to get off the freeway at the next exit. As we wound our way through the busy streets, the houses became more impressive. She kept giving me strange looks, and I was trying to keep a poker face. "Turn left at the next street," I instructed. "Just under a mile to go."

"This is a really nice neighborhood. Are we going to meet someone?"

"Yes."

She frowned. "Well, I wish you'd quit being so secretive and tell me already. I don't like being unprepared."

There was no way to prepare her for this, not really. If I'd told her ahead of time, she'd be even more apprehensive. "Don't worry, just be yourself."

If looks could kill, I'd be a pile of bones on the floor of the car. I had a slight moment of panic that she might not react the way I'd envisioned, but we were already approaching the gate at the driveway. I told her the code, she punched it in on the pad, and we were climbing the steep drive up to my parent's estate.

There was no turning back now.

173

Chapter Twenty-Two

Sacha

oly frickin' hell.

I had no idea who we were about to meet, but whoever it was had money. Plenty of money. The climb up the driveway had taken us about a quarter of a mile up a hill, on top of which stood a sprawling mansion. Fountains, statues, and topiary graced the front grounds. Then there was the house itself—a Mediterranean style three-level masterpiece. Glowing a rose-golden hue in the afternoon sun, with white-trimmed windows, which were adorned with boxes overflowing with plants. It was the very picture of a Tuscan tycoon's retreat.

"Who do you know that lives here? A client?"

Gib smirked and shook his head. "Nope. My parents live here."

"What?" I'd emerged from the car and stood staring at him, unable to stop my reaction. "Your parents live *here*?"

"That's what I said. Come meet them."

My legs wouldn't move. There was no way this could be true. My brain was trying to reconcile everything I knew about this man with what he was telling me, and it did not compute. "No."

He walked to where I was, next to my car. "Sacha, it's okay. They are going to love you, I promise."

His casual demeanor was pissing me off to no end. "You lied to me. You pretended to be some low-income handyman recluse, but your parents live *here*? The least you could have done is told me we were going to meet them. What the hell is going on with you?"

His cheeks grew red above his beard, but before he could answer the front door opened.

"Gib? Oh, Lord. Mamma is gonna have a fit." A young woman with short, bobbed hair the color of Gib's stepped onto the front step. She looked over her shoulder then back at us. "Too late."

He nodded up at her. "Thanks, Audrey," then turned to me. "My sister."

All I could do was arch a brow and wait to see what would happen next. I wanted to kick him for springing this on me. My back was aching fiercely now, and I needed to lie down, not get involved in someone's family drama.

Audrey moved aside as an older woman came out onto the step. She was dressed in a red Chanel-styled suit, and her blonde hair was piled up on her head in a neat bun. Her eyes widened when she saw me then narrowed, as she looked at her son.

"What's going on, Gibbie? You showing up out of the blue with a lady friend must mean God heard my prayers."

Gib took my hand, and I reluctantly let him pull me forward. I so wasn't dressed to meet his parents. It was one of those days when I felt fat, so I'd thrown on yoga pants and a long tee, topped with a thin sweater. Thankfully, it was one of those warm Georgia winter days, and I was wearing slip-ons, not gym shoes. My swollen ankles couldn't accommodate anything stylish at the moment, anyway.

"Mamma, this is Sacha Rowan. Sacha, my mother, Angela Colebank."

There was no way I was getting out of this, so I smiled and extended a hand. The woman shook it. Her delicate fingers were adorned by several clunky but gorgeous rings. Her demeanor was also cool, and I had the uncomfortable sensation of being sized up.

As soon as I was alone with Gib, I really was going to kick him.

"Well, come in then. We just got home from church and had lunch. But there's some leftover cake and pie."

It took a concentrated effort not to gape as we entered the grand house. The décor was a mix of traditional southern and Mediterranean that somehow blended. It was simple, yet elegant. I still couldn't reconcile the Gib I knew with the family that lived here.

Mrs. Colebank led the way to a huge sunroom at the back of the house, filled with white wicker furniture and soft yellow pillows. It

175

overlooked a gigantic pool flanked by two built-in hot tubs. There was an arching stone bridge suspended over the pool for easy access. My breath caught in my throat at the view of the Atlanta skyline in the distance.

Angela's voice was warm, but her tone was pointed. "Please, sit. And tell us why you're here, Gibbie." She sat in one of the chairs and gestured to the table next to her, which was laden with an assortment of desserts. She nodded directly at me. "And help yourself, if you like. There's sweet tea in the pitcher."

So far, his mother hadn't had a fit, as Gib's sister had warned. She seemed pleasant enough, if a bit reserved. Which was understandable, with her son bringing home a strange woman. I smoothed the front of my shirt, aware that no one had noticed the slight baby bump. Yet.

I declined the tea and dessert, and sat back on a wicker bench next to Gib. I was as interested in his explanation as his mother was. "Yes, Gibbie, tell both of us why we're here."

He cleared his throat, and the ruddy color had returned to his cheeks. "Well, I wanted you to meet Sacha, and for her to meet you. I apologize to both of you for not planning this in advance, but it suddenly felt like the right thing to do. I've wasted so much time already."

His mother sat like a statue, except for the slight inclination of her head. My stomach fluttered as I realized he was about to tell her about the baby. Coupled with the ache in my lower back and belly, I thought I might throw up.

"They're in here," Audrey was saying to someone as she entered the room. Then a man appeared next to her, followed by an older man. They were all extremely good-looking people, and I had the crazy idea that maybe I was on some warped reality show.

"What's going on?"

The older man had asked, his face ruggedly handsome despite the frown. He must be Gib's father, as the other man was introduced as Audrey's husband, Richard. The older man extended a hand to me and introduced himself.

"John Colebank. The father of this young man here, who'd better start talking."

All eyes were on Gib, so he stood and pulled me up with him. He faced the group and held my hand tight.

"I was about to tell Mamma, but you all should know. I'm in love with this woman, and she's having our baby."

For a moment, there was no sound except the faint hum of the swimming pool motor and the gentle splashing sound of water in the nearby fountain. Then everyone talked at once.

"Baby? You've got to be—"

"So that's what you've been doing all this time."

"Just like you to disappear and then—"

I wanted to kick him and run out, but then I would miss his family putting him in his place. I'd come to feel something for him, maybe it was close to love. But for him to announce he was in love with me, without telling me first, was unacceptable. To announce the pregnancy without my consent made it worse.

All I could do was stand there while he argued with his family. They were all talking at once, and when I tried to pull my hand from his, he gripped it tighter.

This was ridiculous. It was as though I didn't exist. "Excuse me," I ventured. When they kept on blathering, discussing how the child would be raised and where he would live, I lost it. "I said excuse me!"

They all turned to stare in my direction, including Gib. They were stunned silent, so I took a deep breath and let go. "You can all stop arguing about this, because your son and brother has misjudged the situation. He may be the father of my child, but we are not in love. And I will have the final say on what happens to this baby."

I pulled my hand from Gib's grip and left the room.

Gibson

I moved to go after Sacha, but my father grabbed my arm.

"Come with me."

His tone was deadly, his face dark with anger. I'd only seen him this angry with other people, and it never ended well for them. I looked at Audrey and cocked my head toward the living room.

"Audrey, see that she's okay."

I followed the older man down the hall to his office, glancing in the living room as we passed. Sacha was nowhere in sight, but Audrey was in pursuit.

I closed the office door behind me and leaned against it. John Colebank II sat on the edge of his desk and folded his arms.

"So, who is this woman?"

Right to the point. The heat of defensive anger washed over me, making it hard to maintain calm. "You know, I didn't have to come here, or tell any of you what I'm doing, or who I'm seeing. But I came here out of respect."

"Respect for who? You certainly didn't respect that young lady, judging by the way she reacted. It was disrespectful to your mother and me to spring this on us. What were you hoping to accomplish, son?"

Crap. What had I been thinking? Now all I had done was piss off everyone. I guess I had seriously misjudged Sacha's reaction and my family's.

What should have been a joyous moment was ruined, and I wasn't even sure why I had been so wrong. I dismissed his comment with a wave, and my sinking feeling of guilt along with it.

"She's in shock. She didn't know we're rich, and it stunned her. Maybe I should have told her about the money before this, but I thought if she saw for herself what we have here, she'd be thrilled to discover I wasn't a bum, after all."

Dad shook his head and laughed, but it was a rueful sound. "You put yourself in that position, Gib. Running away from your responsibilities might have eased your pain for a while, but you've been living in a fantasy. And now you don't know how to get back to the real world."

His words held some truth, but the problem was the pain was still there. It hadn't really eased much. The few moments of joy I had found were when Sacha was around. Now I was afraid that even if I went back to my old life, even the money wouldn't erase the crushing guilt and agony over the role I played in Bianca's death.

I had no clever retort to what my father said. He had a point. I had been living in a fantasy world, and it was time to face reality.

But how?

Somewhere deep inside, I knew Sacha was the key. What could I give her that would really matter?

The only thing that would save me was saving someone else. The problem was, the woman I wanted was convinced she didn't need me, or anyone, to save her. Maybe she didn't, but I was determined to be there if and when she did.

I straightened my shoulders and stood tall. I knew that if there was even a small chance, I had to take it.

"Well, Dad, during my time away I've learned that what you call 'the real world' is highly overrated. I'm sorry if I mishandled things here today. Now, if you'll excuse me, I have to go apologize to the woman I love."

~*~

Sacha

My heart was racing. It occurred to me that might be dangerous, coupled with the ache in my lower belly. Something was wrong, and the stress of all the things that happened this weekend didn't help. All I wanted to do was go home and lay down. Then I would call Dr. Kapoor if I didn't feel better.

I had to get out of this place. I almost made it to the car when Gib's sister, Audrey, came running out of the house.

"Wait up, Sacha. Please don't go."

Because I'd been raised to be polite, even under the worst circumstances, I stopped to hear what the woman had to say. It wasn't going to change my mind, in any case. "I really need to get going. Coming here was a mistake."

The woman was beautiful and impeccably dressed. She resembled her mother but exuded more warmth. She touched my arm and gave it a quick squeeze.

"No, the mistake was my brother's behavior. Sometimes he can be a clueless ass, but he means well."

"I'm sure that's true, but this has been a rough weekend. Frankly, I'm too exhausted to deal with family drama. And Gib is the last person I want to see right now."

Audrey gave me a sympathetic smile. "I get it. You two have some things to discuss. Why don't you come back inside? You can lay down in one of our guest rooms."

It was a tempting offer, to have the chance to see more of this gorgeous house, if nothing else. But the sight of Gib coming out onto the driveway fueled my anger once again. "Thanks, but, I think I'll pass. I just want to go home."

"Okay. Well, it was nice to meet you, Sacha."

The car door was open and I slipped inside before Gib reached me. Audrey watched from the front door for a moment then closed it, leaving us alone.

He knocked on the driver's side window. "Sacha, we need to talk."

I turned on the engine and lowered the window halfway. "I'm

179

not in the mood to talk to you right now. Besides, you don't give a damn what I think. Or how I feel."

"That's not true, and you know it. I'm sorry, I spoke before thinking. I should have discussed it with you. But I meant what I said."

His words hit me in the gut, though I still didn't believe him. I wanted to believe him. I had really begun to like the guy. But I opened my heart to him and look what happened. He blew it again with his "big man in charge" routine.

All the money in the world was not worth losing the freedom to raise my child how I saw fit. But that wasn't the worst of this situation—it was Gib's lies. To me and to himself.

"No, Gibson. You're not in love with me—you're in love with idea of replacing your lost family."

His mouth hung open, but I didn't wait for his response. Escaping down the steep drive, I looked in the rearview mirror. He was standing there, watching me leave. Then he went back inside the house.

Hot tears threatened my eyes, but I refused to cry. I had to get home, to get away from Gib, and think things through. My carefully constructed world was coming undone, and I wasn't even sure who I was anymore.

Chapter Twenty-Three

Gibson

"Audrey—car keys!"

My sister was in the sunroom, talking to Mamma. She looked up as I entered and reached out her hand. In her palm was the electric key fob to her husband's Audi. "I'm way ahead of you, brother. Bring it back spotless, or don't bring it back. You know how Richard is."

"Thank you."

Ignoring the disapproving look on my mother's face, I raced to the front door. In seconds, I was in the car and heading down the driveway. Hopefully I was only minutes behind Sacha.

I made it out of the neighborhood and headed toward the freeway. She said she was going home. I had to get to her and convince her she was wrong about me. It was true I saw our situation as the chance to have a family again, but that wasn't the only reason I wanted to be with her.

It was *her*, Sacha. Her spark, her fire. The way she pushed back at me and wasn't afraid to argue. She was not like the other women I had been with. Even Bianca, God rest her soul, had deferred to me in most things. The money changed people. It colored their perceptions. I could never trust that it didn't influence friends and lovers, at least to a degree.

181

Renee Regent

Sacha and I had met and grown to know each other on equal ground. Until today, she saw me as an average guy, and that was who she had made love to, whose shoulder she cried on last night. Yes, I qualified for the term "billionaire," but that was only my financial status. I was still the same person I had been all my life, so her accusation that I had misrepresented myself wasn't entirely true.

She wasn't without her faults, either, but I didn't care. The way she told me to go to hell when I needed to hear it, like today, only made me love her more. Sacha was a strong, independent woman. For her to leave the way she did, knowing I was heir to my family's fortune, spoke volumes about her integrity.

"She's also stubborn as a mule," I muttered, turning onto the freeway onramp. Dodging trucks and changing lanes, I drove as fast as I could, keeping an eye out for state troopers and for Sacha's car. I saw neither.

My stomach churned as I reached Sacha's street. I was trying to imagine where else she might have gone, when I saw her car parked in front of her building. As I came to a stop behind it, I noticed a figure on the grass a few feet away.

It was Sacha, on her hands and knees, with one hand on her stomach. Her pretty face was contorted, and her eyes were shut tight. I was out of the vehicle and at her side in an instant. Placing a hand on her back, I pulled my cell phone out of my pocket with the other.

"I'm calling 911. What's wrong?"

She gasped in a lungful of air and blew it out. "It hurts. I threw up, and my pulse won't slow down."

No. This can't be happening.

The call went through and I described the situation. I stayed on the line, keeping the dispatcher informed and attempting to calm Sacha at the same time. I was outwardly placid, but my insides were at war. Once she was safely on her way to the hospital, I was sure I was going to puke. But for now, I had to be in control.

It seemed an eternity had passed before we heard the sirens. I had her lay on my lap, and kept stroking her hair, talking to her. Coaxing her to breathe slowly, hoping her heart rate would ease. A small crowd gathered as Sacha's neighbors came out from their apartments. A few rushed to her side to see if they could help, but most hung back, curious. Melanie was not among them, and I wished she was. It would help to have a friend nearby.

The medical team arrived, and within minutes, they had Sacha in the ambulance and on her way to the emergency room. I hadn't dared to ask the questions that were foremost in my mind—would she be okay, and would she lose the baby?

Both thoughts consumed me as I followed the ambulance to the hospital. Had I caused this to happen? If I hadn't insisted on going to my parents' house today, maybe she would have gotten help sooner. Maybe the stress of the surprise had affected her health.

My own heart was beating furiously. I had so damn much to make up for. If they lived through this, I was going to make sure Sacha and our child never wanted for anything. Even if she no longer wanted to see me, I was going to make things right.

~*~

Sacha

The pain in my belly had finally begun to ebb. The emergency room doctors and nurses had been great, keeping me calm while they poked and prodded. My anxiety level had gone astronomically high as I imaged all sorts of problems with the baby, and how I might have been the cause. They had determined I was not in immediate danger, which was a huge relief, but had moved me up to Labor and Delivery for observation.

When Dr. Kapoor, who had been visiting another patient in the hospital, stopped by my room, I burst into tears. "What have I done? Please tell me the baby's going to be okay."

If anyone else but Dr. Kapoor had rolled her eyes just then, I would have wanted to smack them. But I trusted the woman implicitly.

"Don't worry, it'll only make things worse. The baby's fine. You have gestational hypertension. This happens, especially at your age. It can be serious, but we'll keep monitoring it, and you'll have to rest in bed for at least a week. Can you do that?"

"Yes, of course."

I didn't like the idea of lying around doing nothing, but sacrifice was what motherhood was all about. *Better start practicing now.*

Dr. Kapoor was still examining me when a familiar face appeared in the doorway.

"They said I could come in for a few minutes."

It was Gib. The concern on his face was genuine, and I warmed a little inside.

Dr. Kapoor glanced at him then back at me. "It's fine by me. We'll be keeping you overnight for observation. If all is well, and your heart rate stays closer to normal, you'll be released in the morning."

"Thank you, doctor."

"My pleasure." As she passed Gib to exit the room, she wagged a finger at him. "See that she does nothing but rest."

"Yes, ma'am."

He came to my side after I motioned for him to do so. I moved to sit up straighter in the bed, and he helped by putting the pillow against my back.

"Thank you, Gib. For everything. I don't know what I'd have done if you hadn't followed me."

He shrugged. "Someone would have called the paramedics. But I'm glad it was me. Audrey gave me her car."

His hand reached for mine, and I clasped it. The warmth of him calmed my nerves. Thinking about what happened made me realize how foolish I'd been. Yes, he'd been presumptuous to assume I would be thrilled to find out who he really was, but I had overreacted. He hadn't ever lied, he'd just not told me all the details.

And he'd been there for me in more than one way this weekend.

"I'm glad too." I squeezed his hand and smiled. His brows arched, and the relief was obvious in his voice.

"I meant what I said earlier, Sacha. I'm sorry for how I handled it, but I really am in love with you. *You*. Sacha, with her sharp mind, quick temper, and gorgeous body. It's not only the idea of having a family with you, although for that, I am overjoyed." He leaned over and kissed the back of my hand. When he looked at me, his blue eyes glistened with tears. "I thought I'd lost you. And the baby."

The last words came out in a hoarse whisper, and he closed his eyes, bowing his head.

Still holding his hand, I shook it. "But you didn't. We're going to be fine. I have to take it easy, that's all."

I had underestimated the impact losing his wife and baby had on Gib. He was a strong man and could no doubt hold his own in just about any situation. But he also felt deeply, maybe too deeply. His guilt had consumed him and drove him into exile. But being with me, and now the impending birth of our child, had brought him back. He looked at me, blinking to stop the tears that threatened.

"I'm so glad. I want to help, if you'll let me." He released my hand and took a step back. "I understand if you don't feel the same about me. It's okay. Even if you never fall in love with me, I promise to take care of you and our child, to the best of my ability. I swear it."

My heart thumped. My greatest fear had been becoming involved with him, making a family, and a home, only to have it ripped from me when he left. Like my father, like Kevin.

But despite those fears, I believed him.

I was still trying to come to grips with the fact he was a freaking billionaire. It didn't really matter because I knew who he really was, inside. Plus, he was insanely hot, friendly, and talented. Not to mention romantic, strong, and sweet. The truth was, Gibson could have any woman he wanted, and he wanted *me*.

What was not to love?

I crossed my arms over my chest. "Well, you're too late."

His mouth hung open in the most adorable, surprised way. "Too late for what?"

"Too late to give up on me. I already fell in love with you. I just didn't want to admit it."

His bottom lip trembled as he stared at me. Seconds later, his mouth was crushing mine. We were making out in my hospital bed, with the door wide open. And neither one of us cared.

~*~

Gibson

I walked back to the waiting room, fighting the urge to dance my way there. Sacha loved me. I wasn't sure I believed in fate, but if Dahlia hadn't given me the free drink ticket that fateful Friday, I might not have gone to the Frisky Beaver and met Sacha. Whatever it was, whether serendipity or divine intervention, I owed it a world of gratitude.

As I entered the room, my mouth fell open in surprise for the umpteenth time that day. Audrey waved, and the rest of my family turned their faces toward me. As I reached the group, Mamma grabbed me in a hug.

"Oh, Gibbie. Tell me she's all right."

"Yes, she's going to be fine, and the baby is fine. She just needs some rest."

Murmurs of relief came from my father, my brother-in-law,

Richard, and from Audrey. I had called her on the way to the hospital, never expecting them all to rush down here. To be truthful, I was glad to have them here. I had pushed them all away over the past few years, but when I needed them most, they came through.

They all began asking questions about what had happened. Reliving it was the last thing I wanted to do, but they needed to know. It helped to pass the time, anyway, because I wasn't going anywhere until Sacha was released.

When my sister and Mamma finally sat down, my father pulled me aside.

"Listen, son. If you need a bit more time to settle things with your…with Miss Sacha, I understand. Take what time you need. I only pushed you because I hate to see your time and talent wasted. It's not the money, you know."

It was the first time my father had ever been so understanding. Even after we had buried Bianca, the man had prompted me to get back to work. It occurred to me now that perhaps it had been a way of helping me to cope, by forcing me to focus on something other than feeling sorry for myself. But it had only made me hurt more, so I rebelled by running away.

"I know, Dad. And I know why you pushed me so hard. But I had to figure things out for myself."

"Yes, I get that now. But we'll manage. I'm sure Spencer can continue filling in until you work things out."

"That won't be necessary. I'm coming back."

I'd already decided what I needed to do on the drive to the hospital. Sacha and the baby were no longer in immediate danger, and my promise to myself if they were safe and healthy was to take care of them to the best of my ability. Which meant making a good living and relocating to be near them.

I had a purpose and a challenge—to take responsibility for my new family. I no longer needed to hide away and pretend to be something I wasn't.

I was John Gibson Colebank III, and damn proud of it.

My father was looking at me now with trepidation. "Are you sure? When?"

"As soon as I can wrap things up in Tilly. Maybe a few weeks?"

"Sure, that'll work."

The thought of Marvil gave me a chill. It wouldn't be the same living in Tilly, anyway, without my grouchy old friend. But I still needed to do what I could to sort things out with the cabin and Marvil's belongings. It was the right thing to do.

Then I'd move back home or stay with Sacha, if she'd let me.

Just then a nurse appeared, pushing a wheelchair. Sacha waved from her seat, her smile lighting up the room. Everyone went to greet her, and I stood aside.

"Sacha, oh my gawd."

A woman's voice was loud above the din. I looked up to see Melanie running to the wheelchair. She hugged Sacha then released her.

"I came as soon as I heard. My neighbor told me they took you away in an ambulance. I about had a heart attack myself."

Sacha patted her friend's hand, which was still on her shoulder. "It was a false alarm. I'll mend. They're keeping me overnight for observation, so while they moved me to another room, I asked to come down here, hoping you'd arrived."

"Well, thank God you're okay. I'm sorry I wasn't home to help."

Melanie was then introduced to everyone. As I stood back, watching, a warmth filled my heart. I pictured family gatherings and holidays, with Sacha, me, and a bunch of kids. Maybe the events of the weekend had made me maudlin, but it had been so long since I dared to dream again.

This time, I'd make sure our dreams came true.

Chapter Twenty-Four

Sacha

*T*hat night in my hospital room, I called my mother. I couldn't put it off any longer without the risk of upsetting her even more. When she answered, I put on my best happy voice so she wouldn't panic.

"Hi, Mom. Don't freak out, but I'm in the hospital."

Then I held the phone away from my ear to avoid the inevitable shriek, which came in two seconds. It was followed by a barrage of questions. "Oh, no. What happened? Are you still there? Is the baby—"

"It's fine, I mean the baby's fine. It was gestational hypertension, and it can be managed. I have to rest up for a week, that's all."

I went on to describe the details of escalating pain, my heart rate problem, what the doctors had said, and how I planned to recover. As expected, she had plenty of advice in between her questions.

After promising to call her the next day, I hung up. It wouldn't surprise me to find her at my door the next day, despite repeated assurances that the baby and I were in no danger.

The next morning, I was released with orders to stay in bed for a week, except for a visit to Dr. Kapoor for a follow up examination. Gib had stayed the night, sleeping in an uncomfortable chair at my bedside.

Melanie returned in the morning to drive us home from the hospital. I described my conversation with Mom as we left.

"She'll be checking flights right about now," I informed Gib and Melanie. He was at my side in the backseat and would not let go of my hand. He kept smiling, that same smile he'd had on the way to his parents' house. He had something to tell me, but it would have to wait. Melanie had met my Mom once before, and the two had hit it off.

"Great, I hope she does. Her mom's a hoot," she said, glancing at Gib in the rearview mirror.

"I'd love to meet her, if I'm still here."

We hadn't discussed any plans yet. I wanted him to stay, not only to be sure I had recovered, but because I would miss him. Melanie had agreed to stay with me when he left, in any case.

"Can you stay tonight, at least?" I'd lowered my voice, although it didn't matter if Melanie heard. I wanted him to know I liked the idea.

"I'd like to. I want to make absolutely sure you're going to be okay."

I sighed and rested my head on his shoulder. I caught sight of Melanie's dark eyes in the mirror, and the knowing smile my best friend gave me showed she approved. And Melanie didn't even know his secret yet, that he was actually a billionaire.

Well, so do I. I'm Sacha Rowan and I approve of this relationship.

~*~

Gibson

Once Sacha was settled in her bed with a blanket and a cup of chamomile tea, I finally relaxed. I sat on the edge of the bed, contemplating taking a nap next to her. My body was weary, but my mind was still processing all that had happened. Sacha must have noticed my introspection and nudged me with her toe.

"Been a hell of a weekend, huh? I bet you're sorry you didn't go back to Tilly on Friday."

I took her foot from under the covers, placed it in my lap and began to knead. She sighed and moaned, the sound reminding me of my favorite part of the past crazy weekend. The part when she was naked and on top of me.

"Not one bit. There's nowhere else I'd rather be. And I have a

189

private jet at my disposal."

"Yeah, about all that… I still can't picture you, jet-setting around the world while raking in billions of dollars."

I continued to massage her foot, enjoying her occasional "oohs" and "ahhs."

"That's true, but it's not quite as simple as people think. Our company has many investors, and much of our wealth is on paper, at least currently. It's not like we have it all to ourselves. But yes, my family lives quite comfortably, and someday I will inherit the mantle of CEO, unless I make other arrangements. That's why my dad has been so pissed about me being gone."

Her expression was thoughtful as she pondered my description. Most people had no idea how a large corporation really worked. They assumed the money flowed like a never-ending, magical stream.

"So, are you thinking of going back to work in Atlanta? I thought you liked it in Tilly."

"I do, I love it there. But I've already informed my dad that I'd be back to work in a few weeks. I told you, I plan to take care of you and… We still need a name for this kid, you know."

She pulled her foot away and sat up. "I'm not going to quit my job and become a kept woman, so get that thought out of your head right now."

This. This is why I love her. That, and the stern look she gave me when I chuckled at her.

"Sacha, I love your independence. If you want to work, please do. Even if it means moving to Alabama. I only want you to be happy. But it's time for me to come back to the 'real world,' as my father put it. Plus, I'll have to move out of my cabin anyway, since Marvil died. I don't know what's going to happen to his property."

Her face softened. She leaned back into the pillows and placed her other foot in my lap. When I began my ministrations again, she closed her eyes. When she opened them a few seconds later, her face had gone somber.

"Well, I appreciate that you understand how I feel. I want to do what's best for our little one. It's no longer about what we want, is it?"

"Not really. Things are going to work out. I promise."

Her smile, full of acceptance, melted my heart. Then a puzzled look crossed her face. "We do need to think of a name, don't we?"

~*~

Not So Broken

Leaving Sacha the next morning was incredibly difficult. She'd snuggled all night in my arms, and I'd slept like the dead. I made her breakfast, and when she was comfortably situated once again, I gathered my things.

Leaning down for one long, last kiss, I let my hand wander to her breast. Her nipple was prominent through her thin cotton nightgown, and she made a small noise of delight. I reluctantly pulled away, clearing my throat. "I better go before I end up staying another night."

"Yes, that's a possibility if your hands keep wandering like that."

"Doctor's orders are rest only, so it's probably better I leave."

Melanie had promised to stay with Sacha, which eased my mind. I hated leaving her, and it wasn't only because of her physical condition. I was going to miss her, every minute.

Placing a hand under her chin, I leaned my forehead to hers. "I love you."

"I love you too."

Our lips met, and this time the kiss was more emotion than passion. I pulled away, releasing her slowly.

"I'll call you when I get back to the cabin."

I did, but even her voice couldn't erase the sadness I felt knowing Marvil was gone. I kept expecting to see him on the porch of his cabin, every time I passed. My own cabin was too quiet, now that I was alone. I wandered around, making a mental note of what I wanted to take when I moved out. I had rented the cabin furnished but had found some décor items in town that I hated to leave or throw out. Perhaps I would invite Sacha to come up when she was feeling better to see if she wanted anything.

I made some phone calls and formulated a schedule to get my jobs done. I had only one in progress and two upcoming. I estimated finishing all three in the next few weeks, and then I'd be done. I hated to leave anyone hanging, and I was really going to miss working with my hands.

It was late afternoon when my cell phone rang. It was Marvil's attorney, so I took the call.

"Hello?"

"Good afternoon, Mr. Colebank. This is Michael Stazky. I've gone through Mr. Crouch's estate documents, and I would like to meet with you as soon as possible to discuss it."

I had no idea why I would have anything to do with Marvil's estate, but now I was curious. "Sure, let me know when, and I'll be there."

Renee Regent

The appointment was the next afternoon. It was in a nearby town, so I could get some work done in the morning and then grab lunch on the way. I had no clue as to why Marvil would involve me, unless it had to do with his belongings or how long I could stay in the cabin. Whatever it was, I'd do it to honor my friend's memory.

The word "bittersweet" came to mind as I settled in for the evening. Though I was sad to lose a friend, I had so much to be thankful for. I wondered what Marvil would have said about Sacha and the baby. Something told me my old friend would have grumbled something about noisy kids, and then smiled and congratulated us. He hadn't been fooling anyone.

Chapter Twenty-Five

Sacha

On day three of my captivity I was lying in bed, reading a spicy romance novel Melanie had picked up for me at the drugstore. I had quickly learned that daytime television was either game shows or soap operas, and I had no patience for either one. I rarely watched shows or movies when I was working, but now I was seriously considering downloading a streaming service. I decided, though, to wait until I found out about Alabama first.

I'd called Dan on Monday morning to tell him about my health issues. He arranged for someone else to handle my orders for the week, and then asked me how it went with Mr. Redfield.

"I think it went well. He seemed nice, and we had a good conversation. Well, as good as we could have since he was distracted with his daughter's art show."

"So, you're still on board then? I mean, with your situation changing, I wasn't sure…"

I let a beat of silence go by. Was I really sure? Being with Gib now made the move to Alabama, and taking the training position, seem less enticing. But our relationship was still so new, I couldn't determine yet what was best for both of us in the long run. He'd told me to work the job I wanted, and this one was the only opportunity currently on the horizon. After all, I could stay home and let Gib support me, and live in a condo or a large home, all paid for.

But that wasn't how I was raised. Deep down, I still feared being dependent on him, no matter how luxurious that situation might be. Some would call me crazy for feeling that way, but I wasn't ready to throw away my independence yet.

"Sure, if he offers me the job and it's as he described."

"Great. We should know something soon. Get some rest, Sacha."

I hung up, pushing aside the feeling that I'd never make it to Alabama. Then what?

My thoughts were interrupted by the sound of a knock at the front door. I listened as Melanie, who'd been napping on my sofa, went to answer it. Then came the sound of a loud, familiar voice.

Mom.

When I looked up a moment later, she was standing in the doorway to my bedroom.

"Mom, what a lovely surprise," I cooed, knowing the sarcasm wouldn't be lost on my sharp mother.

"Don't be a smart ass. You knew I was coming the minute we hung up."

I had known. She came to my side and we hugged, laughing. Then I lifted my tee shirt to show off my baby bump. Her hands were ice cold, causing me to shriek and pull down my shirt.

"Mom! You need a hot mug of tea to warm your hands."

The next day, we were on my bed, watching some kind of cooking show. Melanie had gone home to get some sleep and whatever else she had to do. I leafed through a magazine as we sat, unable to keep still. I was feeling much better, but still nervous, as I contemplated what was about to happen.

I hadn't told Mom about the text message I'd received shortly after she had arrived. I had initiated the text conversation, knowing I was taking a huge risk. But that seemed to be how my life was going these days.

"So, Mom… There's something you need to know."

Julia had an expressive face, and now fear was etched in the lines around her mouth. "About?"

"The baby's father. His name is Gibson Colebank, and we've become more than friends recently. Actually, it's serious." I lowered my voice, still unable to believe what I was about to say. "We're in love. And he's totally on board with raising the baby together."

Her smile was tentative, reflecting the way I felt. I loved Gib.

There was no doubt about that. But how we were going to live and where had yet to be determined.

"And are you on board with this? I know how set you were to do things on your own."

I leaned back, hugging a pillow. It didn't matter how or where we lived, as long as we were together and our child was safe and healthy. The rest was a bonus.

"Yes, I am. And by the way, he's rich. I mean, wealthy. His family is worth billions. With a 'B.'"

For once, Julia was stunned into silence. Then she smacked my leg. "Oh, good one. You almost had me fooled there. You can be honest with me."

"No, I am being honest. His family owns a major resort and vacation rental company. Huge. World-wide. But he's had a rough past—he lost his wife in a tragic accident a few years ago, and he was in hiding, sort of, when I met him. I had no idea who he really was."

"Wow. That's…stunning. I'm not sure what to think."

"You'll like him. I'll see if we can get together before you leave."

She was thoughtful for a moment, processing what I'd said. Then she smiled. "Well, yeah. I'd like that. Even though he has money, he better treat you right, or he'll have to deal with me."

I patted her arm. "Of course, Mom. He's great. You'll see."

The sound of rapping on the front door cut off any further discussion of Gib. It wasn't Melanie's knock, but the knock of a stranger. My heart leapt, hammering in my chest, as Mom got up to answer it. I held my breath, waiting for the fireworks to begin.

"What the hell are you doing here?"

I was already out of bed and into my robe. I walked slowly to the bedroom door then into the living room. "It's okay, Mom. I invited him to come here."

Garth looked at me through the open door, his face even paler than before. He reminded me of a cartoon cadaver, except his eyes didn't have x's on them yet.

"You didn't tell me you had company, Sacha."

His tone indicated he was unprepared to face both his ex-wife *and* me. Mom's face told me the same. She wasn't prepared to face him, either. This was the gamble I'd taken, but it was an opportunity to clear the air and face the hard truth about our collective past. If I'd learned anything the past few weeks, it was that everyone has a story and deserves a chance to be heard.

It didn't mean the past didn't matter, but running from it or ignoring it weren't solutions, either.

"Well, Dad, you said you wanted to tell me the truth about what happened. I figured she deserves to hear it from you, too."

Julia's arms were crossed over her chest, and her lips were drawn tight. "Yes, do tell. Not that we can believe a word the bastard says." She threw up her hands and went to sit at the dining table.

I prompted Garth by pointing to the empty chair opposite. "Shall we?"

He nodded, closing the door behind him and removing his coat. I was struck by how thin he was, his black polo shirt hanging on his frame, his bony arms covered with faded tattoos. As a child, I'd studied some of those cartoonish drawings with fascination. A few new ones I'd never seen had appeared, and I wondered how someone once so familiar to me could become such a stranger.

I sat down and looked expectantly at Garth. He cleared his throat and began talking.

"First, I have to say I'm sorry for any and all the pain I have caused both of you. Whether you believe me or not, I'll go to my grave knowing I did the right thing. I know that is almost impossible for you to believe, but I hope you'll hear me out."

Mom and I exchanged looks, but there was no reason to stop him now. May as well let him speak, for what it was worth. I nodded.

"Go on."

"I'll admit, I got into some bad stuff back in the day. I drank too much, and I gambled. When you were a baby, I guess I wasn't ready for the responsibility that entailed, and I went off the deep end a time or two. That's no excuse, but that's the truth of it."

"To put it mildly," Julia spat, her tone laced with venom. "I had to beg my sister to bring us food when you were on a bender. We had no money, no way to get around. It was humiliating, to say the least."

Garth's gray eyes had misted over, and his hands were clasped together tightly. "I know, Julia. It was horrible of me. But there's more I need to tell you." She leaned back with a sigh, and he wiped an errant tear away. His voice had gone shaky, but he began to get the words out in a rush.

"I was working for a man who ran a gambling ring on the side. Fights, sports, card games, you name it, he handled it. I started making good money—remember when we replaced our old furniture, and I finally bought you that diamond ring, Jul? Well, I thought I had made it, and that the money was going to continue. I was good at it, so good the guys I ran with called me 'Lucky G.' But then somehow, it all came crashing down on me.

"I never told you what I was doing because I was ashamed and afraid you'd make me quit. It was the only thing I ever felt I was good at. But I wasn't good enough—or lucky enough—because in a short time I owed a bunch of money to some loan sharks, and they wanted me to pay it back."

Julia now had her fingers woven together underneath her chin and was blinking prettily. "Oh, this sounds like a movie I saw once. Or was it a crappy dime store novel I read? I can't recall."

I said nothing, watching the interplay between my parents. My gut told me Garth was telling the truth. If he was dying, what did he have to lose? Lying again wouldn't help his case in the afterlife, would it?

He ignored her sarcasm and continued his story. His voice had turned quiet, barely above a whisper. "When they threatened the two of you, I knew I had no choice. I did everything I could to secure the money, but it wasn't enough. I was truly afraid they'd do something horrible, so I offered the only thing I could at that point. Myself. Mr. Bogelli, the man I worked for, paid them off on my behalf, but in return, I had to work for him. I became part of his gang, which meant traveling wherever he sent me, to do whatever I had to do."

Julia's anger was still barely contained. She rolled her eyes and let out a "shhhsh" sound. "So, you're saying you worked for the mob, eh? You never had the guts for that."

"You're right, I didn't. But my fear for you and Sacha was so strong, it made me turn cold-blooded. I became pretty good at being a thug. I did some very bad things, which I'll regret for the rest of my life. I left because I didn't want either of you to be connected with all that crap. Anyway, about a year after we divorced, me and some of the other guys got popped in a sting operation. I ended up in prison. That's why I never contacted you. I wanted to come back and finally explain everything so many times, but I couldn't bear for both of you to see what I had become. And then it was too late."

Silence filled the room, thick as fog. My head swirled, my mind filled with fragments of childhood memories. I had always known my father had secrets but never expected all this. Though my heart still held anger over his abandoning us, I knew I had to let it go. Holding on to bad memories wouldn't help any of us.

Renee Regent

He bowed his head then erupted in tears. I handed him a paper napkin and dabbed my own eyes with another. Mom's face was red, and she was blinking back tears too. When I looked at her, I saw a softness slowly replace the hard edges around her mouth. When she spoke, her tone was calm.

"Garth, it doesn't matter. Yes, I'm still angry with you. I may never get over that. But we've all suffered enough. Let's agree to live our own lives and be as supportive as we can for Sacha and our grandchild."

He sobbed once and struggled to regain his composure. Wiping his eyes, he reached out a hand to me, his only daughter. "I'd like that. I don't know if I'll be around, but I'm going to give it a hell of a try."

I clasped his hand across the table. "I'd like that. I don't want to hang on to the past. I've learned recently that we can't live life completely on our own. We need each other, and we all make mistakes."

Mom reached across the table to hold my other hand. My smile that followed was prompted by the life inside me, kicking. It seemed someone else approved of our family reunion.

Chapter Twenty-Six

Gibson

Friday morning, I sat in my truck in downtown Tilly, sipping coffee. I'd gone by the diner to tell Dahlia and the others about Marvil's passing, but they already knew. Word traveled fast in Tilly, especially when it was something big. To my surprise, everyone I spoke with said good things about Marvil, despite his reputation for being the town grouch. It seems he really wasn't fooling anyone with his abrasive personality. Almost everyone had a story of something Marvil did to make someone's life better—volunteering, donating, and contributing his money to the needy. He always asked for anonymity, but there was no point now to hide the fact Marvil Crouch had indeed been a man with a heart of gold.

No one knew the truth about Marvil Crouch better than I did, which was why I couldn't wait for Sacha to arrive. I had good news and was itching to share it with her. Tapping my fingers on the steering wheel, I checked my phone again. She was due to arrive in Tilly any moment.

After ten days of rest, Dr. Kapoor had pronounced Sacha fit to return to her normal duties, within reason. Since she had a few accounts to visit in Tilly as a follow-up, I asked her to meet me before she did anything else. I was looking forward to holding her in my arms as soon as possible, but my plans included much more than that. We had talked on the phone early this morning, and it was all I could do to keep from revealing my plans.

I had my parent's blessing, something I was still in shock over. This wasn't how I'd ever pictured my life turning out that day I rode into Tilly, but I was thrilled. Fate had handed me a second chance, and it was more than I'd ever hoped for.

When Sacha's car pulled up alongside the truck, I couldn't get out fast enough. Before she'd opened her door, I was there. I grabbed the door handle and she emerged, falling into my arms. I covered her lips with my own, tasting the sweetness I'd been craving for so long.

"Hello, sexy. I missed you."

She laughed, and looked down at her belly, straining against her coat. "I don't know about sexy, but yeah. I missed you, too."

"Come on."

I took her hand and led her to the truck. Helping her in, I let my hand brush her bottom. She turned and gave me a smile then smacked my hand playfully.

"So, what's your big secret? You sounded like a little kid on the phone. I could hear the giggle in your voice."

I gave her what I hoped was a stern look. "I don't 'giggle.' And you'll see."

We chatted as I drove, but I could tell she was curious. I hoped she was going to react the way I imagined. Sometimes she caught me off guard with her opinions, but I was learning to anticipate her reactions. Still, this was a biggie.

Only one way to find out.

When I turned onto the gravel road, she looked at me. "We're going fishing?"

"Nope."

She shrugged and held onto the armrest as we traversed the bumpy road. When we finally came to a stop, I put the truck in park. I sat for a moment, listening to the roar of the river as it tumbled over the rocks. "Let's take a short walk."

Fortunately, she was wearing sensible shoes. High heels were out for a few months, so she was able to walk through the grass and gravel, holding my hand. When we came to the edge of the river, I stopped.

"Sacha, I have what I think is great news, and a proposition for you."

Her brow arched. "Okay, spill it already. I can't take much more."

Not So Broken

"Marvil Crouch never told me when he was alive, but *he* owned this property. Twenty-three acres of prime riverfront property. And he left it all to me, and the cabins too."

"The one you've been living in? And all this?"

She looked around, up at the hillside, the trees, the river. I nodded, still unable to believe it myself.

"Apparently, he had no other relatives, so he left it all to me. I'm humbled, and thrilled, because I think it will make a fantastic resort. We'll keep it rustic, like a lodge, and cut as few trees as possible. But it will be exclusive, luxurious, and a really great investment. Not to mention, a tribute to Marvil. He loved this place."

She turned in a circle, taking it all in as I described my vision once again, this time in more detail. "Yes, I can see that. It's a great idea."

"And I'll be in charge of the whole thing, from start to finish. I spoke with my father at length, and he agreed. And there's room to build a grand house too. Big enough for all of us to live in."

Now I had her attention. She cocked her head, her eyes going wide. "Us? To live here?"

"Yes. Tilly is a great place to raise a family. And with your experience, you could manage the restaurants. What do you think?"

I held my breath. She was looking stunned, but her eyes held interest. "I'm... That's a lot to think about."

"Maybe this will help."

I went down on one knee, pulling a small velvet box from my shirt pocket. I opened the box to reveal a delicate platinum ring, adorned with a huge sparkling diamond. I held it up to her, watching her hand fly to cover her mouth.

"What the...oh my."

"Sacha Rowan, will you marry me?" Torturous seconds dragged by as I watched her face. It had gone pale. Then her cheeks began to color. A slow smile graced her lips as she stuck out her left hand.

"Yes. Yes, of course. You're the father of my child, and I love you!"

I slipped it on her finger and gathered her into my arms. "I love you too. I promise to be everything you ever wanted in a husband and more."

Our first kiss as fiancées was sweet and gentle. She whispered her response against my lips. "You already are."

201

Epilogue

Gibson

We were married at my parent's estate a few months after our engagement. It was a small gathering, just our families and a few friends. Sacha's parents flew in for the event, and Melanie was her maid of honor. Since everyone was forgetting about the past, I tapped my cousin, Spencer, as my best man. Everyone was together, and somehow, we managed to avoid any drama for the day.

I couldn't believe a bride could be as beautiful as Sacha was, big baby bump and all, but my heart swelled at the sight of her walking toward me on her father's arm. It was a simple ceremony, and the reception wasn't as wild as my first wedding reception had been. But I was a different man now.

I was proud once again of who I was, and everything I had accomplished. More than that, I was humbled and grateful to have found a woman who challenged me to do my best, every day. When our son was finally born, I knew I was truly blessed, and it had nothing to do with being a billionaire.

Well, the money helped. It had been ambitious to build our resort and our new home at the same time, but I welcomed the challenge. The resort was still a work in progress, but we were on schedule to open later in the year. That would give Sacha more time with the baby, before the work of managing the restaurants began. Her former company had been gracious about her leaving, and she was thrilled with how things worked out.

We had already lined up several people in town to work for us. All of Tilly was abuzz about the opening of the Riverbank Resort and Lodge. It was the largest project to come to town in several years, and the Convention and Visitor's Bureau was enthusiastically supportive. I was proud to be able to give back to the community in this way, since they had been so welcoming of me when I was at my lowest point.

But the most satisfying part of the whole thing, for me, was my father's unwavering support.

"I guess I should have let you run things your way sooner. I'm impressed."

His words when I showed him the blueprints and the projections still rang in my ears. I couldn't believe I was finally free to do the work I had been born to do and still benefit the family business. But I couldn't take all the credit. With Sacha as my partner, I knew we could have it all, do it all, be it all.

Standing on the deck of our new home, looking down at the rushing river below, then out at the deep green mountain range in the distance, I couldn't have been happier. She walked up next to me, with little Jonathan Garth Colebank in her arms.

"Daddy's dreaming again," she cooed. Wrapped in his blue blanket with a white beanie covering his pink head, baby Jon cooed back. The name was a compromise, but it suited our son. He wasn't exactly "the fourth" but his name still honored his ancestors.

I wrapped an arm around my wife, pulling her close. Nothing could be better than this. I told her what I truly believed in my heart.

"It's amazing what two people can do when they share a dream."

A Note To My Readers

I hope you enjoyed Gibson and Sacha's story as much as I enjoyed writing it. I write romance novels because I am fascinated with stories of how couples came to be together, especially when there is an element of fate. The idea of two people who barely know each other having to face together the greatest responsibility a couple can have, intrigued me. I never had children of my own until I became a stepmother, so taking my characters on this journey was a challenge for me. But it was also fun, and I plan to explore the lives of other mismatched couples in the Love Grows series. Book Two, Not So Wrong, (Spencer and Melanie's story) will be released in 2019. Stay tuned!

I always appreciate honest reviews, so thanks in advance to any readers who take the time to write a review.

For news, exclusive content, and special promotions, (and a free mini e-book) join my newsletter at http://www.reneeregent.com/newsletter-sign-up

About the Author

A true believer in the power of love, Renee writes stories of mismatched people who fight the odds to be together. Whether fighting the supernatural or their own inner demons, her characters will always find their way to a happy ending.

Renee lives in Atlanta with her husband, three cats and four turtles. When not working or writing, she can be found sitting on her deck enjoying nature. Wine may or may not be involved....

Printed in Great Britain
by Amazon

40793526R00121